There's a palpable buzz in the air around the Nursing Department at Memorial. Phones ring continuously, computer screens glow with facts and figures, women (and a handful of men) rush with folders in hand to meetings, doors open and close. Nurses, regardless of their position on the ladder, so it seems, are temperamentally ill-suited to sedentary behavior. So there's a hum in the air, too. It's the sound of clicking heels and moving feet. "We were always taught," says a seasoned night nurse, "that a sitting nurse was not a working nurse." Clearly it was a lesson that was never lost.

Nursing is the heartbeat of the hospital. Without nurses, the hospital cannot run. If doctors do the curing, then nurses do the caring, and caring is the primary service that is rendered "day-to-day," "minute-to-minute." Patients come to hospitals to be nursed.

# RN

## The Commitment, the Heartache, and the Courage of Three Dedicated Nurses

## JANE CARPINETO

ST. MARTIN'S PAPERBACKS

R.N.

Copyright © 1992 by Jane F. Carpineto.

Cover photograph by Tom Rosenthal/Superstock.

Library of Congress Catalog Card Number: 91-33234

ISBN: 0-312-92918-8

Printed in the United States of America

St. Martin's Press hardcover edition/February 1992
St. Martin's Paperbacks edition/August 1993

10  9  8  7  6  5  4  3  2  1

THIS BOOK IS DEDICATED TO
JESSIE, DOMINIQUE, AND GINA, AND TO
PRESENT AND FUTURE NURSES
EVERYWHERE.

# CONTENTS

# ACKNOWLEDGMENTS

HAD I NOT the good fortune to have Jane Dystel as my agent and Tom Dunne as my editor, this book would not have been possible. From beginning to end, it has been a labor of love, so it is to both of them, first, that I want to offer my heartfelt appreciation.

A possibility would not have become a reality, however, without the support and encouragement of Memorial Hospital (not its real name) administrators. They gave me permission to see whatever there was to see and to write whatever I wished to write, with only minimal conditions. In return, I promised the administrators an advance look at the manuscript, signed authorizations from patients to use only the content of interviews and not their real names, and an assurance that the name of the hospital and the names of its employees would be fictitious. The last condition resulted from the desire of some of the nurses to remain anonymous rather than from an administrative concern that the hospital could not withstand close scrutiny. Like every institution, it has its flaws, but these are far outweighed by its achievements. Memorial has earned a well-deserved reputation as a leading teaching hospital that delivers high-quality patient care.

To everyone in this book, I owe a debt of gratitude, but to the three nurses, Jessie, Dominique, and Gina, I owe an enormous one. Instead of paying a debt, however, I have received a bonus. I have three new friends who, in the time that they've known me, have every right to regard me more as an obtrusive shadow than as a friend. Throughout the project, I was regularly impressed with their ability to accept my symbiotic attachment to them with humor and grace. Gina often introduced me to people by saying, "I'd like you to meet my shadow." Jessie, when she was especially busy, would say, "You're a really nice person, but don't let my good opinion of you give you the idea that I can spend all of my time entertaining you." Dominique, always behind schedule, would say, "No one has ever asked me as many questions in my entire lifetime as you have in a few months. It's flattering, but how do you expect me to get my work done?"

Other people in the book deserve honorable mention for their extensive contributions. They will recognize themselves by their fictitious names. Jessie's, Dominique's, and Gina's families and friends were crucial to this project. Without them, I never could have obtained a close-up view of the nurses' personal lives.

For the professional perspective, I want to give special thanks to several people who, by the time I began writing, knew themselves almost as well by their fictitious names as by their given names. I am grateful to Nicole McClean, who served as my able mentor throughout the project; to Colleen Lindstrom and Pauline Irving, the nurse directors in charge of the oncology units and the Surgical Intensive Care Unit (SICU) and were generous with their time; to Jean Pirelli, the acting vice president of nursing, who made the arrangements for my participation and gave me the benefit of her expertise whenever I needed it; to Ben Callahan, who not only taught me a lot about health care but offered invaluable assistance in the final preparation of the manuscript; to nurse managers Caroline O'Rourke, Wendy Fleming, and Judy LaVigne, who went out of their way to answer my innumerable questions and to accommodate me in their schedules; to

Drs. Sandra Wilder, Paul Donaldson, and Clifford Siegel, who gave me much more than my fair share of their precious time; and to all of the nurses, physicians, and clerical staff on 5B, 5C, and the SICU who do appear (or do not appear) in the book. I am grateful to them for allowing me to intrude in their activities. To Alice Cochran and Dr. George Tirrell, also, I owe special thanks for making room for me in their crowded schedules.

The one person in the book whose name is not disguised is Dr. Lucie Kelly's. With very short notice, and in the midst of a national convention, she rearranged her schedule to meet with me and to introduce me to people who could be helpful in my research. I value her friendship and her knowledge of nursing.

As with the writing of any book, there were people on the periphera of this one whose help was invaluable. I want to thank Memorial's director of gastroenterology for paving the way for my initial entry into the hospital, and the hospital's vice president of Corporate Support Services for granting me official permission to conduct the project there and for giving me so many thoughtful editorial suggestions. For her expertise on nursing unions, I offer my appreciation to the former official of the state's nursing association who met with me at Dr. Kelly's suggestion. I am indebted, too, to Dr. Brenda Millett, assistant professor of nursing at the University of Massachusetts, Amherst, for her reading of the manuscript and for her thoughtful commentary. My friends June and Dick Wolff, Linda and Bill Green, Frank Wright, and Judy Quain read all or parts of the manuscript and contributed helpful advice, editorial assistance, and encouragement. I owe special thanks to Mary Lou Delacey for sharing her professional wisdom with me. My husband Joe accompanied me to several social events in connection with the book, gave me ideas about content, lent me his cherished art studio to use for writing, and assumed both his own and my share of domestic responsibility during the project. To my friends Sharon Shay and Wayne Workman and Rita and

Harry Pothoulakis, I offer herewith an official acknowledgment of my appreciation for the use of their splendid homes
in various stages of preparing the manuscript. Finally, I
want to thank the daytime attendant in the hospital parking
lot who never failed to give me a cheery greeting every
morning when I arrived at the entrance booth.

# INTRODUCTION

TWENTY-FIVE YEARS ago, long before I had any inkling that I would be writing a book about nurses, I was employed as a social worker in a teaching hospital. My memories of nurses from that early stage of my professional life are sketchy. I remember a sea of faces belonging to women in white caps, starched white uniforms, white stockings, and white "nurses'" shoes. A few first names come back to me—a young nurse named Joan, an older one named Pearl—but their last names escape me. Even though nurses were everywhere around me, I didn't know many of them well. Neither did I know, nor was I inclined to ask, how well they liked their jobs or how much respect they felt they received from hospital administrators or physicians. Nurses in those days appeared to me as shadowy figures, women working behind the scenes in service to the men in the vanguard—the physicians. It was physicians who had all of the glory and the power. That was the way it was, or seemed to be, back then, and to the best of my recollection, no one challenged the status quo.

If that was the way it was then, it isn't that way now. I have tried in this book to demonstrate that today the professional lives of nurses bear little resemblance to those of their predecessors. The three nurses, Jessie Concannon, Dominique Raza, and Gina Rossi, are not just subjects of a book, they are characters in a much bigger story—the story of the renaissance of an entire profession.

The action that surrounds them speaks to the enormous changes that have taken place in nursing. Among these, one of the most significant is the introduction of a modern model of practice known as primary nursing, in which a patient is assigned to one nurse for the duration of his or her hospital stay. Although other nurses attend the patient on different shifts, the primary nurse is the coordinator of the patient's care.

The nurses here are the new breed: they are managers and expert clinicians, executives and creative thinkers, strong patient advocates and skilled caregivers. They are full-fledged members of clinical teams. They work hand in hand with physicians and sometimes overrule them when nursing priorities prevail over medical ones in the process of making clinical decisions and clinical policies or procedures. They are professionals in every sense of the word.

The achievement of genuine professional status is the exciting news from the nursing front. But for every victory there is a price to be paid. Three dark clouds hover over nursing these days. First, primary nursing, just as it has begun to take hold, is becoming endangered because it is seen by many administrators as a high-cost care delivery system in an era of tight money. To implement it successfully, nursing and hospital administrators and staff nurses have to be committed to it wholeheartedly. For some administrators it is difficult to make a commitment to a system that, in the final cost analysis, may prove to be unaffordable. Second, a nationwide shortage of nurses, more serious in some regions than in others, represents a current crisis for those hospitals where it exists and a potential crisis for all hospitals. The shortage is exacerbated by fluctuating enrollment at nursing schools, and by the elimination of some baccalaureate nursing programs due to university budget cuts. And third, nurse ''burnout'' is an omnipresent threat, made worse by the shortage of new people entering the field, by financial limitations that prevent some hospitals from replacing departing nurses, and by a concomitant demand for more nurses to care for a growing population of critically ill people. In general, nursing is a profession that requires hard work and dedication from its practitioners without sufficient resources for reward. Nurses' salaries and status are higher than ever before, but there are never enough nurses to handle the load. For the typical staff nurse, relief time from relentless pressure is in short supply, and there are insufficient variations and new challenges to interrupt the monotony of daily routines. Opportunities for advancement are increasing, but more are needed. Add to all of these problems the scarcity of on-site child-care services and flextime possibilities, benefits that many other professionals take for granted, and it becomes easy to understand nurses' dissatisfaction.

While writing this book, I had the opportunity to meet Dr. Lucie Kelly, a well-known nursing leader and a professor emeritus at the Columbia University School of Public Health and School of Nursing. She is the author of two widely read nursing texts, *Dimensions of Professional Nursing* sixth edition (Pergamon Press, 1991) and *The Nursing Experience: Trends, Issues and Challenges* (Macmillan, 1987). Dr. Kelly has an abiding principle for nursing administrators:

> I preach it regularly. I tell them to listen to the grass roots people. They'll give you all the answers you need to all the problems you're experiencing if you take the time to ask them questions. Top-down administration never works. If you're on top, it doesn't do you any good to act like an autocrat. You have to mingle with the staff nurses yourself instead of leaving it all to a nurse manager on a unit. Staff nurses are smart and career oriented nowadays. They need to be heard. There's been lots of research on how to keep nurses happy, but hospital administrators don't always

listen. Nursing administrators need to educate them.
It's important to know about management and finance,
because they're crucial skills in health care today, but
nothing is more important than keeping in touch with
the grass roots people, the staff nurses.

It wasn't until I had spent time with Dominique, the staff
nurse in this book, that the wisdom of Dr. Kelly's principle
came home to me. As an outsider looking in, I could see
the signs of burnout in the words and the body language of
Dominique and her colleagues. They talked about it with
one another but didn't discuss it with their administrators,
the people who most needed to hear.

Dr. Sandra Wilder, a physician in this book, is the daughter of a nurse. Among the many physicians I interviewed,
she stood out for her knowledge and appreciation of nursing
and for her popularity with nurses. Like Dr. Kelly, Dr.
Wilder worries that nursing administrators are out of touch
with the day-to-day activities and attitudes of their staffs
and may not be able to respond to nurses' needs. Dr. Wilder
believes that even though it demands more from nurses,
primary nursing increases job satisfaction.

I'm an advocate of the concept of primary nursing,
the idea that one nurse follows the patient from admission to discharge, but it's a hard concept to implement.
It's an expensive way to deliver care, and it requires
flexibility on the part of the nursing staff. They have
to be eager and willing to adjust their schedules to
maximize their availability. To be an effective primary
nurse, you can't work a twelve-hour shift three days
a week. You have to be there every day. There have
to be incentives to make nurses want to do it. If you
conducted a survey of patients and doctors, I think
most would say that primary nursing is the optimal
way to deliver care. Nurses who are serious about
their careers would have more job satisfaction because

they'd feel that their impact on patients was greater. I think that the primary nurse should serve as the team leader who coordinates regular conferences between herself, the physician, and the patients' families.

On the Surgical Intensive Care Unit, we have a modified form of primary nursing. It's hard to get critical care nurses to sit down with families to discuss the impact of a patient's critical illness. They see the blood-and-guts stuff as their first priority. I don't think that nursing directors have in-depth knowledge of the daily operations of their units. They're not close by. They're afraid that if the nurses and doctors on the units are able to work out an effective collaboration by themselves, then they'll be out of a job. There seems to be a feeling in nursing that if you want to do something new, you have to meet from now 'til next year to get it done. What they don't understand is that the more decentralized the administrative structure is allowed to be, the more likely it is to meet the patients' and the nurses' needs. The ripple effect will be that nursing will look more attractive as a profession. As it stands now, nursing is having difficulty recruiting new people.

Despite all of the problems, however, I believe that there is more good news than bad. One of the most encouraging developments is the increasing number of people entering nursing as a second career. They represent a constituency of mature individuals who have tried their hands at other careers and have determined that nursing offers them greater job satisfaction. They can enter the field with the assurance that today's nurse is so far removed from yesterday's doctor's handmaiden that that dark chapter of nursing history can be closed. Nurses have proven their worth. No hospital can function without them. Doctors cannot deliver treatment without them. And patients cannot recover without them. The demand for nurses is so great, in fact, that they are in an ideal bargaining position. Jobs in the public and private sector are plentiful for nurses, and the terms attached to them are growing increasingly more favorable.

Memorial Hospital, where this story takes place, is a very desirable place to work. It does a better-than-average job of keeping nurses happy in the face of mounting financial constraints. The nurse vacancy rate is low. The hospital's nursing administrators are farsighted and enlightened, and they wield considerable influence in the overall governance of the institution, lending a strong voice to the cause of maintaining high-quality patient care. For them this means keeping as many well-trained nurses on board as is financially feasible and enough nurse extenders (patient care technicians and nursing assistants) to free nurses from time-consuming menial tasks.

The three nurses in this book are among Memorial's best and brightest, and their stories reflect both the triumphs and the troubles that are indigenous to the nursing profession.

# WHY A NURSE?

*Why be a nurse!!! I'd like to help people like parents and sisters, brothers and relatives, friends and dogs. I'd like to care for them in a certain way, like nursing! I'd especially like to help young children so that they will live to see the wonderful world that God made, just like he made us, though the world was made long before we existed. I'd be like Clara Barton, only in a hospital and not on a battle field. Many people feel that they would get sick if they went to work with sick, dying people, but, I feel that I would rather die myself than see other people suffering or dying.*

*—Jessie Concannon, grade seven*

## JESSIE CONCANNON

**S**O JESSIE CONCANNON knew at the age of twelve that nursing was her destined career. Perhaps her immature decisiveness had its roots in the comfort and stability offered by her family, as if the predictability of family life afforded her the psychological security to predict her own future. The elder Concannons parented a jolly band of nine children and occupied a big red colonial house in the suburbs of a small New England city in which both parents had been raised. Dad owned a mechanical contracting business and Mom stayed home to raise the kids. She would have chosen nursing as her own career had marriage and children not interfered. They were as close-knit and traditional as an American family can get. Hardworking, hard-playing, trouble-free, and Irish Catholic to the core. With a hint of pride, Mrs. Concannon described them as a normal family, and Jessie as a normal child.

From the time she was ten years old until she went to college, Jessie shared the junior-mom role with her next-youngest sister, Claire. "She was the softhearted one and Claire was the disciplinarian. They made a great team. Jessie seemed to enjoy caring for her younger siblings," her mother recalls. "It made perfect sense that she'd become a nurse. She told us so in junior high, and we knew she meant it. It fit her personality. She liked people and liked to be helpful. She never had any problem getting along with people."

The Concannons saw to it that all of their children received a Catholic education for at least a portion of their school years. Mr. and Mrs. Concannon are not in total agreement in recalling Jessie's overall performance in school. Her father saw her as a good student but not spectacular in any area, with the possible exception of mathematics. Mrs. Concannon feels that Jessie was better than average—a solid B student. Jessie's parochial education began in high school, at the same school her mother had attended. When it was time for her to go to college for nursing, her mother felt strongly that it, too, should be at a Catholic institution.

> I wanted her to have the values that I have as far as nursing goes. If we had sent her to a nonparochial nursing college, she might have gotten into the abortion thing. I don't know how she feels about abortion now, but I don't think she'd work in a place that gives them. We worked hard to steer her toward certain values, and although she may be slightly more liberal than we are, for the most part she seems to have accepted our values.

According to Jessie and Claire, accepting family values meant drawing a clear line between that which was private family business and that which was public family business. "The bad news—the fights or arguments stayed in. Only the good news went out," explains Claire. "I was a lot more rebellious than Jessie. Our father had a temper and was very strict. I'd go out and get in trouble and get punished for it. Jessie would go out and do whatever she wanted, but then she'd come home and confess it all to Mom and Dad. She never got in trouble.'' In fact, Jessie enjoyed enough favor with her father to earn the nickname ''Her Royal Highness, Princess Jessie.''

From all accounts, then, the only significant incidents that would qualify as bad news in the Concannon family were Mr. Concannon's occasional outbursts of temper. Sometimes he appeared to be intolerant of behavior or life-styles that were distinctly different from his own. ''Jessie was rarely on the receiving end of his anger,'' says Claire, ''but to this day she hates to be yelled at.''

Nursing was the most ''acceptable'' career choice a Concannon daughter could make. It was an affirmation of family values almost as rock solid as motherhood and as enduring as marriage, and there was no reason then to believe that Jessie would not embrace the entire package.

True to her preadolescent word, Jessie Concannon did become a nurse. This ''normal'' daughter from the ''normal'' family, the child who never made waves, was to become an extraordinary nurse—a natural leader, a fighter, a boat rocker, and, in the words of a senior oncologist colleague, ''the most knowledgeable oncology nurse I've ever met.''

## DOMINIQUE RAZA

Dominique Raza set foot on American soil for the first time when she was six years old, but the ground beneath her was nowhere near as firm as it had been for Jessie. There was no clear consensus about family values, and the values that did exist—such as her father's stringent Muslim attitudes—were the source of so much noisy friction that domestic privacy was impossible to maintain.

Before her marriage, Dominique's mother had found her way to London from a convent school in rural Ireland in search of work and her father had emigrated from his native Pakistan in the hope of pursuing an education in engineering, in accordance with his father's wishes. But he did not complete his studies. He met his future wife in a London movie theater, where she worked part time and he was the evening manager. It was a lopsided three-year courtship— Omar Raza in hot pursuit of the young, naive, and reluctant Mary O'Malley. "Finally he just chased me down," says Mary, betraying through the inflections in her Irish brogue a disbelief that must have been lingering for all of these twenty-five years, that she actually had relented to such a suitor. "After all, we had nothing in common really—neither religion nor culture. He believed that women should be totally submissive to men, just as they were in Pakistan."

The couple married without fanfare or family blessing. By the time Mary was twenty-four, she had two daughters, Dominique and her younger sister Sabrina, all of the accompanying child-care burdens, a demanding husband, and a full-time job. Except for the joys her children brought her, Mary's was an unfulfilling married life, and the eventual emigration to the land of opportunity did little to improve it. Some measure of solace was derived from the fact that Mary had three sisters who had preceded her to America, and it was with one of them that the Razas stayed until they could establish their own household.

Omar Raza, like many an immigrant before him, came to America with a dream—to open a restaurant. But once again, hope did not materialize into reality. Mary's life of toil and trouble continued, to be interrupted only by the joy surrounding the birth of the couple's only son, Sharif. Omar brought his old-world and Muslim values with him to the new land, and the more he found them out of step with the prevailing culture, the harder he pushed them. They were supplemented by strict parenting (especially of his two daughters) and a fondness for alcohol.

"You were physically abusive to Sabrina, me, and Mom," Dominique reminds her father one afternoon.

"No, I only remember hitting you once, and I'd call that discipline. I was strict. I was a good father but not a good husband to your mother. I drank too much, but I wouldn't say I was sick or an alcoholic like you say. I was domineering. I just liked to drink. I was never abusive to you, Dominique."

"You can't remember what you were like when you were drunk," she replies.

The standoff between father and daughter is characteristic of their relationship. When Dominique turned eleven years old, she started to defy her father openly. She pursued an active social life and did as much as she could to escape her father's overprotective clutches. Finally, during Dominique's freshman year in high school, Mary, with the support of her sisters, mustered the courage to leave Omar for good. After their separation, Omar continued to pursue Mary, but by then she had gained enough confidence to stick to her guns and follow through with a divorce.

So childhood was a chaotic time for Dominique. The mercurial atmosphere within her family coupled with their acclimation to a new country took their toll on her. "For the first few years here, she had this habit of rocking herself to sleep at night," remembers her mother. Fortunately, she was a bright and friendly child by nature, so once she finally settled in to her new surroundings, she did well in school and made friends easily. With every passing year, though, her friendships served as a replacement for her family.

"She was always out," says her friend Pam at one of the regular evening gatherings of Dominique's old gang. "Her mother cared about her, but she had enough of her own troubles coping with her husband to really see how Dominique was being affected. So *we* were her family. We all had very different personalities and different backgrounds, but we had in common the fact that we all had divorces or other burdens we were carrying. We talked a lot about our problems.''

Another friend, Cleo, pipes in, ''Dominique's bedroom was the metaphor for her life. It was always chaotically messy. It gave a clue. She kind of walked right through it, and didn't notice it. That's the way she handled the confusion in her life. She was always helping other people with their problems, but she couldn't sort out her own. Her mind was, and still is, in a perpetual whirlwind.''

The momentum of the conversation among her friends gathered intensity as they recalled what Dominique was like during high school.

''She was a mess her first year,'' says Liza, punctuating the air with a cigarette. ''She'd miss classes, get in trouble, and get called down to the housemaster's office. She was always worried that she'd hurt someone's feelings or had said the wrong thing to somebody. It didn't matter who it was. Then she'd call all of us and get five or six different opinions about her behavior.''

It became a family joke, too. Her mother often would say to her, ''Dominique, I'd swear you were born with a phone attached to your ear.''

''And you know what,'' adds Virginia, Dominique's ''artsy'' friend, ''she's still calling us. Doesn't she call you every time she and Mark have a lovers' quarrel? To anybody else, the things she calls us about would be nothing, but to her, everything is a big deal. She analyzes everything.''

''Yeh,'' her friends chime in unison.

Dominique became serious about school toward the end of her sophomore year in high school. By then she had a steady boyfriend, Jason, who had become the mainstay of her adolescence, her safe harbor. It wasn't until the end of her senior year that she confided to her friends that she was going into nursing. When the announcement came, it didn't surprise any of them. They remembered how she had dropped everything to help them whenever they'd had a problem. She was always there, even if she'd only had two hours sleep the night before. She'd run herself ragged to be helpful. She couldn't say no. Of course she'd become a nurse.

Her mother was pleased with Dominique's decision, although there were no financial resources to support it. Dominique would have to borrow heavily to put herself through school, but at least her mother could be assured that in the end, her daughter would have a stable career and a guaranteed income. Like Jessie's mother, Mary Raza also had wanted to be a nurse, but family problems and lack of money had prevented it. "I think it was her father who influenced Dominique to make an early career decision," says Mary. "He was always pushing her to figure out what she wanted to do. I just wanted her to be able to earn a decent living."

Actually, Dominique's father had grander notions for his daughter. "She was so smart," he said. "I thought she should become a doctor. Of course, I'm proud of her now, but if she decides to continue her education, I hope that she'll choose to become a doctor."

For the year and a half that Dominique has been a staff nurse, she's "run herself ragged to be helpful" to her patients. Says Dominique,

When I started out, I was so idealistic. I thought that I was really going to make a difference in the quality of my patients' lives. I still believe that I can make a difference, but I'm not as idealistic now as I was then. I have so many very sick patients to take care of, and very often we're so short-staffed that I don't have time to get to know the patients as well as I want to. I'm too busy, and I have less stamina now. When I'm being brutally honest with myself, I feel that my job makes it difficult for me to be the kind of nurse I want to be. I'm pretty sure I'll go back for more nursing education, but I don't know where I'll wind up. There are so many choices. I get confused.

It could be said, then, that Dominique is a nurse on a journey, still growing and emerging, finding her way to a landing in a professional territory that is expanding in new directions every day. For the little Irish-Pakistani-American kid from London, it's second nature to be heading toward an unknown destination.


## GINA ROSSI

Gina Rossi wanted to become a doctor. For most of her childhood, the winds seemed to be blowing in her favor. She was the shining star, the embodiment of her family's dreams, the one who would make a mark on the world. Had she come from more privileged circumstances, her childish achievements might not have been so embellished with parental pride and expectation, but she was the oldest daughter of working-class parents, a Lebanese-American mother and an Italian-American father.

Carla DiTullio, Gina's mother, looks as motherly as she sounds. "I was an old-fashioned girl. I didn't know much about pregnancy and delivery, and Gina came rushing into this world. She came out almost at the same time that my water bag burst. I told the nurse I'd wet my bed. That's how much I knew about what was happening to me, but the next minute there was Gina, easy as one, two, three. What a beautiful, delightful child she was."

At the time that Gina was born, Carla and her husband Anthony lived on the outskirts of the city in a two-family house owned by one of Carla's sisters. The sister lived upstairs with her husband, and Carla, Anthony, Carla's mother, and Gina lived downstairs. Gradually the downstairs occupants multiplied to include Gina's two younger sisters, Catherine and Marie, and another of Carla's sisters. It was a jumble of generations all under one roof, and for Anthony, especially, it must have seemed that marriage was a two- rather than one-family matter. He supported his nuclear family first as, at various times, a roofer, a tow-motor operator, and a wallpapering and painting contractor. For all of his travails, he never was rewarded with the fulfillment of that most American of dreams—home ownership. Later, as adults, his two oldest daughters would express compassion for this disappointment in his life. As a husband and father, however, he was less than ideal, alternating his behavior and occasionally his women like so many changes of clothes.

But home felt like home to Carla, with or without her husband, and she remained there to care for Gina and her own elderly mother until her death and then for Gina, Catherine, and Marie until they married. Carla still resides there with her sister.

The child who "came rushing into this world" has been in perpetual motion ever since. "Gina never had anything less than an A in school," boasts her mother. "She went to the local public schools, and when it came time for high school she was asked to apply to the city's most competitive exam school, but I felt that she'd be better off in the local high school. At the exam school she would have been one of many bright students, but at the neighborhood school she would stand out." And stand out she did. From freshman through senior year, she was a straight-A student. She excelled in all subjects, but in science she was exceptional. She won first prize in two science fairs, one of which was a statewide competition. At graduation, she ranked sixth in a class of 440. No doubt about it, Gina was headed for a career in medicine.

Like many a seventeen year old, Gina had arrived at one of life's crucial crossroads without benefit of parental privilege or guidance, and immediate needs in the minds of most teenagers are apt to take precedence over long-range considerations. Left to her own devices, Gina decided to reject the almost full scholarship offered her by a prestigious private university for entrance into its six-year medical program. She told herself that at the better school, she'd be only one of the talented throng. She wouldn't stand out. To

go there would mean, also, that she would have to supple-
ment her scholarship with four hundred dollars annually of
her own or her family's scarce resources. She chose instead
to enroll in the least expensive, alternative premed program
at the local branch of the state university.

Probably there was another, less conscious force conspir-
ing in this decision. She was in love. Gina and Carl's romance had begun in high school and continued into college.
His family had all the money, position, and power that her
family lacked. Gina was impressed, and she felt proud to
be the object of such high-placed affection. Looking back,
Gina recalls this time in her life as the first harbinger of a
self-esteem problem that she hadn't known existed. Carl
was a student at another, better-known university in the city,
and the Vietnam War loomed on the horizon. Gina and Carl
married and started a family earlier than they originally had
planned. Carl was spared service in the war. By the middle
of her sophomore year, Gina was a college dropout, and the
medical profession had lost one star that might have shone.

"It was a terrible time in our family," explains Gina's
sister Catherine, the pain still etched in her voice.

> I was sixteen then and Gina was nineteen. We hadn't
> gotten along all through school anyway, because our
> parents had always compared me unfavorably to her
> and so did the teachers we both had. Gina was the
> perfect one, the goody-two-shoes, the compliant one,
> and I was the brat. Believe me, I did all that I could
> to live up to my reputation. Even though we fought
> our way through the school years, underneath it all
> we loved each other, but when she married so young,
> she made my life a living hell. She had burst the
> family's bubble in one fell swoop. Our father became
> a total maniac then, punching walls and drinking. Our
> mother was more despondent than ever, and I had to
> listen to both parents refer to Gina in the most de-
> meaning language. "Don't you be like her," they'd

repeat over and over again. "She ruined us, now don't you do that, too," they'd say. She didn't have to listen to any of this, and the guilt trip that was laid on me took several years of therapy to overcome. Gina and I didn't get close until after we both were married. Even now, at the age of thirty-eight, I can still feel the anger.

Gina and Carl settled down in an apartment near her family and awaited the birth of their baby. What should have been a celebration became a near tragedy. It began with two attacks of phlebitis in Gina's legs in the latter stages of her pregnancy and culminated in her near death after the delivery of her daughter Kendra. Her mother fights back the tears as she recounts the experience.

She was in a lot of pain and having trouble breathing in the hours after the delivery. Luckily, the surgeon who had taken care of her during the phlebitis episodes was in the hospital. The nurses paged him. He rushed in, took one look at Gina, and told me that he'd have to operate on her that night, as soon as he could get into the operating room. He said that she was critically ill, but God must have been on our side. At midnight, he performed a vena cava plication and Gina was saved. I think that this experience really strengthened her resolve to enter the health care field. She remembered everything that had been done for her.

Whatever foresight her mother had then, Gina's future was far less clear to Gina. She was a wife and a mother, and she certainly didn't intend—nor could she afford—the luxury of staying home, so she took a real estate course and began selling houses. "It didn't last long," says Gina. "I didn't like it. So many of my colleagues seemed like unscrupulous people. I wasn't comfortable in real estate." At about the same time that she was on her way out of the real estate business, her marriage was beginning to go sour. Several more years of enduring an unhappy marriage passed before Gina could reassemble the pieces of her life.

In the organized and orderly fashion that is a hallmark of her character, Gina approached her personal rebuilding process in step-by-step fashion. First she went to a career counselor and relearned what she had known all along: she was best suited for a health care career. For a time, she wavered between returning to a premed program or entering nursing. She talked to many nurses and decided that nursing was the field for her. She entered a two-year associate's degree program, worked for a short time as a nurse, and then returned to get a bachelor's degree in nursing.

In the meantime, her faltering marriage had led her to seek psychotherapy, and that decision as much as any other before (or since) had a profound effect on her life. With nursing she had acquired the financial wherewithal to support herself and her young daughter, and with psychotherapy she regained her self-esteem. The combination enabled her to begin a new life, one that was free of an incompatible marriage.

She was at it again, off and running, rushing out into the world in much the same way she had departed the womb. And it would not be long before she would make her mark on nursing. Today Gina Rossi's curriculum vitae is eleven pages long and growing. "Hell, her CV is longer than mine," confesses her admiring colleague Dr. Clifford Siegel, an associate professor of surgery at the hospital's affiliated medical school. But it is her youngest sister, Marie, who summarizes it best.

A year or so ago, I went with Gina to this huge professional conference where she was going to speak, and all of a sudden I was the little sister again, and there was my big sister up there at the podium all by herself in front of hundreds of people. She wasn't even nervous. She spoke so well. I was in shock. Oh

my God, I said to myself, that's my big sister up there.
I felt so proud.

Jessie, Dominique, and Gina all work in the same hospital,
but the institution that employs them is large enough, and
their jobs different enough, to preclude much interaction
between them other than a passing greeting. Jessie and Dominique are both oncology nurses, but they work on different units. Jessie and Gina are older and higher on the
professional ladder than Dominique, but their paths rarely
cross. So if the three of them have a common connection,
it is their mutual interest in the psychosocial side of nursing.
They all began their careers with the desire to help suffering
people, but it was only when they became practicing nurses
that that desire took any shape, substance, or direction. By
now Jessie and Gina have had years of experience to refine
their definitions of "help."

For Jessie, helping means acquiring expert knowledge in
the field of psychology. It means learning as much as possible about improving the quality of life for cancer patients
so that she can do more to ease their pain, learning all that
there is to know about symptom control, and learning to
teach professionals and families how to help patients live
better and die better.

Gina has similar ideas about the critical care patients
she sees—the heart, lung, kidney, and trauma patients.
She, too, believes that patients and their families need to
be educated, informed, and psychologically bolstered to
prepare them for the impact of a critical illness and the
changes it will bring to all of their lives. Gina is confident
that she has the experience and people skills to be an effective teacher. Jessie and Gina spend many hours of their
working days conveying their ideas and beliefs to junior
staff.

Were she a colleague of either Jessie's or Gina's, Dominique would be an appreciative student of the gospel according to both of them.

I love the part of nursing that involves getting to know
the patients, finding out all about them, their families,
their values and beliefs, and then teaching the families
how to care for them at home. My biggest disappointment in working with cancer patients is that they're
often so sick and needy that I don't have time to get
to know them well, and so many of them die before
I even get the chance. I think I might feel more helpful
as an obstetrical-gynecological nurse practitioner as-
sisting young women with sexuality issues, or as a
psychiatric nurse dealing directly with people's emotional problems.

They drive to work, each of these nurses, from the western
suburbs of the city. Gina has the longest commute, from the
home she shares with her husband of ten years, Terry, and
his son Jeff. It's an immaculately maintained, fifteen-room,
raised ranch set on five acres of land, but Gina does not
return to it until about thirteen hours after she's departed. It
is not out of character for her to prepare the evening meal,
or parts of it, before she leaves. By 7:00 A.M., she's in her
office and donning a white coat in preparation for another
twelve-hour day. There is no guarantee, however, that when
Gina returns home, she will be able to rest, for her house is
a stopover for many an out-of-town friend or colleague or
an assortment of local friends and family members whom
she routinely entertains. "I don't understand how you do it
all, Gina," is a refrain she hears repeatedly from everyone
who knows her. She doesn't understand either, but her standard, hackneyed reply is, "I'm just well organized."

Jessie arrives at the hospital at the same time Gina does
at her office two floors above. She rises at 5:30 A.M. in her
bedroom of the big white Victorian colonial that houses
her, her sister Claire, her brother-in-law Dan, and Dan's
daughter Rebecca. She walks the household's two dogs with
her brother-in-law while Claire and Rebecca sleep. That's

about all that Jessie does by way of domestic activity. "Claire and I pay Dan fifty dollars a week to clean the house. We weren't satisfied with the cleaning people we hired, so we hired him. I pay rent to Claire and Dan. It works out well for me. I don't have time for any household maintenance stuff. Dan does all the cooking, and about all I do is my laundry." There is never enough time for Jessie to do all that she wants to do at home, but she's rarely late for work. Her typical day is as long as Gina's, and often after work she stops at a bar or restaurant to meet her friends. Claire and Dan say that sometimes they don't see her for several days.

If Dominique is working the day shift, 7:00 A.M. to 3:00 P.M., she stops at her locker and is on her unit at the opposite end of the floor from Jessie's unit at the same time that Jessie and Gina arrive. She tries to get there on time, and usually does, but some mornings, she just can't make it right on the button. Her mother and younger brother are still asleep as she prepares to leave for work, and often she finds herself weeding through the piles of clothing scattered around her room. Sometimes she finds at least one of the garments needed to complete her attire in some other room of the family's rented bungalow. It's never easy for Dominique to put a finger on what she wants to wear, and when she finally does, she has to iron it. Fortunately, she has the shortest distance to get to work. She gets there in her nifty red sports car, which is littered with Nicoret wrappers— testimony to her having stayed off cigarettes for several months. Dominique is on her feet most of the day and rarely leaves the hospital at the official ending of the shift. At departure time, she drags her body out of the hospital, heading either for home or for her boyfriend Mark's city apartment. Whatever her destination, she relaxes there just long enough to muster a second wind for an evening out on the town. A few hours' sleep tides her over for the next day's shift.

## MEMORIAL HOSPITAL

The main building of Memorial Hospital, the Pavillion Building, could be mistaken for a high-priced hotel. The imposing two-story glass facade and the comfortable couches and plants in the spacious lobby just inside its entrance appear as invitations to relaxation—a kind of seductive come-on. As Ben Callahan, Memorial's colorful publications director, says, "Why do you think that that new Pavillion Building looks like a goddamned hotel? It's to attract patients, that's why." A minute in one of those couches, though, in full view of the never-ending white-coated pedestrian traffic on the second-story bridge, will suffice to remind visitors that they are not on vacation.

Memorial Hospital is one of the smallest teaching hospitals in a city where there are many similar, but larger, institutions all competing for a share of the patient pool. The hospital has 368 beds and 2,100 people on its payroll. One-third of these employees are accountable to the Nursing Department, making it the largest departmental entity in the hospital. To understand just how important nursing is to the overall operation of the hospital, one need only take a walk through Memorial's labyrinthian administrative corridors. Nursing's administrators, assistants, and educators occupy more office space than any other department, and when the top brass move out collectively from the privacy of their offices, they project an aura of executive power. Gone are the white caps and uniforms of yesteryear. As physician Sandra Wilder once remarked in jest, "Now we have what you might call a cadre of Gucci nurses." Indeed, Memorial's nursing administrators, from the vice president at the top to the several nursing directors on the next level, clad in business suits are symbols of the changes that have taken place in the profession. Providing quality nursing care for patients is still their mission, but economics and management are fast becoming the staples that sustain them in their work. Their jobs are tough. Their days are long. They walk a thin line between advocating for the needs of nurses and patients and responding to the fiscal constraints imposed by the spiraling cost of health care. No one would deny, however, that they are a vastly more sophisticated and powerful force in hospital administration today than they were even a decade ago. Many of the financial rewards and professional gains that nurses have accrued in recent years are attributable to nursing leaders like those at Memorial, who have been persistent and effective advocates for their staffs (even though some staff people may not regard all of the changes as gains).

## THE TOP BRASS

Dr. George Tirrell, like many a CEO, can sit at his desk and look out at a panorama of high-rise buildings, the centers of power in his city, but if he stands at his window and looks down, he can see the benchmarks of powerlessness, a decaying inner city—a sprawling, dilapidated housing project in one direction, an empty, littered lot in another. Some of the people from the power centers and from the housing project have found or will find their way to Memorial Hospital, and with each constituency (but especially with the latter), complex financial and service delivery problems will accompany them through the door. Among those problems are the amount of nursing hours that these patients need and can receive. As the ringmaster of a recurrent circus act, Tirrell directs the consumers and health care providers standing in the center ring, waiting to receive whatever replenishments he can offer, while private and public insurers perform their stunts in the adjacent rings in competition for attention. His is a precarious position, and in some unexplainable way this seems to be reflected in his personality. He is a pleasing exception to the "top-suite" stereotype. A soft-spoken, philosophical, confident, clear, and often humble voice emerges from his tall frame. The vice president of nursing reports to him instead of to the chief operating officer in the hospital because, in Tirrell's words,

> Nursing is just too important to have it any other way.
> It's not just their numbers, but it's what they do. The
> main thing that happens to people in a hospital is being
> nursed. Physicians bring in the patients, but the people
> who take care of them day-to-day, minute-to-minute,
> are nurses. Physicians come to work here because the
> nursing care that their patients will receive is im-
> portant to them. I'm proud of nursing here. I think
> we're perceived very positively by nurses. Our va-
> cancy rate is very low. Maybe we're even number two
> in the city. They've got that Alice Cochran over there
> at the number-one place, a good PR department, and
> a lot more money than we have. They're the best-
> managed hospital in the city, no question about it.

"That Alice Cochran" about whom Dr. Tirrell speaks is a well-known administrator at the "Number One" hospital. Her face and manner radiate kindness, enthusiasm, intelligence, and a notable absence of self-advertisement. What makes her nursing department so exceptional? Her answer:

> We emphasize repeatedly that the care of the patient is
> our most important task. Everything else is secondary.
> Our nurses know how vital they are. They are full-
> fledged members of the health care team. Almost all
> of them have at least a bachelor's degree. In the old
> days, nurses were so frustrated, undervalued, and
> overworked that they weren't nice to each other. One
> of our big operating principles here is, *Thou shalt
> take care of your fellow nurse*. We're a value-driven
> organization. We're not a rich system. We have all
> the financial constraints that every other institution
> has. Our nursing salaries are in the middle range com-

pared to the other hospitals in the city, but we pay salaries instead of hourly rates because we feel that that professionalizes our staff. When I get together with the nurse managers here, we don't talk budgets and money. They have other forums for that. I talk with them on a regular basis about beliefs and values, and sometimes that means shaking off longstanding, traditional practices like fixed visiting hours for families. Instead of telling nurses that they're wrong to want to regulate visiting hours, I ask them what they believe in. The more we talk about it, the more we realize that we believe that whenever we're talking about a patient, we're talking about a family or a network as well. Then we recognize that we can't isolate our patients to suit our own convenience. You can see by this example, then, that all of our discussions come back to our mission: giving the best possible care to the patient.

"Here at Memorial," states Jean Pirelli, the acting vice president of nursing,

our nurses are valuable members of the health care team. Without them, we could not accomplish the primary goal of the department: quality care for our patients. Their commitment and flexibility help us accomplish our goal within a health care system strained by diminishing dollars.

A nursing labor organization represents our staff nurses. They believe that their members should be well paid, and that patients should receive high-quality nursing care. As an administrator, I also share these convictions but my position requires me to balance available resources against institutional goals. Wearing both hats is hard. Frequently, nursing administrators like me have value conflicts with labor unions about wages, merit pay, and career advancement. A lot of my time is spent negotiating, formally and informally, with staff and union representatives to enable the implementation of mutually acceptable programs.

The patient care technician (PCT) program here was instituted three years ago. We decided to embark on it in anticipation of a nursing shortage that never did materialize in our region of the country as it did almost everywhere else. It was our feeling that each PCT would act as a nursing extender for an RN partner. We felt that we were ensuring the continuation of quality patient care. We assumed that our nurses would support the program because it would free them from some of the unpopular, menial tasks that they had traditionally performed. Some nurses did welcome PCTs, but others were resistant. In hindsight, perhaps we made a mistake by thrusting the program on our staff without adequate preparation and processing. At any rate, the union contested our hiring of PCTs on the premises that they would increase the liability of nurses and threaten nursing jobs. Despite some remaining pockets of resistance among our staff, the PCT program has been successful. Even without a nursing shortage now, the use of PCTs has helped us deliver patient care in the face of mounting financial constraints. I doubt if we have seen the end of the shortage, so in the long run I think our decision will prove to be farsighted. Currently, 80 percent of our staff are RNs, but we will need further research and evaluation to determine the optimal mix of RNs and PCTs.

Jean Pirelli will not have to make this future critical decision. It will be the responsibility of the new, permanent vice president of nursing.

# IN PERPETUAL MOTION

There's a palpable buzz in the air around the Nursing Department at Memorial. Phones ring continuously, computer screens glow with facts and figures, women (and a handful of men) rush with folders in hand to meetings, doors open and close. Nurses, regardless of their position on the ladder, so it seems, are temperamentally ill-suited to sedentary behavior. So there's a hum in the air, too. It's the sound of clicking heels and moving feet. "We were always taught," says a seasoned night nurse, "that a sitting nurse was not a working nurse." Clearly it was a lesson that was never lost.

The motion is contagious. It spreads like a virus to the floors above and below and becomes more apparent the closer it comes to the bedside. On the units there is an unceasing whirlwind of activity. The nursing stations are the hub of it, the depots for the incoming and outgoing human traffic. Doctors, nurses, dieticians, pharmacists, physical therapists, and social workers all play musical chairs, taking turns to sit and read and write in patients' records, to use the phones, or to talk with one another. If there is a stationary person at all, it is the unit secretary, who keeps track of and directs the traffic. Transport personnel gather at the stations with stretchers or wheelchairs to move patients to other parts of the hospital or to waiting ambulances or to automobiles. Medical supply salespeople come there to peddle their wares. Families and friends stop there for information about their hospitalized loved ones. The senior doctors rally their trainees there—clinical fellows, residents, interns, medical students—to begin the daily teaching rounds.

Nursing stations could just as accurately be compared to homes in which nurses and their clerical helpers, the permanent "residents," play host to countless visitors passing through on their way to somewhere else. For it is the nurses and their extenders and assistants who are the most visible and mobile. They move constantly from the station to the bedside, back and forth, to secure medications from the locked "med room," to deliver vials of blood to be sent by tube to the lab, to fill out a myriad of forms and requisition slips, to secure supplies for patients, and to telephone for assistance from other hospital services.

Nursing is the heartbeat of the hospital. Without nurses, the hospital cannot run. If doctors do the curing, then nurses do the caring, and caring is the primary service that is rendered "day-to-day," "minute-to-minute." Patients come to hospitals to be nursed. So it is the nurses who are the primary conductors and the coordinators of care.

# CANCER UNIT I

## JESSIE CONCANNON, NURSE MANAGER, 5C

**T**HE INPATIENT FLOORS at Memorial branch out from the Pavillion Building, each unit on every floor being like a limb on a branch stemming from the main trunk.

Surgical oncology is a twenty-four-bed unit on the western limb of the fifth floor. It, along with its counterparts on the floors above and below, is painted in a pleasant emerald green—a considerably more appealing hue than the "hospital green" that was standard fare before hospitals began resembling hotels. Visitors to the unit, whether on foot, in a wheelchair, or on a stretcher, follow a contrasting emerald and gray carpet to the nursing station, there to be greeted by the usual clatter and commotion. On 5C, Lucille, the dry-witted daytime unit secretary whom Jessie refers to as "my boss" is the official greeter. A stocky black woman in her late thirties or so, Lucille is beloved by all of the nurses. In the course of a day, she experiences a full range of emotions, but her facial expression rarely changes to match her mood. She greets visitors, answers the telephones, and directs traffic all at the same time.

"Is Mr. Woodson leaving today?" she shouts into the air. Marcy, Mr. Woodson's primary nurse, bellows out a yes from behind Lucille. "OK, can we get twenty-one ready

for Mrs. Carvallo? She's coming back to us today." Glenda,
5C's loyal housekeeper, obediently scurries to 21.

"Now, listen, Bernice," Lucille says into the telephone
receiver in her best "I mean business" voice. "I called you
people an hour ago to take Mr. Wolff to X ray. You said
you'd be right up. What's the matter with you transport
people? I want you up here, *now*." While half listening to
Bernice's reply, she directs a lab technician to a patient's
room. All day long, within a fifty-foot radius of the station,
Lucille can be heard directing traffic.

While Lucille's voice provides the background music for
5C, Jessie's dynamic energy sets its rhythm. Jessie is the
unit's nurse manager. Five C is her kingdom, and "Her
Royal Highness" prefers to reign over it from a standing
position. She makes her presence felt by being lively and
high-spirited rather than autocratic. Her pretty face and her
tall, slim figure adorned typically in a bright-colored
sweater, white skirt, white stockings, and white sneakers
combine with her manner to draw attention.

As if to insure her visibility, there is the pièce de résis-
tance—her long and lustrous red hair, usually gathered in a
ponytail, occasionally in a French braid, bobbing from side
to side in synchrony with her body motion and the clanging
of the keys pinned to her sweater. Her motions are darting,
with a stop-and-go tempo, but the stops are short and the
gos are frequent. "I've got too much to do to just sit in my
office," she always says, even though many of the tasks
confronting her require her to do just that. In fact, the part
of her job that she likes the least is the sitting part ("I don't
like working on the budget and attending long meetings").
She doesn't take time out for lunch, either, because that,
too, involves sitting.

Any lay observer who happened upon 5C might be surprised at the cheerfulness of the atmosphere. It is, after all,
a cancer unit, and cancer is a disease that gnaws at the
bodies of its victims. But as Jessie frequently reiterates,
"Cancer and death are not synonymous. Everyone who has

it doesn't die from it.'' On 5C, the whole spectrum of cancer patients is present—those who are near death and are hospitalized for palliative treatment, those who are being treated to slow the progression of the disease, and those who are being treated for curable outcomes. The treatment modality may be chemotherapy, radiation, immunotherapy, surgery, or, most likely, a combination of these.

The majority of the patients on the unit who are close to death do not die there, they die in their homes or in hospices. Jessie has long recognized, however, that some discharged patients who are close to death prefer to die in the hospital. Thus, it is her practice to inform these patients and their families that the option to return to the hospital in this final stage is always open to them. Nevertheless, the fact that most of the terminally ill patients die outside the hospital has a great deal to do with hospital constraints on length of stay. Increasingly, hospital practices are dictated by private insurance and Medicare regulations that push patients out of hospitals faster by establishing strict reimbursement guidelines for inpatient services. The whole thrust is to shorten the length of stay as much as possible for every patient.

At the same time, expensive, advanced technology is being introduced that lengthens life and helps to expand the naturally rising elderly population. By the time many patients reach a teaching hospital like Memorial, they are apt to be among the oldest and the sickest in the general population. Doctors are thus placed in the position of discharging very sick patients much sooner than they would otherwise. Many patients on 5C go home attached to a panoply of elaborate equipment that will be monitored and operated by private or public home health agency nurses. Jessie, in her role as nurse manager, does not have the authority to discharge patients, but she frequently must prod reluctant physicians to do so. An overextended hospitalization has a negative impact on her operating budget, and she is well aware that there are patients waiting in the wings who need the vacated beds. In doing this, however, she must walk the thin line between supporting the needs of the patient and the fiscal needs of the hospital. If she thinks a patient should stay longer than the prescribed time, she will not hesitate to advocate for her position.

Still, despite the long shadow of death that hovers around 5C, it is a remarkably pleasant place. The staff, physicians and nurses alike, would say that it's Jessie's example that makes it that way. Dr. Hal Bloomfield, the recently appointed director of gynecological oncology at Memorial, is lavish in his praise: "She runs a well-oiled machine. The staff morale is so high that I often find myself looking forward to going up there, however disheartened I may be about some of my patients. Whenever I can, I send my patients to her floor, even if they don't always fit the exact criteria for admission there."

By the age of thirty-four, Jessie has learned a great deal about dying and living. She can accept death as part of the natural order and even can see it as "right" that one has a privilege to allow oneself a dignified finale to the drama of living. There are times, too, when she can see death as preferable to mere survival, when she wishes that physicians simply would let patients die rather than treat them too aggressively. But when death is not inevitable, she can be determined, too. Then she will use every weapon in her considerable arsenal of knowledge and creative imagination to render a sick patient as much comfort and enjoyment in the act of living as his or her illness will permit. She carries conviction like a grail, and so it passes from nurse to nurse, until they, too, have become believers. Even the skeptical Abby, the newest and one of the prettiest nurses on the unit, has come under Jessie's spell: "By the time I got out of nursing school, I was so disenchanted. My professors made me feel that a career in nursing was going to be an unrewarding experience. I came here with the idea that I'd work a year, save some money, and go do something else. Jessie turned that all around. She made me love nursing, and cancer nursing especially.''

There's an open door to the office that Jessie has so little time to sit in, located off the corridor behind the nursing station. True to her character, the space is so crammed with coffee mugs, books, filing cabinets, and pieces of paper that it invites sitting only as a last resort. The small scraps of paper adorning the walls around her desk form a decorative mural of handwritten maxims: RELEASE ME FROM CRAVING TO TRY TO STRAIGHTEN OUT EVERYBODY'S AFFAIRS; WHATEVER YOU CAN DO OR THINK YOU CAN DO, BEGIN IT; MAKE ME THOUGHTFUL, BUT NOT MOODY, HELPFUL BUT NOT BOSSY. . . .

These maxims are appropriate for one who is as dedicated a nurse manager as Jessie is, for one who is naturally inclined to overextend herself. Nothing, however, arouses the Irish wrath of Jessie Concannon more than being reminded of this facet of her personality. ''Don't you dare say that I give more than I receive,'' she admonishes anyone who attempts to contradict her own self-assessment. Those who don't have the courage to say the unmentionable directly to her don't hesitate to do so out of earshot. Putting aside her personal proclivities, there is no debating the fact that Jessie has a lot to do as nurse manager, far more responsibility than she would have had if Memorial Hospital, along with many others like it, had not adopted a corporate management model. In the old days, her title would have been ''Head Nurse'' and her duties would have been limited to organizing the patient care for the day—assigning nurses to patients, communicating with physicians, and accepting accountability for the nursing care on the unit. She even might have had a few patients to care for herself. Although as nurse manager, Jessie does not have direct patient care responsibility, she assists in it when necessary and otherwise assumes all of the other head nurse duties in addition to a long list of important administrative functions. In short, she is the overseer of the unit—the financial manager, the employer, the quality assurance controller, the policy implementer, the long- and short-range planner, the nursing role model for the nurses, and the staff evaluator and developer.


## HER FINGERS ON THE PULSE

Says Jessie,

> No day is ever the same for me, because the pulse of the unit changes daily. The first thing that I do when I come in every morning is to take that pulse. It dictates my priorities for the day. If the pulse is slow and there's not much activity, I'm likely to concentrate on paperwork, but that kind of day is the exception rather than the rule. There's always something important happening.

Lucille's voice from the nursing station is as good a pulse indicator as any. When Jessie can hear her directing traffic early in the morning, she knows that she can look forward to an arduous day.

One such day begins with the news that a patient fell on the floor by her bed during the previous night. Apparently, the patient forgot that she was supposed to ring for the nurse to be helped to the bathroom. Angela, the patient's primary nurse, presents Jessie with an incident report to sign. (These reports are filed whenever there is even a remote possibility of legal liability.) Jessie reads it over to make sure it's stated factually. It cannot read, for example, "Patient fell out of bed last night," because that suggests that someone might have been negligent. Satisfied that it is worded correctly—"Patient was found on the floor by her bed last night because she attempted to go to the toilet alone''—Jessie signs the report and reassures Angela that no nursing error has been made.

Meanwhile, Lucille is attempting to move the traffic, but she's having trouble on the phone with Clara in the Transport Department. Clara can't seem to understand that the people she sends up to move the patient with OXR (oxycillin resistant staph infection) have to wear masks and gloves. Twice already this morning Lucille has sent them back for the precautionary equipment, and by now she's exasperated. Jessie offers to help, but Lucille refuses the offer. Mary Lynn's patient also needs to be moved to the SICU (pronounced "sick you," it stands for Surgical Intensive Care Unit) with all of his medication and monitoring hookups, but there are already too many problems with transport this morning, so Jessie, Mary Lynn, and Mary Lynn's PCT partner, Jean, move the patient themselves. They place the stretcher next to his bed and a long plastic board underneath his body, and with one person pushing from one side and two people pulling from the other, the patient lands on the stretcher. Jessie tries to explain to him what is happening, but since he is attached to so many tubes, he's unable to speak. She explains anyway and asks him to move his head if he understands. He does. Off they go to the elevator.

When she returns to the floor, Jessie realizes that she's twenty minutes late for the meeting she's supposed to attend in the Materials Management Department. She will end up arriving thirty-five minutes late, because first she has to stop in to see Mrs. Cummings, a patient who spent several minutes with Jessie after she broke down uncontrollably at the time of her admission two days ago. Jessie hasn't seen her since and feels she must check in on her. She's delighted to find her on the telephone and in good spirits.

"The big cheese just walked in," says Mrs. Cummings into the telephone, "I haven't seen her for two days, so now's my chance. I'll talk to you later."

"If you didn't have your own primary nurse, I'd have been here a lot, Mrs. Cummings, but it gets too confusing to have so many people coming in and out." Before Mrs. Cummings can interrupt, Jessie adds, "I'm glad to see you looking so well, and I wanted you to know I hadn't forgotten you."

Mrs. Cummings thanks Jessie and assures her that she is pleased with her nursing care.

Jessie stops at her desk to take an aspirin for the mild headache she feels coming on and retrieves some money from her purse for the peanut butter crackers and Diet Coke that serve as her daily equivalent of lunch. On her way to the Materials Management Department, she walks quickly down several flights of stairs and climbs just as quickly up several more. Waiting for elevators is a waste of time.

By 2:00 P.M. Jessie has returned to her office. Angela comes to the door to ask about a certain medication that is being given to one of her patients. She wonders whether another one may be more effective. Jessie consults one of her reference books, agrees with Angela that a change is worth considering, and suggests that Angela call Susan in the pharmacy for a second opinion. In short order, Angela reappears at Jessie's door with Susan in tow. The threesome agree that Angela will call the physician for authorization to change the medication. Susan likes these consultations on 5C. "Jessie is so curious, creative, and resourceful that it's always a challenge to work with her. She really makes you think. It makes my job more interesting."

The day ends at 3:00 P.M., four hours earlier than usual. Abruptly Jessie departs for an appointment outside the hospital, but it makes her uncomfortable to leave. There's too much action today. On the way out, she announces that she may return if she has time.

Another hyperactive day starts on a light note and gathers momentum as it progresses. Jessie's friend Kristen, a surgical research nurse, peeks her head in the office door. It's rare for Jessie to talk about anything but business on the job, but this morning she tells Kristen about a one-bedroom condo for sale in her neighborhood.

"I need two bedrooms," says Kristen.

"Convert the dining room," suggests Jessie. "The price is right, and we'd have so much fun if you lived in the neighborhood."

"I'll think about it," promises Kristen.

The social banter is interrupted by Mary Lynn, described by Jessie as a "wonderful nurse who's not always the most tactful in her dealings with doctors." Frustration is written all over her face as she explains that she has several patients who are ready to leave, but their doctors won't discharge them, despite Mary Lynn's admonitions. Jessie recognizes this as a call for help and moves out to the nursing station to hold a mediation pow-wow with Mary Lynn and the residents on duty. She agrees with Mary Lynn that the patients should go, and she knows that today there are others awaiting beds. However, the nurses cannot discharge a patient without the consent of the "attending," the senior staff physician.

Mary Lynn pages the two physicians. Neither are in the hospital. Eventually one of them responds, but he refuses to discharge the patient. Finally, as a last resort, Jessie goes to her office and calls Memorial's chief of surgery.

"We've got a problem," she says, explaining the situation. He agrees to do what he can. Back to the station she goes to inform Mary Lynn that the problem is being addressed from on high.

In the meantime, she does what she can to make room on the unit. Lucille, in her usual, very audible voice of authority, tells Jessie, "Look, all you have to do is move Mr. French to room sixteen, and you've got two beds." With the help of four nurses, Toni, Angela, Jeanette, and Mary Lynn, she moves Mr. French from his semiprivate room to the full privacy of room 16, explaining the transfer to him as it's being accomplished. She summons Glenda to prepare Mr. French's old room for two new female admissions. This still leaves her three beds short, and the woman in admitting is none too pleased when Jessie calls to inform her that she

can take only the two women. By the end of the day, the
shuffling of the deck will have produced the required empty
beds.

In the time between the onset of the traffic problem and
its resolution, there have been other problems. There's a big
one still brewing, a leftover from the night before, and Jessie
now turns her attention to it while alternating bites of peanut
butter cracker with sips of Diet Coke. Mr. Carvallo was
scheduled for the operating room (OR) at 9:00 this morning
and had to have an electrocardiogram (EKG) done during
the night. Memorial's EKG technicians leave the hospital
at 4:00 P.M., so any EKG's done between then and 8:00
A.M. the next day are the responsibility of whoever has the
time (either a nurse or doctor). Last night the intern asked
the two night nurses to do it, but they said they were too
busy, so at 3:00 A.M. the intern woke up Mr. Carvallo to
do the EKG himself. Mr. Carvallo refused to oblige.

As many possibilities as there are for costly errors in
a hospital, none is worse than holding up the expensive
personnel and machinery that constitute a modern operating room. If the preoperative workups have not been
completed on schedule, thereby necessitating postpone-
ment of the operation, there are a lot of wasted dollars
on the line. As it turned out, at the eleventh hour, Mr.
Carvallo did get his EKG, but his cardiac status wasn't
stable enough to allow the operation. In a good-faith effort
to replace Mr. Carvallo on the operating table, Jessie
decides to send down a preoperative female patient, but
just as she's prepared to have her moved, she notices that
she's not yet on the proper preoperative medications. It's
no go. Five C and the OR are on a rocky course today.
Eventually the fallout from this episode centers around
the issue of teamwork and the nurses' claims that they
were too busy to perform the EKG. Jeff, the intern, had
felt that he was too busy, too. He was angry and reported
his sentiments to Jessie.

"I agree with you, Jeff, that whoever is available should

do the EKG,'' Jessie tells Jeff when she catches up with him in the afternoon, ''but I can't believe that any of the nurses would say that they were too busy just to get out of doing it. If they refused, I'm sure they felt they had more pressing priorities. I'm going to see what I can find out about it, but I will get back to you after I've had a chance to research it.'' True to her word, she attempts, then and there, to find out what happened but is unable to reach the nurses who were on duty at the time. It will have to wait until tomorrow. Mary Lynn will be the ''charge'' nurse on the evening shift, and Jessie knows that she can trust her to handle it. ''Just make sure that you reinforce the point that no one should use the 'too busy' explanation simply as an avoidance strategy. If you hear, as I expect you will, that they really were too busy to do the EKG, you can be supportive to them,'' she instructs Mary Lynn in the corridor. ''Oh, and by the way,'' she adds while moving toward her office, ''don't forget to review documentation [nursing notes in patient records] again. Make sure the evening and night people are doing it correctly.''

Wendy Fleming, another nurse manager, comes over from 5B, Dominique Raza's unit. She and Jessie are ten minutes late for the opening celebration of Memorial's new hospitality suite, an overnight accommodations area in the hospital for the families of out-of-town patients. Still thinking about the OR fiasco, Jessie talks as she walks. ''The trouble with working in a hospital is that everybody is so busy that blame becomes part of the daily dialogue. When you're overworked and things go wrong, the first thing you do is find someone to blame, and if you don't intervene soon enough to work things out, it escalates easily into a team crisis.''

On one occasion in early July, things do escalate into a team crisis. July 1 is the day in the United States when the medical guard changes in teaching hospitals. New interns and residents arrive to begin or wind up another year of their postgraduate medical training. Already Mary Lynn has become a thorn in the side of the Surgical Oncology Department because of her assertive advocacy on behalf of her primary patients. This crisis begins with a simple surgical procedure that an intern is performing on one of Mary Lynn's patients—the insertion of a chest tube. The intern has been at Memorial for only a few days and is still learning the ropes. Mary Lynn has told him prior to the procedure that if he has any problems, he can give her a yell. He does his procedure and leaves the used equipment on the bedside table. In a wrapped parcel on the table, he has left sharp objects that may be injurious to someone. Later Mary Lynn approaches him and says, ''Next time, don't leave that stuff in the patient's room. Put it in the dirty room.'' The insulted intern reports the incident to the director of surgical oncology, Dr. James Morley, but decides that he won't pursue the matter further with Mary Lynn. If he makes a big deal out of it, he reasons, she may take revenge by calling him all the time in the middle of the night when he's on duty. The matter does not rest there, however, because Dr. Morley asks other interns and residents about Mary Lynn, and many of them attest to her assertiveness.

Jim Morley has come to Memorial from a hospital in another section of the country, but he's been around long enough to have developed strong opinions about the different regional nursing practices.

Where I come from, nursing is not as strong as it is in this part of the country and certainly not as strong as it is at Memorial. They get their two cents in but there's more inequality. For a surgical procedure like inserting a chest tube, those nurses would have the equipment ready for you, would be standing by to hand you the tools, and would have cleaned up after you. Don't misunderstand me now, I think that the nursing care on 5C is very good, but their ideas about their job and my ideas about it are often antithetical.

We don't do these simple procedures very often, and I think that when we do them, our way is the right way. Some of those nurses on 5C, not just Mary Lynn, are ultra-assertive. They think of the patients as "theirs," not "ours," even though we're the people who bring them in. I'm glad that they're interested and concerned. It's entirely possible that they may see something I've overlooked, but there's a line there. A lot of these assertive nurses are doctor-wannabes. They ought to go to medical school if they're so smart.

He pauses to reflect and then continues in another vein.

They've got this thing here called primary nursing. They really believe in it. I never heard about it in my former position. I don't think it really works. I had this patient who I wanted admitted to my floor [5C] because I know the people there, and I know that Jessie maintains excellent staff morale. Lo and behold, just as I was about to admit the patient, Jessie comes to me and says there's a problem. My patient has been on 5B once before for chemotherapy, so she has a primary nurse there. Jessie informs me that she will have to go back there. Every time I went over there afterwards to talk to the primary nurse, she wasn't there. It was always her day off. Now, I'll be damned if I can see what's so great about primary nursing.

Jessie and I have a polite stand-off about my walk-ing rounds, too. She thinks it's a bad idea to have a bunch of doctors talking about patients outside their rooms. I tell her that that's the best way to teach—right by the bedside. After all, nurses have their spe-cial places, too. They don't want physicians in their glass bubble where they keep their coffee and donuts. The corridors are my turf, and from what I hear, it will stay that way, because there's a rumor circulating that Jessie wants to leave to go to graduate school in psychology. If it's true, I hope it's the right move for her. Maybe she ought to go to medical school instead.

So the intern's remarks about Mary Lynn find a sympathetic listener in Jim Morley, who brings the matter to Jean Pirelli's attention. The end result is a meeting between Jim, Jessie, and Colleen Lindstrom, the nurse director to whom Jessie reports. Jessie, in the meantime, has heard Mary Lynn's side of the story, and knowing her to be, if not the most diplomatic, certainly one of the most tireless and intelligent nurses on the unit, she finds little justification to fault her. According to Mary Lynn, she had offered the intern the assistance of her PCT partner, Jean. True, Mary Lynn probably could have spoken more politely to the intern, but in Jessie's mind, the infractions seem minor given the unceasing pressure on the unit and Mary Lynn's numerous patient responsibilities. Jessie sees no reason why Mary Lynn herself should stand by the intern's side during the procedure. It's not her job, except in the unlikely event that she has nothing else to do, and worse still, it smacks of the old-fashioned doctor's view of nurses as handmaidens, a perception that nurses have fought hard to overcome. Colleen, she's sure, will agree. Colleen and Jessie, each in her own way, is a clever and articulate spokesperson, but put them together and the resulting alchemy can disarm any opponent. By the conclusion of their three-way meeting, Dr. Morley has every reason to believe that the good old days will never return—never, at least, in the Nursing Department at Memorial Hospital.

There are days, though, that are not as high-pulse and highly charged as the ones described above, days when there are long slow periods. These usually come when the census on the unit is relatively low. Jessie makes good use of these quiet times, either for the ever-present paperwork tasks or for the planning and implementation of special projects on the unit.

One such project now in the works involves Abby in partnership with Jill, the stunning, youthful, and very popular unit social worker. Jessie has encouraged their interest in forming an ongoing weekly support group for patients on the unit. Today the three of them are available to meet with Betsy Langley from the Development Office. Jessie knows that a donor has given a small fund for oncology nursing and that Betsy's office controls and distributes these monies. Jessie, Abby, and Jill want financial help to provide "healthy snacks" for the group. According to Jessie's calculations, they'll need about a thousand dollars to pay Memorial's Food Service Department.

Like everything else that happens in a hospital involving the spending of money, this small-scale project is not a simple matter. Betsy, with the help of these nurses, will have to write a proposal justifying the need for the expenditure. She must, therefore, be informed about the project and its purpose.

Betsy listens as Abby explains, "We want this group to be a relaxing experience, but not just a social hour. It has an educational function but shouldn't be uptight. They will educate each other, and we'll be the facilitators. As health care professionals, we don't really know what they're feeling like and what they're going through. They need to be with other people like themselves who are all experiencing the same thing."

Jill seconds Abby's statement, "Yeh, it's isolating being a patient here."

"What's really good about it is that patients with different kinds of cancer can see each other and learn from one another about how to cope with their conditions," adds Jessie.

"That's right," continues Abby, "like we have four or five people on the unit now who have ovarian cancer, and we always have several laryngectomy [removal of all or part of the larynx] patients on the unit. It's great for these people to meet each other. Sometimes it happens spontaneously."

"I can remember times when discharged laryngectomy patients have come back to visit the still-hospitalized laryngectomy patients that they happened to meet while they were here," says Jessie for emphasis.

Betsy listens, takes notes, and occasionally interrupts with a question.

One of Jessie's idiosyncrasies emerges in this meeting, as it does in many meetings. Her tolerance for reflecting on and processing information lasts only so long before an internal alarm goes off compelling her to put talk into action. The gear switch is startling because it comes so quickly, preceded only by a slight body movement, a hand gesture, or a shift of position. This time it's her hand reaching for the telephone in the middle of one of Betsy's questions.

She's got the food service woman on the line. "Hi, this is Jessie Concannon, nurse manager on 5C. I wonder if you could give me an estimate for a weekly snack of crackers, cheese, fruit, and beverages for ten to fifteen people plus delivery, cleanup, and removal. Let's say we're going to offer this fifty-two times. Would a thousand dollars cover it? Can we pay for it up front?" She taps the phone with her pencil while she waits for the woman to do the calculations. "Thanks so much. I'm glad we can handle it that way. I thought I was on target about the cost, too, but I'm glad to have it verified." Jessie gives an affirmative nod to Betsy.

She hangs up, and in rapid-fire delivery dispenses assignments to Abby and Jill. Abby is grateful. She confesses that she hadn't known what she should do next. As Betsy prepares to leave, she mentions that there are other funds at the disposal of nurses. Jessie then reels off a shopping list for the unit: textbooks for the staff and tape recorders, relaxation tapes, and headsets for the patients. Betsy advises her not to be shy about making requests for these things if she needs them. The meeting has been more productive than Jessie had anticipated.

For most of the remainder of this day, Jessie stays in

her office to concentrate on paperwork. She is interrupted
regularly. As they do every day, fast-paced or slow, in
or outside her office, the nurses solicit Jessie's advice.
Today they come in and out asking questions about
medications and treatments, talking about handling disagreements with doctors, seeking Jessie's opinions or
relaying information to her. Jeanette, for example, comes
in to show her an order that a physician has written in a
patient's record. "Ambulate without excuses," it states
in large print. Jeanette exclaims, "Get a load of that, will
you? I have to go to her and tell her to strike that from
the record. It reflects badly on nursing. Makes us look
like we're not walking him. Don't you agree?" Jessie
does. Later Jeanette comes back to report that the physician
hadn't meant it the way it sounded. She simply had meant
that the patient may try to avoid walking. Jeanette has
succeeded in getting the ambiguous message removed
from the record.

## THE PAPER CHASE

One of Jessie's greatest accomplishments in her three-year
tenure, the one in which she takes the most pride, is the
development of a self-contained unit, one of the few in the
hospital. When she took the job, the unit was dependent on
the Nursing Department to fill the staffing holes with per
diem nurses or "floats"—nurses from other floors. Jessie
was philosophically opposed to this system.

I didn't want orthopedic nurses caring for cancer patients, and I believed that every patient was entitled
to his or her own primary nurse. I was lucky because
when I came here there were some wonderful nurses
who wanted to stay and a lot of vacant positions. I
could hire the people I wanted—people who had been

or hoped to become dedicated oncology nurses. This
meant that I could build the unit in my image.

But there was more to becoming a self-contained unit than
just hiring the right people. The nurse manager had to have
the support of the Nursing Administration, enough leeway
in the budget to permit it, and a staff that was willing to
make the sacrifices it would entail.

It was the last criterion that put Jessie to the severest test.
Colleen Lindstrom remembers,

> Jessie was so enthusiastic and so eager to get it done
> that she'd forget that everybody couldn't move as fast
> as she could. Her staff really liked her and wanted to
> please her, but for them it meant agreeing to fill in or
> work extra hours when their colleagues called in sick,
> came in late, or needed a day off. She had such a nice
> way about her that she got away with the pushing and
> prodding that it took to bring the staff around. She
> succeeded because people responded to the kindly side
> of her personality as much as to the forceful side. It
> was an amazing feat. Nurses in general are resistant
> to change. Jessie accomplished her goal in such a
> short period of time. What she really did up there on
> 5C was build a culture. Her standards of practice and
> her beliefs became the core of it.

As a partial result of the self-contained "culture" that
Jessie has built, she spends some portion of every Monday
morning ensuring her three-shift coverage for the week.
Sitting at her desk in her cluttered office, she pencils in the
week's schedule on a huge lined chart. Several times she
picks up the phone to call one of her nurses to fill in a hole,
or to ask a nurse to switch a slot or work extra hours. When
the patient census is low, she may ask someone not to report
to work as scheduled. Because she has been so flexible and
accommodating in meeting people's requests for time off or

for schedule switches, she receives nothing but cooperative responses to her own requests.

Jessie devotes a part of every working day to nurse-patient assignments. She stands at the nursing station with a pen and yellow legal pad facing the board on which all of the patients' names are listed along with the names of their physicians and their primary and backup nurses. The primary nurse, usually either a day-shift or an evening-shift person, coordinates the patient's care and leaves orders for the assigned backup nurses on the other shifts. Those patients who are on the board already have their nurse assignments, but in the course of every day, names will be erased for the departing patients and new names added for incoming ones. Jessie tries to keep each nurse's primary patient load to three or four if she has sufficient staffing for the day, so she watches the board to see who can pick up additional patients. Frequently an incoming patient will be someone who has been hospitalized on the unit before. Whenever possible Jessie attempts to reassign patients to the same nurse they had during previous hospitalizations. She is so adamant, in fact, about having her primary patients returned to her floor that she checks with the Admissions Office on a daily basis to see if she recognizes the names of incoming admissions. When she does, she instructs admissions to send that person back up to her. Likewise, if an admitted patient has to be moved to another unit for procedures not performed on 5C, Jessie will request that the patient be transferred and then sent back following the treatment. She gets her way, but not always without irritating the physicians and residents who have their own ideas about where they want to locate patients. "I don't tell them how to practice medicine, and I don't believe that they have the right to order nursing priorities," she states emphatically. So when Clark, a handsome senior surgical resident, asks Jessie one day for a favor—to keep one of his patients on 5C, a patient who in her opinion doesn't need to be there, she responds with a smile and a firm grip on his shoulder, "Sorry, Clark, I'd like to help you out, and I would if I could, but we're just too busy.'' Clark appears slightly startled by her response, but he accepts it without argument.

Once her daily nursing assignments are completed, Jessie removes the yellow sheets to her office, where they will sit on her desk until the next day—when the same process begins again.

Staffing is Jessie's big-ticket budgetary item. Her budget allows her a fixed number of nursing hours per patient per day (HPPD). This figure is based on an estimate of the number of hours of nursing care that each patient on the unit will require in a given period of time. It, in conjunction with an estimated patient census, helps to determine how many full-time equivalent (FTEs) positions she can have on her floor. On high-acuity units (those with very sick patients) like Jessie's, the nurse-patient ratio will be higher than it is on lower-acuity ones. Throughout the course of the fiscal year, Jessie needs to monitor her budget constantly and keep tracking it on the computer printouts that are sent to her on a weekly and a monthly basis. It is her job to be within or very close to her fixed budget. There will be some periods when the census is either lower or higher than the estimate. In a low-census time Jessie's staffing budget should be ''flexed'' downward, and at a high-census time it should be flexed higher. Her goal is to balance the low and high times so that they cancel each other out at the end of the fiscal year.

While staffing consumes the lion's share of the unit budget, there are other items to be monitored as well. The supplies on Jessie's floor, everything from toothbrushes to rubber gloves and plastic ''chucks''—the pads used for incontinent patients—are allotted to her on the basis of preestablished estimates of the quantity she will require. So Jessie takes regular supply inventories to make sure that that portion of her budget is not overspent. Then there are the other expenses on the unit, less problematic perhaps but still demanding her attention. Telephone calls and secretarial supplies are also budget items, and occasionally their misuse or overuse may provoke warning memorandums from Nursing Administration.

While Jessie does not attempt to conceal her personal loathing for the budget part of her job, she holds fast to the conviction that the control of the budget should be in the hands of the nurse manager.

> I don't like doing budgets and never will. It's not what I went to nursing school for and certainly not the reason I went and got a master's degree in nursing. There are a lot of nurse managers, quite a few in this hospital, in fact, who love the budget stuff. It's a game for them, juggling the numbers. Several of them have or are now getting MBA [masters in business administration] degrees instead of MSNs [masters in nursing]. Maybe it is the wave of the future, but it's not for me. I'm afraid that if I stay around much longer, I'll begin seeing a lot more staffing cuts, fewer RNs, more patient care technicians and nursing assistants, and even though I've been a strong proponent for using nurse extenders, I just don't believe that you can provide quality patient care without a high RN-patient ratio. I'm so convinced about the value of primary nursing that I don't want to be around to see it compromised for lack of money.

Just as Jessie's distaste for the budget is common knowledge among her colleagues, so is her propensity to be over budget. "She's always having to justify her expenditures, mostly those related to staffing," explains Colleen. "But most of the time she has such good justifications that it's hard to argue with her. When she has very sick patients on her unit, she feels that she has to provide them with the nursing care that she thinks they need, even if it does stretch her budget. She is an effective advocate for patients." Colleen believes, nonetheless, that Jessie's budgetary attitudes may rankle some of the other nurse managers at Memorial, especially those who always keep within their fiscal parameters. "On the other hand," Colleen continues, "she's got this sweet way about her and such strong principles about nursing that maybe they overlook it."

Maybe because of her "strong principles about nursing," Jessie approaches the required writing of staff evaluations with considerably more enthusiasm than she does the budget reviews. Once a year, she sits down individually with each of the nurses on the unit and reviews her or his progress before committing her thoughts to paper. As she sees it,

> the biggest part of my job is empowering the staff, making sure that nurses feel vital, confident in their clinical abilities, and capable of disagreeing with or making recommendations to physicians. I expect a lot from them. I treat them like adults, and I expect that they will behave accordingly. I'm not like Florence Nightingale. I don't hover over them, and I'm not a big stickler for strict obedience to rules. When people are treated this way, they rarely let you down.

The real testament to the efficacy of Jessie's philosophy is contained in her scrupulously honest nursing evaluations. She thinks that they are one of the most important components of her job, as helpful to each nurse's professional growth as they are to her in gaining an overall perspective on her staff and her own leadership. The more progress she can document for each of her nurses, the more confident she can be that she has been on course.

If ever she needs evidence, she has it in the example of Toni, a tall, pretty brunette in her twenties, who listens attentively to Jessie's assessment of her. She gets high praise. In Jessie's opinion, Toni has met most of the short- and long-term goals documented in her previous evaluation. The one weak area is that Toni seems to have difficulty initiating "patient care conferences" with the staff—presenting patients for group discussion. She fumbles for reasons, says she really ought to do it but just hasn't gotten around to it. Jessie gives short shrift to Toni's fumbles except to say that Toni seems to prefer informal consultations with her colleagues. They move on to how well she does with patients—follows up on them when she's been away, responds well to emergencies, and asks to be assigned primary patients with complex physiological and psychological problems. "Toni," says Jessie, "you're a leader in every way, not only with patients but with their families, too. You're an active participant in our unit committees and in hospital meetings and national conferences. Your sense of professionalism is strong. There's no better way to say it than just that you're a superb nurse and person." Embarrassed but proud, Toni beams as brightly as the big diamond on her long, manicured finger. To wrap things up, they discuss future goals: to further develop Toni's expertise in cancer and cancer nursing, to pursue additional nursing education, and, yes, definitely, to initiate patient care conferences. When Toni leaves the office, Jessie remarks, "You've just seen an exceptional person. I have encouraged her to go to graduate school, and I know she will. She has the potential to be a major change agent in the world of professional nursing. I want you to understand that every nurse is not a Toni, but almost all of them have or will have superior evaluations." With a twirl of her chair to face her desk, Jessie begins writing this down.

In the course of a year, she will have completed and submitted to the Nursing Department evaluations on at least twenty nurses and several clerical personnel and PCTs. That's a lot of sitting for a woman as poorly disposed to it as Jessie is.

And the posterior portion of her body, however much it may protest, will have to locate itself in that swivel chair for yet another vital writing assignment—the preparation of her annual report. To make the task less onerous, Jessie begins several months before it's due—a page here, another

there, an hour here, an hour there. The annual report is the
saga of the nursing philosophy and culture on 5C and the
record of the year's events on the unit, including the accomplishments, the disappointments, the goals met and unmet,
the operational assessment, the nurse manager's self-assessment, and the directions for the future. In its final form,
Jessie's annual report is chock full of unit accomplishments—self-containment, the establishment of an ongoing
staff journal club (to review the current literature on oncology nursing), the inception of a support group for the families of cancer patients and a social group for the patients
themselves, the completion of a booklet by the unit's primary nursing task force. The disappointments list is short:
the task force booklet remains unpublished; the patient care
conferences are not a regular occurrence. Jessie's nemesis,
the budget, is humorously referred to as both an accomplishment and a disappointment—an accomplishment when it's
been on target, a disappointment when it hasn't been. Most
of last year's goals have been met, and the listed goals for
next year are exciting and ambitious. The finished document
justifies Jessie's pride in the collective achievements that
the year has produced.


## ROUTINES
### Report Meeting

April 24, 1990, is the day that Jessie Concannon selects to
announce to a variety of individuals and groups in the hospital that she will be leaving Memorial to return to school to
obtain a doctorate in clinical psychology. She will have four
months to tie up the loose ends of her job as nurse manager
of 5C, a position that she has held for three years. She
chooses this Thursday, 7:00 A.M., report meeting to tell her
staff because she usually holds staff meetings at this time,
when she can catch two shifts at once, the outgoing night

shift and the incoming day shift. On this day, they gather as usual in the enclosed glass "bubble" just behind the nursing station. Some of the night nurses are not yet in the bubble but are out on the floor completing their tasks. The tape recorder is on, and the day-shift nurses, pens and paper in hand, are writing the night nurses' oral accounts of the patients on the unit. Jessie keeps a daily record of the reports for all of the patients on the floor, but the staff nurses take notes only on those that apply to their own assigned patients. A succession of monotone voices can be heard from the machine: "Mrs. Flaherty was depressed and crying most of the night. I think she wants to see the shrink. I don't know what's bothering her, but somebody better call Marty [the psychiatrist] today," says one voice at the end of her reporting. Jessie stops the tape to remind Toni, Mrs. Flaherty's primary nurse, to make the call to Marty. The tape continues.

Another voice comes on, saying,

Sally Carmichael, a DNR [do not resuscitate] patient in room nineteen had stainage on the tracheotomy sponge all night long. We suctioned her. Her output is low. She's expressive but very sick. Her IV [intravenous] morphine bag will run out soon. It's going at one and one-half milligrams per hour. Her heart rate is way up. Temperature going up, too. We gave her Tylenol, and she sweats it out. There's rectal and vaginal oozing. The colostomy is OK. Lungs have rales. Respiratory rate is thirty-two. Bloods are OK. We're talking hospice care for her. Can't tell how she's dealing with the idea. Maybe she's worried about how her mother is coping with it.

We had a new admission at twelve A.M. Her name is Marsha Simpson, but it's not the same Marsha Simpson we all know. The new Mrs. Simpson is a seventy-six-year-old preop. The intern was called and came to do her workup.

The nurses listen and write until the tape ends. Gradually all of the night-shift nurses have straggled into the bubble, as has Lucille, one of the PCTs, and a nursing assistant. There are fifteen people sitting or standing. Jessie regularly uses this time to make general announcements, so she starts the meeting out on a cheerful note by stating that May 31 has been designated as Nurses' Day. This year, she has arranged to take the entire staff and their "significant others" to a comedy club in celebration of the event. She says that she will arrange coverage for evening-shift people who want to attend. Having thus completed the easy part of this morning's assignment, she moves into the hard part in a voice so controlled that it almost completely conceals the emotion behind it. "I've resigned," she begins. "I'm leaving in August. I'm going to get a doctorate in psychology, but I'm not leaving nursing. I want to use what I learn to help cancer patients and their families." There's a momentary hush in the room.

Lucille breaks the silence. "This is a bomb," she says, putting her head in her hands to stifle her sobs. From another corner of the room, someone says, "Oh, shit."

Others start crying as Jessie leaves the room. "Who's going to be our next boss?" asks one of the nurses, directing her question to no one in particular. More silence is followed by more questions about who will succeed Jessie, and the discussion ends with a comment from Mary Lynn. "I should have guessed it. She's been more relaxed in the last month."

Lucille and the night nurses drift out, and those who remain appear to have entered a denial stage. The conversation turns to gossip about patients and doctors. Gradually the room empties and the active day begins. From that day until her departure in August, there will be few public utterances about what it means to the staff to lose Jessie, but privately, they all know that they are not likely to see her kind again.

Jessie will repeat her dramatic announcement individually to all of the other nurses on the other shifts. Predictably, the news is greeted with shock, disbelief, anxiety about the future, and tears.

Jessie routinely attends the 7:00 A.M. report meeting. When she conducts the weekly staff meetings, the agenda usually is devoted to unit matters or hospital-wide policy and procedure changes that will affect the unit. The announcements that she makes at these early-morning meetings are repeated by the charge nurses whom Jessie appoints to take over in her absence on the evening and night shifts and on the day shift when she has to be off the unit for a block of time. For two months now, she has been spending a good deal of time at the report meeting on documentation.

Currently a hot issue in the Nursing Department at Memorial, nursing documentation—the notes that nurses write in patient records—is one of the criteria used to determine a hospital's standing with the Joint Commission on Accreditation of Health Care Organizations (JCAHO). On their last visit to Memorial, the JCAHO's panel of evaluators found nursing documentation to be wanting, and they gave the department an indefinite time period to bring it up to snuff. Ever since, there has been a mad scramble to change the documentation system. The primary complaint about Memorial's system was that the nursing notes did not reflect the outcomes of the nursing care plans. Daily notations on patients' problems were recorded, but the resolutions of the identified problems were not documented. Committee after committee of nurses was formed to address the problem and meeting upon meeting was conducted to correct it. New and more-detailed documentation forms were devised and numerous directives about their proper usage were issued.

Jessie has toiled long and hard in the documentation trenches, so she has a big investment in seeing that 5C is implementing the new regulations. Time is waning. Soon the JCAHO panel will return. Jessie, therefore, makes routine checks of the patient records on the unit and uses the report meeting time to cajole and reeducate the staff to iron out any documentation glitches she finds. For the most part

5C has performed admirably, but not without resistance. Time is the scarcest commodity of all in the working life of a nurse, and the new documentation procedures extract a bigger chunk of it than anyone wants to give.

## Rounds

In a teaching hospital like Memorial, rounds are the modus operandi for educating the professional health care team. Jessie attends as many as time will allow. Rounds come in two varieties—the field trip model, wherein a senior guru in a medical or surgical specialty leads a pack of junior trainees around a unit, stopping at the doorways of patient X and patient Y to learn about the diagnosis and treatment of their diseases; and the classroom model, wherein a senior guru lectures to a pack of seated trainees about the diagnosis and treatment of the kinds of diseases seen on any given unit. In a less liberated era rounds would have been the exclusive province of physicians, but nowadays they are attended regularly by nurses, sometimes co-led by them, and often conducted for their benefit. Frequently, too, nurse managers and clinical nurse specialists conduct their own nursing rounds. Jessie has her favorite rounds, the ones she rarely misses. Dr. Martin (Marty) Rosenbaum's Monday morning psychiatry rounds on 5C fall into this category. Marty is Memorial's director of psychiatry and his is a ubiquitous presence on 5C. His teaching style, at least in this arena, is an exception to the usual lecture format.

On this Monday morning the topic is death, the setting is the glass bubble, and the participants are all 5C nurses. Marty listens as Paula, one of the senior staff nurses acclaimed for her professionalism and nursing competency, describes a patient who is near death. She explains that the patient's wife asked not to have him placed on beeper code (emergency resuscitation). Marty knows the patient and reminds Paula that the wife's request may have an unconscious retaliatory tinge to it. The patient, it seems, was abusive to his wife before his illness. The nurses begin to talk about former patients who have died recently. Marty listens. Jeanette, one of the more humorous nurses on the floor, goes off on a tangent about a patient she has now who has a serious form of cancer:

> I've never met anyone quite like her. Yesterday, when I knocked on her door, she told me that she was sorry but she was indisposed. She was on a long-distance call to Europe. The calls keep on coming in from around the world, so she's frequently indisposed. I'm not sure what she thinks we're doing here. I think she has her own alternative ideas about healing.

Marty chuckles and directs the discussion back to the topic. "It's pretty clear that you all have a lot of feelings about death today," he says in his inimitable, mild-mannered way. They all agree that it is hard on them when there are a lot of deaths at once. They admit that they remain attached to patients, even if they haven't been in the hospital for awhile, and it saddens them to realize that there are some whom they never will see again. Their grief is expressed sotto voce, in a kind of choral sigh, rather than in solo eulogies to the dead patients. Marty empathizes, Jessie remains attentive but silent, and the rounds conclude.

Dr. Hal Bloomfield's rounds with the 5C nurses also are popular with Jessie and the staff. This morning Hal is coming to talk about cervical cancer, and the nurses await his arrival enthusiastically. Hal, in his brief tenure at Memorial, has become one of Jessie's strongest admirers.

> She's phenomenally resourceful, both for the patients and for the staff. That's what makes her stand apart from other nurse managers. She really cares about her staff and gives them so much support that it helps to compensate for working in such a tough specialty

area, where patients stay long enough for nurses to grow attached to them. Caring is important in all aspects of nursing, but in oncology it's crucial. The primary nurses will see much more of my patients than I will, and it will be to her that they turn for help. They, in turn, will go to Jessie for help, and she always delivers. She's a master at human interaction, and on top of that, she's got a great head on her shoulders and amazing organizational ability.

Perhaps because Hal is married to a nurse and has a personal fondness and respect for them and their work, he and they constitute a mutual admiration society. It doesn't hurt his cause, either, that he is young, attractive, and witty. He lights up the bubble with his entrance.

Paula, intermittently spooning yogurt into her mouth, says jokingly, "Speak to us, Dr. Bloomfield."

"Paula," he responds with a smirk, "did you know that a British medical team has found a possible link between yogurt consumption and ovarian cancer?"

"You're kidding, really?" says Paula placing the yogurt on the table.

"See what we're coming to? You can't do anything fun or eat anything anymore," says Hal.

The jocular atmosphere in the room changes to serious and then to depressive as he launches into his talk on cervical cancer.

"Invasive cervical cancer is on the wane, but preinvasive cervical cancer—dysplasia—has reached epidemic proportions. To make matters worse, it can appear shortly after a normal pap smear. People are getting it at younger ages now, and the female lower genital tract is much more susceptible to the bad HPV [human papiloma] virus than [is] the male lower genital tract. So far, there's no documented evidence that promiscuity or a high level of sexual activity is the cause of the virus."

The hush that falls over the assembly of nurses is interrupted by Jessie. "Is promiscuity a risk factor, nonetheless?"

"Yes," responds Hal. "Nuns don't get cervical cancer. Early sexual activity with multiple partners increases the risk. If you get cervical cancer in your twenties or thirties, the tumors are more aggressive than if you get it postmenopause. Treatment is complex. Young women of childbearing age are not good candidates for radiation because it damages the vagina and makes intercourse more painful. Surgery makes it possible to move the ovaries up so that they can function, so it's preferable for this age group, but it is terribly painful postoperatively."

Jessie's expression provides no clues as to whether or not Hal's words have given her personal reassurance or heightened anxiety, but the group expression is silent and somber. Each participant is a woman in her twenties or thirties.

Hal winds up the discussion with a compelling soliloquy on the importance of frequent pap smears. Women neglect them, he says, and some doctors give them only every three years. He launches into a story about two women from a graduate business school who have come to him for help in developing a home-use pap smear kit. He has agreed to help them because he thinks the idea has merit, but there are kinks, especially in the areas of laboratory testing and in obtaining deep enough vaginal specimens. Jessie volunteers that she would have many reservations about the do-it-yourself variety.

By the conclusion of rounds, the level of depression and anxiety is visible to Hal. "Let's face it, GYN oncology is a depressing service to work on."

Abby laughs nervously.

"Why are you laughing? I go home in tears every night," he tells her.

"I laugh so that I won't cry," she answers.

* * *

Laughter is standard fare at Dr. David McGuire's Friday medical oncology rounds. This Friday afternoon they are held in his office, as usual, and Jessie arrives late, as usual. A bald, bespectacled man in middle age, David somehow succeeds at retaining his good looks where others of his vintage often fail. As the director of medical oncology, his and Jessie's professional lives interface regularly. They have a special bond, perhaps the kind that belongs only to the Irish. Like select members of a private club, they speak a common language distinguished by mutual respect, quick-mindedness, sociability, and wit. As accomplished and well respected a physician as David is, he is easily distracted by the effect that his charm has on his audience. He's a natural raconteur on everything from European soccer, especially of the Irish variety, to the personalities and idiosyncrasies of his patients, and he is incapable of separating entertainment from medical education.

"Didn't you know?" he asks his assembled staff, "that the patient in room twenty is a big shot? He likes physicians a lot. Something's wrong if you guys haven't gotten a case of wine from him."

"We'll go to see him right away," they promise.

They attempt to get him back on the track of reviewing all of the patients on 5B, his unit, and on 5C. For a short time, they succeed. One patient, says the senior fellow reporting to David, thinks his cancer is all cured. "He's playing games," says David. "You'd better straighten him out." They go down the list of patients, smiling when they come to those who are responding well to treatment and frowning about the less fortunate. Intermittently they stop to ask for Jessie's concurrence on their assessments of the patients on her unit. She concurs. More names, more discussion of cancer of every variety—breast, neck and head, liver—and of treatments and procedures, including chemotherapy, interferon, radiation, the CAT scan, surgery for lesions. Then, out of nowhere, comes David again, reminding them all to tune in to cable TV on Sunday for the Irish soccer match.

"Cancel all your plans," he instructs.

"OK, OK," they chime, "let's finish this list."

"If we must," says David.

## EVENTS
### Cancer Awareness Day

Jessie is this year's chairperson for Cancer Awareness Day, an annual event held just inside the lobby of the Pavillion Building. She and Colleen are holding a planning meeting today, a few weeks in advance of the event, to review the posters about cancer that will be displayed. The posters' graphics are supposed to make it clear that Cancer Awareness Day has a twofold purpose—the raising of public consciousness about cancer prevention and detection, and the advertising of Memorial Hospital's services for cancer patients. Essentially the message is: Here are the things you can do to prevent cancer and to detect it as early as possible, but if, despite your best efforts, it should strike, this is the place to come for treatment. We've got it all here—nurses, doctors, social workers, pastoral services, every kind of therapist imaginable, administrators, and pharmacists. Jessie and Colleen concentrate the most on the interdisciplinary cancer team at the hospital. They want to make sure that no one is excluded on the posters. Having satisfied themselves in this regard and in general matters of layout, they agree that Jessie's next task will be to assign nurses and doctors to work at the Cancer Awareness Day booth for hour-long intervals to answer questions from passersby.

May 2 arrives—the big day. Jessie is dressed up for the occasion, no hint of the nurse about her, not even the jingling keys. The booth was set up the night before. In one

area there's a long table topped with several hundred brochures on every type of cancer, along with rubber models
of breasts and testicles to encourage tactile exploration in
search of tell-tale lumps. Behind the table, the on-duty
nurses and doctors, all in street clothes, stand ready to
dispense information. The carefully crafted posters rest on
tall easels opposite the table and next to a TV monitor that
shows men and women in various states of undress feeling
their bodies for lumps. Simultaneously an unseen narrator
with a soothing voice offers hints on how to conduct these
self-examinations. He advises men as well as women, to
feel for lumps in the breast region, because, as he goes on
to explain, once in a while a case of breast cancer turns up
in a male. Every so often the narrator and the body checkers
are interrupted by a kindly doctor in a white coat who comes
on screen from behind a desk and talks in lay language,
with the aid of statistics and graphs, about the prevalence,
prevention, and treatment of all kinds of cancer. Then the
whole video repeats.

When it's Jessie's turn to be on duty, there's not much
action at the booth. A few stragglers pick up brochures.
Hospital personnel and lay people alike glance at the monitor
and a few of the more adventurous visitors experiment with
the breasts and testicles. Overall, the audience for whom
the day is intended appears to respond to it in hit-and-run
fashion, perhaps operating collectively under an unspoken
illusion that in avoiding in-depth information they also may
be avoiding the disease. By contrast, David McGuire and
most of the other members of Memorial's cancer team are
everywhere in evidence in the area of the booth. In clusters
they joke and banter and recount their on-duty experiences
to one another, as if drawing strength from camaraderie that
they can use to advantage in their daily battles against this
formidable disease.

## Free Lunch

Almost as ubiquitous as physicians in a hospital are the drug and medical supply salespeople and the health care service vendors who roam the corridors regularly. Dressed in street clothes, the peddlers often are distinguishable from other visitors by their large, square briefcases. Usually they come to the nursing stations bearing gifts for the nurses and secretaries—pencils, rulers, protractors, pens, pads of paper, all emblazoned with product names and company logos. Once the goodies have been dispensed and they have secured the attention of the nurse manager or the charge nurse, they display their sample products. The products, of course, are accompanied by sales pitches to demonstrate the superiority of their wares over those of their competitors. These informal drop-in sales visits are daily rituals in any hospital.

Once in a while a vendor hosts a sumptuous catered lunch on the unit and invites the entire on-duty nursing staff to attend. Today a home-care vending company places a lavish spread on the table in the 5C bubble, and Jessie and the staff sit and eat while the sales representative explains that his company is expanding and wants to provide home health services to discharged patients from 5C. It takes him about a half hour to describe the services that his company provides. His monologue is greeted by a skeptical audience, whose spokesperson is Jessie.

"I don't understand why you subcontract your respiratory therapy services to another agency," says Jessie. "Why don't you use your own therapists? Isn't the contracted therapist insulted by the fact that she's being supervised by your people?"

"If you're asking whether or not it would be better for us to provide all the care ourselves, then the answer is yes," the sales representative replies rather defensively as he watches Jessie munch on chicken teriyaki, "but the reality is that we can't afford to be totally self-sufficient."

Jessie leans forward. "Excuse me for asking a direct

question, but aren't you owned by two other hospitals in the city?''

''Not exactly. We own ourselves, but those institutions have invested some money in us, and they receive a return on their investment.''

''Then, aren't we helping them when we call you?'' asks Jessie.

''Yes, but you're not hurting yourselves,'' comes the reply.

''Well, I can tell you that we've had good reports about the agency you're using as the subcontractor, so that's the good news, but to be fair to you, I'd have to say that you have a lot of competition. Since we know some of your competitors well, and have been satisfied with them, we're unlikely to stop calling them.''

The chicken teriyaki and the salad are disappearing fast, and some of the nurses are beginning to reach for the fresh-smelling bakery goods. They're growing restless, and the representative looks discouraged.

''We'll certainly keep you in mind, though,'' adds Jessie, standing.

''I want to thank all of you very much for your time, and I do hope you'll call us,'' replies the beleagured salesman as he forces a smile and individual good-byes to his departing guests. As soon as he is out of sight, doctors, social workers, Lucille, and anyone else who happens to be around enter the bubble to devour the remnants of the banquet.


# PATIENTS

Walter Green is one of the few patients on 5C who does not have cancer, but four years ago, when he first came to Memorial Hospital, he was admitted to the unit. Now, whenever he returns to the hospital, he goes to 5C. It's like home to him. He's been there longer than Jessie has. On this last admission, he's been in for almost seven months.

At the age of fifty, he lives with a chronic, recurrent stomach disease that necessitates all manner of medical and surgical procedures, emergency measures, and nursing care. Because of his illness, he's been unable to work for four years. Having lived so long on 5C, he is more familiar with its operation than any other patient.

"You couldn't ask for a better floor," he says in an animated voice.

> The nurses treat me like a father or a brother, like a member of the family. They understand how sick I am, and they do everything to make me feel good. If you've gotta be sick, this is the best place to be. Once I had to leave here to go temporarily to another hospital. You might not believe this, but the nurses called me over there all the time to see how I was. It almost brings tears to my eyes when I think about it. They even give me parties on my birthdays. And that Jessie, she comes in whenever there's a problem. She stands there and explains what's happening to me when I'm in a lot of pain or if I'm going for another operation. Then she gives me a big hug and a kiss. It's like she's a daughter. She makes this floor the way it is. There's never any tension here. They all work so well together.

All of his positive comments about nurses lead Mr. Green to express his feelings about doctors.

> I don't think that they understand. I don't mean my own doctor. I mean interns and residents. They want the patients to get well too quick. They don't come in and explain what they're doing. They leave most of that to the nurses. Like they'll have me on a pain medication, and all of a sudden they'll take me off it without telling me why. It makes me think maybe they don't care how I feel after I'm off the medication.

What they should do is talk to you before they make
a change like that. What happens is the nurse comes
in, and she's surprised that you didn't know you'd
been taken off the medication or been cut back to a
lower dosage. I have to say that I have many more
positive feelings about nurses than I do about these
young doctors.

His expression turns to sadness as the subject changes to
his upcoming discharge.

When I go home, it will be like leaving part of my
family behind. I've gotten used to waking up and
having them [the nurses] come in to say, "Come on,
Mr. Green, it's another day." You just don't get this
kind of treatment from your real family. They try to
be as good as they can, but they give you the impression that they're helping you because they feel they
have to, not because they want to. They're willing but
hesitant. These nurses here, they want to take care of
me.

Mr. Green's sentiments are echoed by Mrs. Fisher, who
occupies a room two doors down. This is her second admission, and now she's here for a short stay to receive chemotherapy. A year ago, she was on 5C for ten weeks for surgery
on her cancerous bladder.

When I came here the first time, I was terrified. To
me, having cancer meant that I was going to die. I'd
never been sick before in my life, and I was only in
my fifties. I certainly wasn't ready to die. The nurses
were wonderful. They told me that I had lots of reason
to be hopeful, and that I needn't assume that I was a
terminal case. Jessie frequently came in and talked to
me, too, even though she wasn't my nurse. She knew
how traumatic the experience was for me. On that first

admission, I had round-the-clock nursing care. The nurses gave me drive and motivation. Their approach was always positive. I liked my doctors a lot, too, but they didn't have the day-to-day contact with me that the nurses had. The nurses were my inspiration. Jessie runs this floor on a personal basis. They save a bed for me whenever I need to come back. There's always a personal touch. I love going back to the same floor and the same primary nurse. I tell everybody what a wonderful experience I've had here. If it weren't for my nurses, I wouldn't feel as secure about my illness and my life as I do now. My daughters are nurses, and they were thrilled with the care that I received here. That counts for a lot when it comes from fellow nurses.

Mr. Green and Mrs. Fisher have left the hospital now, but they will return in the future. Each time they do, they will be coming "home" again to 5C—to the unit with the personal touch.

Meanwhile, Sally Carmichael—a woman in her mid-thirties—is dying. Day by day, whatever vestiges of youth and health she clings to are disappearing. Her cheeks are pallid. Flesh and bone are almost indistinguishable from each other. The fight has gone out of her. She wants the nurses to do her fighting for her, and if not them, then she wants medicines and machinery to do it—painkillers and oxygen equipment. Her mother keeps constant vigil, and she, too, wants the nurses to "do things" to make Sally better, but there is nothing more that they can do. Paula is her primary nurse, and God knows, she's done everything she can to make her comfortable. All day long, every day, she walks in and out of Sally's room to attend to her. When Paula is off-duty, the other nurses take over for her.

Sally never goes to a hospice. Her time is measured, first in days, then in hours. Death's shadow stalks the nursing station and the corridors on 5C, and this is reflected in the faces and the voices of the nurses. Lucille is quiet and somber. The air is filled with the kind of expectancy that muffles sound and makes activity unnoticeable.

"It will be some time today," Mary Lynn tells Lucille softly in response to a mood rather than a question.

"I know," answers Lucille. "I know."

The day after Sally's death, what remains of her on 5C is a vivid memory, for those who saw it, of one scene from her last full day of life. Toni had wheeled her out into the corridor to give her a change of scene, and there she sat, expressionless, as pale as the white johnny and the sheets that covered her. Toni, only a few years younger than Sally, was combing Sally's long auburn hair and talking quietly to her as she combed. The visual contrast between the pale, wilting patient and the rosy, blooming nurse was more sensory stimulation than some eyes could tolerate. Most people passing by smiled at Toni, glanced at Sally, and quickly looked away. They did not see the faint smile that suddenly appeared on Sally's face, nor did they see her hand rising to meet Toni's from underneath the sheet. A red ribbon lay in the hand. Toni took it, tied it neatly around the ponytail she had shaped with Sally's hair, and moved away to better visualize the results of her handiwork. What the eye beheld then was beautiful and ineffable, at once as despairing and redeeming as the sight of a solitary cardinal on melting snow at the end of a long, hard winter.

# THREE

# CANCER UNIT II

## DOMINIQUE RAZA, STAFF NURSE, 5B

**T**HE EASTERN LIMB of the fifth floor houses the twenty-six-bed Medical Oncology, Hematology Unit—5B. Because it is closer to the elevators than 5C is, the corridor leading to the nurses station is not as long, but rounding the corner from the elevator, the walls and the carpeting change color. Michael, the rather stout, ponytail-coiffed daytime secretary on 5B, refers to the shade of the eastern limbs' walls as "industrial blue"—darker than sky blue, less vivid than royal blue, kind of a blah blue. The companion carpeting is a blend of gray and a textile facsimile of blah blue. Michael's style as the unit host is more subdued than Lucille's. He is the quiet traffic cop at the opposite end of the fifth-floor block. Instead of staying seated at the station and relying on his voice to keep the traffic flowing, he moves around the corridors himself, looking for the appropriate nurses to assist him in orchestrating the arrivals and departures. The patient traffic is slower there than it is on 5C, because the patients are often sicker and remain in the hospital longer. And Michael and Wendy Fleming, the nurse manager on 5B, create a different atmosphere on their unit than Lucille and Jessie do on 5C. Both Michael and Wendy are less visible and audible than Lucille and Jessie. Preferring the sidelines to the center of the stage, they seem content to let the staff nurses assume the lead parts in the unit drama.

On 5B, the motion that strikes the eye of the observer is the bustling of the nurses who form a steady, ever-moving line in and out of the locked med room located at a right angle to the nursing station. If one listens carefully, one can hear the constant clicking of the code buttons that must be pushed in order to gain entry to the room. For the most part, though, the din on 5B is the chatter and clatter of the nurses talking to one another as they retrieve armfuls of medications, needles, blood vials, and medical supplies to carry to their patients' rooms.

The day-shift nurses on 5B, like most of their counterparts on 5C, are young, but on this unit there is a more tightly knit alliance between them. Friendship and collegiality among peers is the top layer of it, but it has an underbelly, too. There's a rumbling there, a collective waning of youthful idealism, and a hint of impending burnout. In short, all is not well on 5B, and Dominique Raza is one of those who has been bitten by the gloom bug.

Dominique, with her dark coloring, dark eyes, and long, naturally curly brunette hair, is as striking in the uniqueness of her appearance as Jessie Concannon is in hers. Dominique's is a youthful, exotic, and ethnic beauty that conceals its Irishness as effortlessly as Jessie's brand reveals it. Although the younger nurse is as intense and energetic, Dominique's activity is not mirrored in her body language in the obvious way that Jessie's is. Dominique's battery is charged by introspection. The outlet for Dominique's energy is talk. She is an open book. Jessie keeps her selfhood to herself. So while Jessie is darting from place to place on 5C, Dominique is striding in time with her internal drummer on 5B. Sometimes the drummer bids her to move in lilting giant steps. Other times it coaxes her body forward with the aid of a weary shuffle.

Although Dominique is primarily a day-shift nurse, she,

like her daytime colleagues, rotates on the other shifts. Once a month, she takes the night shift for five consecutive days. Intermittently, she works a weekend (day, evening, or night) shift for two days or for several weekday evening shifts. On some weeks, she may work three consecutive twelve-hour shifts, which earns her four days off instead of the usual two. Regardless of her rotation, Dominique never finishes her work within the parameters of the eight- or twelve-hour schedule. One, two, or three extra, unpaid hours per shift are standard practice for her. The reason for this is one-third the nature of the nurse and two-thirds the nature of the job.

## DAY SHIFT

There is a sameness to the routine that begins for Dominique every morning at approximately seven o'clock (give or take a few minutes, but usually on the late end). She arrives at the door to the fifth-floor locker room and pushes the code buttons to open it. From the waist down, the uniform she wears is as everyday as the routine—loose-fitting white pants, white socks or stockings, and white sneakers. Only the tops of her outfit vary—a different brightly colored T-shirt, lightweight sweater, or neatly pressed blouse. She shuns such adornments as jewelry and makeup in deference to her fondness for the au naturel. It's summertime, so there are no jackets or coats to put into her locker, just her purse and whatever additional extraneous belongings she has brought with her. She closes her locker, clips her ID badge to her T-shirt, stops to look in the bathroom mirror, walks out, and takes a right turn down the corridor leading to the nurses' station. A quick stop there to fetch a pen and piece of paper, to say good morning to Michael and whoever else is at the station, and to check the board to see how many patients are assigned to her that day—sometimes five or six, often four or five, rarely the optimal three. Some of these patients will be primary patients. Next she retraces her steps partway back down the corridor to the nurses lounge, where one of the recording machines is located. More than likely, other nurses are already seated around the table listening to the night reports. Dominique pours herself a cup of coffee, sits down, and waits her turn to listen to the reports on her patients. Usually she is halfway through her second cup of coffee before she starts taking notes on all of her patients. The information she obtains will help her decide on care plans for the patients and on the order in which she will attend to them. By 7:45, she has slipped her notes into the pocket of her pants and is on her way to the med room to begin the morning's tasks.

### July 12

This morning in mid-July begins like all of the others, with one noticeable exception. The entire staff is wearing Hawaiian shirts in honor of Denise's upcoming two-month leave of absence, which will take her halfway around the world— everywhere, that is, except Hawaii. During part of her leave, she and Dominique, good friends on and off the job, will join forces to volunteer their services for three weeks to a nursing organization. All they know now is that they will be sent in November to a rural clinic outpost somewhere in the Caribbean. Today Dominique's thoughts are about her patients and the anticipation of the lunchtime send-off party that the staff has planned for Denise. At this early hour of the morning, even the party seems a long way off.

Each visit to the med room is an exercise in efficiency and time management. There usually are long lists of medications and accompanying supplies that must be taken to every patient's bedside. Forgetting items on the list means wasted steps and time, so the nurses check and double-check to make sure that every item is included. Then the medications they remove have to be recorded in the med room ledger for the hospital pharmacy. At some point in the day, the administered medications also must be noted in the individual patient's records. If, in the process of retrieval, any narcotic medication is spilled or wasted, the nurse notes it on another ledger and gets the required witnessing signature from a second nurse.

For Dominique's upcoming visit to Mr. Riley's room, the list of supplies is short—a few test tubes and a syringe.

"How are you today?" she inquires of him.

"Doing good," he answers lethargically.

"Are you having any problems?"

"No."

Dominique talks to Mr. Riley while she first puts on her rubber gloves and then draws blood from the portacath (an implanted device used to receive medication and draw blood) inserted in his chest, a painless procedure.

"I wanted to ask you about your family. Am I right that you have two brothers?"

"Yes, and one of them is home five days a week, and my sister can come on weekends."

"OK, so it's alright for me to tell the social worker that you won't need any assistance when you leave the hospital?"

"That's right," Mr. Riley says agreeably.

Two vials of blood are now filled, and Dominique has thrown the rubber gloves into the wastebasket and the needle into the disposable needle container. Before she leaves, she explains, "You'll be going home today or tomorrow, but you'll be coming back once in a while for chemotherapy. They're going to leave the catheter in your chest, and a nurse will come to your house every day to take care of it."

"Every day?" Mr. Riley sounds surprised. "I hope she'll tell me when she's coming."

Dominique assures him that she will. As she's about to leave the room, Peggy, a nursing assistant, enters. Mr. Riley, ignoring Dominique, asks Peggy to change a bandage. Peggy agrees, and Dominique bids farewell to Mr. Riley. She feels ambivalent about Peggy's intervention. Granted, there is now one less thing for her to do for Mr.

Riley; still, in her opinion, his bandage change could wait. She has other patients for whom Peggy's services would be far more beneficial, but Dominique resists asking for help. ''It's a stupid nursing trait that I've acquired. I tell myself that I'm incompetent if I can't handle everything myself. I wait until I'm totally in the weeds before I scream.''

Dominique stops at the station with the blood, fills out requisition sheets, wraps them around the vials, and places them inside the automatic tube that sends them to the lab. Back in the med room, she retraces all of the step-by-step procedures she went through in preparation for Mr. Riley. This time her list is longer. She organizes all of her materials on the counter, then loads her arms with tablets, syringes, and plastic containers of liquid medication. In the process, she talks about the new needles they're using to draw blood from catheters.

These are being tested now. They're supposed to be less risky. They're really needleless, more like tiny spouts, and they're supposed to cut down the risk of nurses getting AIDS or hepatitis. If they work well, the hospital could get a discount on its liability insurance. It takes awhile to learn how to use them and the companion equipment that goes with them.

Temporarily placing her armful of supplies on the nursing station counter, Dominique stops to call the lab to check on a patient's potassium level. If the potassium level is running low, she will have to administer it, but she can't do it until she gets the results. Too much waiting around can foul up her schedule. While she's waiting on the line for the test results, she sticks labeling tape on the plastic containers of IV medications that she will be taking to Mr. Stafford's room. ''Oh, the results aren't ready yet. I was afraid of that,'' she says into the receiver.

Mr. Stafford is an older leukemia patient. He's asleep when Dominique comes in and doesn't stir as she moves the equipment around his bedside. It bothers her that it has taken her so long to get to him today. He's been hospitalized for seven weeks. For the first two weeks, he couldn't keep anything in his stomach. He lost thirty pounds, but now, with the aid of intravenous TPN (total parenteral nutrition), he's gaining again. Dominique goes right to work, hanging several fluid-filled plastic bags containing antibiotics on the IV rack by his bed. Along with the medications, she hangs a bag of sodium chloride, which will open up the line if something goes wrong. If Mr. Stafford has an allergic reaction, the sodium chloride will inject automatically to counter it. She explains,

> Sometimes patients get rigors [shakes] as a reaction to strong medication or to transfusion. If I think there's a risk of that, I can inject Demerol or Benadryl into part of the main line to control the reaction to medication. I always use a main line just in case, but that's my decision. Some nurses prefer to inject it into the patient directly. It isn't hospital policy to do it my way, so Wendy Fleming has to approve it as an exception to policy procedure.

Having hung all of the medications, Dominique turns her attention to the time-consuming job of checking and untangling all of the lines that are going into Mr. Stafford's body. This activity arouses him and he awakens in a cheerful mood, made all the more cheerful by the entrance of his wife.

"Don't you look colorful today?" she says to Dominique.

"You see, we're all wearing these Hawaiian shirts for a party we're having for one of the nurses who's leaving," responds Dominique.

Mrs. Stafford, readjusting her husband's head on the pillow, is pleased to hear him say that he is feeling better. Addressing Dominique, she says, "Yesterday he was feeling awful from that medication you gave him."

"That's Amphotericin. It fights fungal infections, but it does produce reactions. Your husband was a little faint and dizzy earlier this morning, but I think he's feeling better now. His blood sugar will go up because of the TPN we're giving him."

"How long will they keep him on that?" asks Mrs. Stafford.

"Until he has enough calories."

Dominique is still untangling Mr. Stafford's tubes, all of which are marked at intervals with light-blue latching gadgets. While Dominique converses with his wife, Mr. Stafford watches her work. "You know, they should have color coding for all these different tubes," he says.

"Great idea, Mr. Stafford. You ought to get to work on that when you get out of here," Dominique responds.

"He won't be leaving for at least two weeks, though," says Mrs. Stafford, beginning to look and sound slightly fainthearted. "I want you to know that I cleaned the microwave oven myself yesterday," she tells Dominique. "The housekeeping people just weren't doing it. They were drinking coffee and standing around talking loudly in the hallway. It's annoying."

As she exits, Dominique promises to tell Wendy Fleming about Mrs. Stafford's complaints. The clock at the nursing station surprises her. Its hands are moving ever closer to the eleven o'clock mark. Dominique has not had time for a midmorning coffee and breakfast break, and she has more patients to attend to before the party.

Bypassing the med room, she heads straight for Tom's room. Earlier in the morning, before her first trip to the med room, she stopped there briefly in response to his call button to move him from his bed to a chair. It had been a rushed encounter with few words exchanged. Dominique habitually refers to younger patients by their first names, reserving a more formal greeting for older patients like Mr. Riley and Mr. Stafford.

"Hi, Tom. Howya doing?" she asks the seated patient. Tom appears to be a well-built black man in his mid-thirties whose voice reflects his mood more than his affect does, and whose illness, a blood disorder, strikes black people disproportionately.

Rather than answering Dominique's question, he says, "Take that sponge thing off the bed."

Dominique feels Tom's crankiness. Guessing that he's probably annoyed with her because she hasn't had much time for him, she chooses to ignore his mood. "OK, I'll take it off. I'm surprised you don't like it. Most people say it makes them more comfortable."

She removes the big blue sponge, goes out into the corridor to the linen cart to get clean blankets, sheets, and pillowcases, and returns to change the bed. Tom sits silently in his chair, occasionally focusing his eyes on the overhead TV set without showing any sign of interest in what he's watching.

Bed making is Dominique's last priority, but today she senses that clean sheets might lift Tom's spirits a bit. She works rapidly, making tight, perfect corners with the sheets and blanket at the end of the mattress, fluffing up the newly covered pillows, and, finally, placing a single sheet horizontally across the bed ("in case I need to boost him up in bed or move him around"). With Dominique's help, Tom is returned to his freshly made bed.

It's now time to change the dressing on Tom's chest cavity, a ritual that takes place for every patient every seventy-two hours. Neither PCTs nor nursing assistants are permitted to change dressings whenever there is a risk of infection. Dominique ties a mask around Tom's face and one around her own, then dons a pair of rubber gloves. After the bandage is removed, she looks for signs of infection. This time she doesn't find any. With a cotton swab, she applies Betadine to the area to "kill any potential bugs" and places a clean dressing over it. Gently she records with a magic marker on the dressing's taped border the date that it was changed and D.R., her initials. Throughout all of this, Tom has remained quiet and expressionless, as if he were alone in the room. Dominique would like to have more time to talk to him, but it will have to wait.

On the way to the med room at 11:50, she pops into Mr. Stafford's room to start the Amphotericin IV. Mrs. Stafford takes this opportunity to ask Dominique if she can "clean him up a little bit."

"Sure," replies Dominique, even though it's the last thing she wants to do. She will have to do it in a hurry because, except for delivering tablet medications, she hasn't done anything all morning for one of her sickest patients—Arthur. Meanwhile, Denise's party down the hall is beginning. She turns Mr. Stafford on his side, opens his johnny, and, after donning another pair of rubber gloves and grabbing a washcloth, proceeds to clean his unsightly buttocks. Once again, she disposes all of the used materials, hastens to the linen cart, and returns with a clean johnny for Mr. Stafford. Both patient and wife express their thanks.

Arthur is about the same age as Tom. Lymphoma has eaten away at his flesh, reducing him to near-skeletal proportions. He is in constant pain and today is having constipation problems.

Without even waiting for a greeting, he questions Dominique. "How long does that laxative take to work?"

"If I don't get better results by tomorrow, we'll have to try something else. Moving your bowels would give you a lot of relief, but I don't want to give you an enema because your platelets are so low that it could cause bleeding." Exhaustion is creeping up on her. She shuffles as she walks and her sentences are clipped. "Now we have to change two dressings," she tells Arthur perfunctorily.

Dragging herself between the room's cabinet and the bedside for gloves, dressings, cotton swabs, and masks, she repeats the routines that she has just performed on Tom. The exception, in Arthur's case, is the necessity of rolling him over onto his side to change a dressing on an infected-looking bed sore at the base of his spine. To this ominous-looking lesion, she applies a medicated cream, the dressing, and the standard markings. The task completed, she uses one quick swoop to toss the soiled equipment into the appropriate waste containers. A wave and a "See you later" accompany her departure.

At last she'll be able to sit down, have some fun, eat some badly needed food. It has been four and a half hours since she's felt the contours of a chair. The anticipation of it prompts her body to relinquish the shuffle in favor of a stride, but as she approaches the nursing station, Michael calls out to her. "You've got a new admission—Mr. Donnelly in room twelve."

From under her breath comes, "Oh, no. I can't stand it. Just when I'm ready to relax a little." She knows she's only got enough energy left to offer a simple greeting to Mr. Donnelly. The admission workup and all of the documentation that goes with it will have to be put on hold. The detour to room 12 is a quick one. "Hi, Mr. Donnelly, I'm your nurse. My name is Dominique. I'm going to let you get settled. Make yourselves comfortable," she tells him and his worried-looking wife. "I'll see you again in a little while."

At 12:20 the party is in full swing in the tiny lounge—a tightly packed congregation of attractive Hawaiian-shirted nurses. Dominique sandwiches herself in between two people on the loveseat. Three half-eaten pizzas are on the table along with soft drinks and a sumptuous chocolate cake. The conversation is about drug salespeople. Karen says she can't stand them.

"What do you mean?" says a blonde nurse named Debbie. "I'm married to one, you know."

"Well, I like them when they bring those lunches," Dominique injects. "That last guy brought some good chicken." The group agrees that they like the lunches.

Nancy, a four-year veteran on the unit, says, "Let's face it, caregivers are all oral types."

"Well, that's better than being anal," says Dominique's good friend Katie.

Dominique, playing dumb, asks what the difference is between the two types, and Katie responds that anal personalities are uptight, while the oral ones are forever giving to themselves. They reach another consensus that being oral is a lot more fun and then amuse themselves briefly by placing one another into categories. Denise, they say, is definitely not anal, but neither is Debbie oral. Tiring of trying out the labels on themselves, they switch to the patients on the floor. Arthur is anal for sure, and so is Katie's patient, Mrs. Thompson. They start in on the doctors next. Doug Simpson, a new intern, is anal.

"No he's not," says Dominique. "He's passive-aggressive. He smiles while he lectures at you. He's condescending."

A chorus of people disagree—Lila, Nancy, Barbara. "He isn't like that with us."

"Well, what about David Benton?" Lila asks the group. "I think he's a nice guy."

"I think he's a little bit anal," says Debbie, "and obsessive-compulsive, too. He gets too depressed over here. He wants to get off this unit as fast as he can. A lot of interns are like that. They don't understand how we work here."

The discussion of orality and anality ends with a discourse from Lila about how anal her step-grandmother is. "She's anal personified," she concludes.

Denise has barely contributed to the frivolity that is taking place in her honor. Now, while they're all eating thin slices of cake in homage to the maintenance of their figures, she explains that she's not feeling well. Besides, she's worried because she doesn't see how she can finish everything today, and she certainly doesn't want to come back tomorrow to do it. But she wants everybody to understand that she's not depressed about leaving. On the contrary, she can hardly wait. One by one the nurses wish her well and reluctantly filter out to the unit. Several of them look as weary as Dominique.

The brief interlude of R and R has done little for Dominique's spirits. At 1:15, she sees more than an hour and three-quarters' worth of work ahead of her. There is still the workup on Mr. Donnelly—taking his vital signs, obtaining his medical history, implementing the doctor's orders, issuing the patient's personal supplies. All of this will take at least an hour of her time, and thereafter, she will need to make the rounds again on all of her other patients, many of whom will have to be remedicated. That will still leave her with all of her documentation duties and the tape recordings about her patients for the evening shift's report meeting.

Dominique hates the new documentation regulations.

> It takes us so much longer to do our nursing notations now. We have enough paperwork as it is, and this system just adds more. Within forty-eight hours of each new admission, we're supposed to have it completed, and that doesn't include the daily notes we have to record. We're always so short-staffed, and most of the time our census is high, higher than it is on 5C. It becomes impossible to keep up with it all, and the worst thing about it is that you don't have the time to relate to the patients the way you want to. I'd like to be involved in research projects, educational activities, and hospital committees, but I'd never get my work done if I did. Eventually, it gets to you.

These comments are overheard by Katie and Denise, who have entered the bubble, where Dominique is taking a brief time-out for documentation while an intern examines Mr. Donnelly. They echo Dominique. "Yeh, we're all taking LOA's [leaves of absence]. We're exhausted," says Katie. "A month after Denise is leaving, I'm going, and when I come back, Dominique is going. Besides being good friends and needing each other, our leaving makes it harder on one another. It adds fewer hands to the already short supply.''

At 5:00 P.M., two hours after the shift has changed, Dominique's day ends.

## July 13

A unit staff meeting follows report this morning. Wendy holds these weekly at different times. This morning she's listening to complaints from the staff. Dominique and Katie say they feel like they're running around frantically but getting nothing done.

Wendy tries to be supportive. "Look, you're not doing anything wrong. You have so much to do. We have more leukemic patients now than we've ever had, and they all have central lines to be maintained. Then there's the increased number of portacaths. All the new technology has increased your load. We could try becoming self-contained, but it would mean some longer shifts, and people would have to be willing to work them. Also, if you were willing to take them on as partners, we could hire a few more PCTs to help lighten the load. There are some things we can do to make it easier.''

"In order to do all this, though, we have to have a good, strong team. I'm not sure that we have that now,'' says Dominique.

"Well, you ought to think more about your options,'' Wendy responds on her way out the door of the lounge.

Several nurses linger for a few minutes, finishing their coffee. Dominique says she'd rather have nursing assistants than PCTs. (In taking this stand, Dominique is expressing the union's position. All of Memorial's staff nurses have some affiliation with the union. Debbie, in fact, is the union representative on the unit.) "They're more under our control. They can bring water to the patients, do their baths, answer their call lights. With PCTs, you have to take a lot of time to train and evaluate them. I don't know. Maybe

I'm wrong. Maybe I should reconsider, but that's how I feel now. And I don't think the self-containment idea will work here, either. The census fluctuates too much. The staff would have to increase their hours and fill in for each other. They won't buy into it. There are too many people with kids who want to come in, work their eight hours, and go home.''

The subject shifts to a topic introduced by Barbara, an especially articulate and thoughtful person, about nurses feeling more like engineers. "It makes me sick to see nursing becoming ever-more technical. All the relationship stuff that I went to school for in the first place gets lost. By the time you finally get to know the patient, he or she has died or left the hospital.''

"You can say that again," says Katie. "There's something special about giving someone a shower or a bath. You can complete a skin assessment and talk to a patient while you're doing it. The patients appreciate that kind of stuff— a walk, a bath, a conversation, a bed change. No one thanks you for the technical stuff. They don't say, Gee, thanks for the chemotherapy, thanks for flushing my central line.''

Barbara and Katie's remarks seem to revitalize the group. They are followed by a chorus of approval and an apparent renewal of physical energy. With their last sips of coffee still warm in their bellies, they file out into the corridor.

Today's activities are a repeat of yesterday's but a little less high-pressured. Mr. Riley has left the hospital. Arthur has developed another bed sore on his hip, and his entire back is bright red. Dominique applies lotion to his back, explaining as she does so that chemotherapy causes immunosuppression (decreasing of the capacity of the immune system to combat infection), which, in turn, increases the probability of bed sores and infections. Furthermore, the skin is affected by the diminished supply of nutrients that can be ingested by a patient whose appetite is as poor as Arthur's. Yesterday's bed sore is still a problem and now requires a change of dressing every twelve hours in addition to a high-sodium-concentrate application that acts faster than

Betadine to kill bacteria. In addition to these difficulties, Arthur still has the bowel trouble and a host of other complaints.

"Who's my primary nurse?" he asks wearily.

"I am," replies Dominique.

"Well, I lost my appetite again, I have a headache, and I'm in a lot of pain."

"I'll see what I can get for you."

She returns to the nursing station and pages the resident in charge of Arthur. She receives authorization to go ahead and administer morphine, and when she suggests a change of laxative, the resident agrees to come to the unit to see what she can do about it. Dominique hurries to the med room and back to Arthur's room with a full syringe.

Much to her surprise, Dominique finds that this morning, she has time for a coffee break. Actually, it's a breakfast-lunch combination. After taking food orders from everybody on the unit, she rides the elevator down to the cafeteria to bring back a tray of juice and bagels. On the way to and from and then back in the lounge, she talks to me about herself.

> I'm one of those people who always tries to plan her future course. I planned to put in a year or a year and a half here, then take a break to do some volunteer work, because I've always wanted to do that. I'm not as driven now as I used to be. I feel less energized and enthusiastic. I will probably come back here after my LOA to earn more money so that I can go to graduate school in some area of nursing. On this job, I feel I'm too busy to think, and I like thinking about things. It's only the people on the upper levels in this profession who get to do that. Sometimes, here, I feel like a peasant on the job, like I'm just surviving. Even if I have an easier day, like today, I'm stressed from the accumulation of stress.

Today will turn out to be one of those rare ones when she has time to take care of her patients as well as spend several hours on paperwork. Except for occasional interruptions, she is able to get caught up. By 3:30, she is on her way out of the hospital.

## July 17

At 11:00 A.M., the unit resembles a beehive swarming with doctors, dieticians, social workers, Sister Eileen—the hospital's peripatetic chaplain—and families, all converging at once at the nurses' station. More doctors arrive to join forces with the ones already present, and they reassemble to form a subgroup by the doorway of a patient's room. Dominique is visibly exhausted. She welcomes the opportunity to take a newly vacated seat at the station desk for a lengthy conversation with the Medical Intensive Care Unit (MICU) about Arthur. A stethoscope is draped from her neck and she is wrapping a requisition slip around a urine sample to be sent to the laboratory.

Today's fatigue is partly due to yesterday's activity. Arthur's mental status deteriorated, but the night-duty nurse mistook his agitation and disorientation for "tiredness." By the time Dominique arrived, he was extremely agitated. With the assistance of an intern and the weight of her full body, Dominique had to help hold him down so that she could draw his bloods, examine his portacath, and enable the intern to perform a lumbar puncture. After all of that they worried that he might have a cardiac arrest, so they sent him to the MICU. There the staff thought that they might have to intubate (resuscitate) him, but first they tried to give him chemotherapy through his spine. This killed the cancer that had spread to his spine and prevented the necessity of intubation. The feared cardiac arrest also was averted.

No sooner did Dominique complete this physically draining activity than she was greeted with the arrival of two new admissions. She didn't leave the hospital until 6:30.

Today she has four patients, and as she talks with the SICU nurse, she realizes that Arthur will be returning to the unit shortly. She believes that there is little more that 5B can offer Arthur. His downhill course has been rapid. He needs hospice care, and at the doctor's instruction, Dominique and Lucia, the unit social worker, begin the discharge process. After the last Tuesday morning unit discharge conference, at which Dominique discussed Arthur's condition with the health care team, there was a consensus that he was ready to leave the hospital. A bed awaits him in another facility. Until he is transferred, however, he will remain on 5B.

While waiting for Arthur's return, Dominique looks in on another patient who is not one of her "primaries," but someone she's caring for in the absence of the primary nurse. Mrs. Richards, a middle-aged woman, is sitting in a chair when Dominique appears. Although diagnosed with leukemia, she looks healthy in comparison to the other leukemic patients on the unit. On her lap are the week's menus, and she is devoting considerable energy to analyzing and documenting all of her complaints about the food on a separate piece of paper. Apparently, she and Memorial's Food Service Department have enjoyed a less-than-cordial relationship since her arrival. So preoccupied is she with culinary matters, in fact, that Dominique has difficulty diverting her attention from the menus to the bruise at the base of her neck. Dominique does not like its looks and announces that she will telephone the hematologist immediately. Returning to the room a few minutes later, she explains to this obviously intelligent patient that when her platelet count decreases, the tendency to bruise increases. The doctor will arrive soon to take a look. Mrs. Richards is one step ahead of Dominique. A former nurse herself, she already has detected the bruise, guessed its cause, and noted it in the ongoing record that she keeps on her condition.

"Oh, and by the way, Dominique, I've left quite a mess in there in the toilet," says Mrs. Richards.

"Good, I can do a stool test," responds Dominique, putting on rubber gloves and sticking the paper stool tester into Mrs. Richards' deposit in the aluminum pan over the toilet.

The completion of these nursing tasks allows Mrs. Richards to return to her favorite subject. "You see here where it says chicken cacciatore on this menu? If that was chicken cacciatore, then my name's not Dorothy Richards. All it is is a piece of chicken with a slab of cheese and a little tomato sauce thrown over it. I need to talk to those food service people again, Dominique."

"OK, I'll tell them to come in to see you," Dominique assures her as she tidies up the room in preparation for her departure. "I'll see you before I leave for the day."

As morning progresses into afternoon, Dominique is both exhausted and frustrated, and so are all of the other nurses on the unit. Today is one of those days when morale is so low that it seeks a scapegoat. Wendy is today's target. Katie, Dominique, Ann, and Maggie, two slightly older, more experienced nurses on the unit, talk about Wendy in hushed tones outside the room of one of Dominique's patients. From their disgruntled perspective, Wendy doesn't get involved with patient care even when they are up to their ears in overwork. She figures that the nurses will come to her if they need her, but they don't do so very often. They feel that Wendy should try to interest them in activities off the unit, both for a change of pace and for their own educational advancement. They wish she would show more leadership.

Right now they could use an extra pair of hands. One of Dominique's new admissions from the day before is a very heavy woman who needs to be transferred from her bed to a stretcher for transport to X ray for an MRI (magnetic resonance imaging, a high-powered imaging device that can detect anatomical abnormalities without using radiation). The MRI machine does not hold patients weighing more

than three hundred pounds, and this patient, they suspect,
may be borderline. Even with four nurses and the aid of the
plastic board, moving someone this heavy puts a strain on
the back muscles. Dominique, in her short career, already
has experienced back problems from so much lifting. After
all their effort, it may well be that the patient won't be able
to have the MRI anyway, will return shortly to the unit, and
will need to be moved again. Luckily, the man from transport arrives just as they are preparing to transfer the patient.
With his help, the job is easier. He promises the nurses that
when the patient returns, he will stay to help put her back
in bed.

Meanwhile, things haven't gone smoothly between Mrs.
Richards and food service. Now they've forgotten to bring
her lunch, so Dominique has to go down to the cafeteria
herself to fetch the cheese sandwich that Mrs. Richards
ordered. When she returns with the sandwich, it contains
the wrong kind of cheese. Another call to food service and
another head-on encounter between Mrs. Richards and the
department produces the desired sandwich. Dominique,
however, has more important things on her mind. Mrs.
Richards' platelet count is below 10, which means that she
needs a transfusion. In the meantime, Dominique must
change a dressing. The old one partially concealed the bleeding under the patient's skin that now becomes apparent in its
naked state. She goes through the usual change of dressing
motions and then decides to change Mrs. Richards' sheets.
Mrs. Richards, still stewing about the cheese, musters
enough gratitude to acknowledge what Dominique is doing
for her. "The nursing care here is excellent. You're all so
dedicated. You always make an extra effort. If only food
service was half as good as you nurses."

At last Mrs. Richards has her cheese, the platelets have
not yet arrived for the transfusion, the obese patient is the
responsibility of the MRI technicians, Arthur has not yet
returned from the Intensive Care Unit (ICU), and her other
two patients are not in need of immediate attention. Domi-

nique can take a late lunch break and relax on the loveseat in the lounge following another round-trip excursion to the cafeteria. She is feeling every bit the philosophical, martyred nurse.

There's something weird about this profession. They get you at eighteen. At nineteen, they start you in a hospital. Right away, you're dealing with life and death. At first, you're very emotional about it. I had a favorite patient when I first came here. He was a cop, and I went out of my way for him because we hit it off so well. I even got an ambulance for him for his son's wedding, an arrangement the family usually makes. When he died, I took it hard. I felt that I should have saved him. Sooner or later, you learn that you can't take it all to heart. It's probably not a good idea to work on a unit like this right out of school; better to wait until you're more mature. None of your friends on the outside see death as an everyday occurrence. For them, it's an extraordinary event.

She pauses to remember how she used to be.

I used to be so idealistic. I took the toughest cases. I was always revved up. Everything I did was accompanied by enthusiasm, even a trip to the pharmacy. I'd speak in an excited Miss Nancy Nurse voice. Now I speak in a monotone.

The day ends, late as usual, after Arthur has returned to the unit. Dominique has transfused Mrs. Richards. Arthur has not yet been placed on DNR status, but his prognosis is very bad—he's a step away from death's doorway. Dominique thinks Arthur's mother should be told that if he is put on a resuscitator, he'll never revive, but that the doctor is afraid to say, Look, if you want us to resuscitate him, just remember that if we ever take him off the machine, he'll be a vegetable. "It's not my place to advise the family about what to do unless they ask for my advice, but I think I have a responsibility to advocate for the patient with his physician. I intend to tell the doctor that I think Arthur should be DNR instead of full code."

## July 18

Another bad day. The unit resembles an airport in bad weather. Crowds milling around. Internal vehicles clogging the corridors. Too many patients being transferred to stretchers for journeys to different parts of the hospital. Some of these patients are Dominique's, some are assigned to other nurses, but either way, she must lend a hand. There are not enough transport personnel to do the job. Arthur is one of those being transported. This time, he's going for a colonoscopy, a test that will detect any obstruction in the bowel. Now the doctors are suspicious that an infection may be developing. If they are correct, his discharge from the hospital will be postponed further.

Today's activities pile on yesterday's as representative of the downside of nursing. "These transport problems are a good example of the kind of stuff we didn't want to hear about when we were in school. We wanted to be in love with the profession. Practicing nurses warned us about the scut work, but we paid no attention," explains Dominique while contributing to the traffic jam by pushing a stretcher up the corridor to a patient's room.

From 7:00 to 9:30 A.M., Dominique has done nothing for her patients except move them around. She hasn't even listened to report. It is 11:00 before she finishes report and begins seeing those of her patients who are still on the floor.

Mrs. Golini, in her fifties, has liver cancer and needs blood drawn—a daily occurrence for most patients. The bulk of the blood drawing is done during the day so that the doctors can receive the lab results and direct the patients' care. Tests are run for counts on hematocrit (percentage of red blood cells), platelets (type of blood cells responsible for clotting), electrolytes (important body substances), BUN, and creatinine (measures of kidney function). With a central line in place, the patient can sleep through the blood-drawing procedure. Mrs. Golini does, and she continues resting peacefully as an extra tube of blood is drawn as a "waste tube" to extract the chemotherapy and clear the lines. On a daily basis, too, each patient's vital signs are taken—temperature, pulse, blood pressure, and respirations. Mrs. Golini awakens but remains drowsy during the vital signs. Her eyes close again as soon as Dominique is finished.

From Mrs. Golini's room Dominique wends her way in search of vital signs and medication recipients to Mr. Donnelly and then to Mrs. Driscoll, a slim woman in her mid-fifties. There are no unusual problems with Mr. Donnelly, but when she enters Mrs. Driscoll's room, she finds her moaning and crying. Dominique is not sure whether the sounds she is making are indications of pain or a degenerating mental status brought on by sepsis (a general blood infection that can affect the brain). The mere touch of Dominique's hand on her body stirs Mrs. Driscoll to invoke aid from higher powers. "Try taking a few deep breaths, hon . . . ," advises Dominique. Mrs. Driscoll is in no mood or condition to take deep breaths or medications; nor can she tolerate the checking of her vital signs. Dominique exits quickly to call her doctor.

By the end of another extended day, Arthur has not returned from his last excursion off the unit, but Dominique's other patients have. There are the usual routine tasks to close out the day plus a final indignity at the hands of Mrs. Driscoll's daughter, who makes an untimely appearance at the nursing station. Michael summons Dominique to answer the daughter's numerous questions about her mother. Politely, she does as she is bid, and after her lengthy explanation, the daughter says, "I want to see the doctor. Can you page him for me?" Dominique leaves the hospital feeling that her words fell on deaf and unappreciative ears.

## July 20

A fairly typical day. In the med room Barbara and Dominique are engaged in a long conversation. Their doubts about nursing are the focus once again.

Barbara begins the conversation. "I think I might go back to graduate school in philosophy. Maybe I'll go for a Ph.D. Let's tell it like it is, nursing is a troubled profession with a high physical and emotional burnout rate, and it's not well regarded by the public or by other professionals. In my nursing school in the Midwest, they taught us a lot of theory. They didn't want to graduate a bunch of task-oriented nurses. I don't know about you, but for me, the disappointment came when I got into practice. I wasn't treated by patients, doctors, managers, or peers like I was a knowledgeable person. There are some patients I've helped. Those who accepted their death and resolved it with their families. Oncology nursing teaches you what's important in life. It's important to do what you want to do, because your time to live is limited. Working with dying people helps you lead a better life."

"I don't know. It makes me feel depressed most of the time," replies Dominique. "Some of my patients stay for a long time, and it's always the same unhappy ending. It's better to work with the surgical patients. At least there's some hope for them. I don't see much physical healing. Maybe I see some emotional healing. When I first came, I wanted to connect with people and help them through the dying process, but frequently I feel dumped on by the very people I want to help.

"Then, there are the nursing administrators. They've turned their attention to financial matters, and they don't inform us about what is going on. It makes me feel like they don't think that we're professionals who could comprehend the information. Most of the nurses here are like me. They have bachelor's degrees, but if the administration doesn't work to maintain the values of our profession, the quality of the people who enter it will decline. It already has, I think. I don't think the doctors are as good as they used to be, either.''

Debbie, the union representative joins Barbara and Dominique in the med room and adds her perspective to the discussion while all three of them retrieve, record, label, and mix their medications. ''There's a lot of apathy in the union, too. People don't show up for meetings because they think that unions have a blue-collar image, but you can bet your bottom dollar that they like the salary increases and the benefits. I think you're right, Dominique, that the best and brightest are leaving the profession. A few of them become private home-care nurses. They feel they'll be more respected that way, even if they make less money. I'm envious of the autonomy they have. I'd like to have more responsibility here, but when I tell Wendy, she doesn't seem very responsive.''

''You know what I hate the most?'' offers Dominique. ''It's when people say, 'Oh, you're a nurse, isn't that nice.' They don't say that to doctors. It's easy to abuse us, just like mothers take more grief from their kids than fathers do. A lot of the abuse is physical—the lifting and transferring of patients. I don't have a lot of complaints about the doctors here, though. I feel that I have good relationships with them. Like early this morning with Diane Dunlop—you know, the attractive new black resident. I told her that I thought that Arthur was suffering more from depression than from physical pain. Let's give him an antidepressant, I suggested. She thought it was a great idea. We worked as a team, and that's when we're at our best. She looks to me a lot because she knows I see Arthur every day. Still, it's rare that I have time to communicate with the doctors, because we're so short-staffed now. When nurses leave, they don't replace them, because of budget cuts. Patients, even if they don't know it, won't go to the hospital if there aren't nurses to care for them. There's a float out on the floor today. She's worked three different units in one twelve-hour shift. Now if that's not nurse abuse, what is?''

The conversation between the nurses has gone on longer than intended. Suddenly all three of them scurry out of the med room with armfuls of equipment. Dominique has five patients today, and she's trying not to feel guilty about having talked for so long. Arthur, she knows, is waiting for the pain medication that Dr. Dunlop authorized an hour ago. Now the nutrition specialist stops her at the station to discuss Arthur's dietary condition.

"We're going to try feeding him with an IV," she tells Dominique, "so he'll worry less about not eating."

"Good idea," replies Dominique. "Thanks for helping."

"Where have you been?" Arthur asks angrily when Dominique enters his room. "The pain is awful."

Last night Arthur was on Narcon, a medication that counters the effect of high dosages of narcotics. Dominique stretches the truth slightly as she explains that she just received approval from the doctor to give him more pain medication. "I couldn't give it to you until I got an OK," she says.

"Well, hurry up, then," responds the annoyed patient. Dominique inserts the syringe in his arm. Without a word of acknowledgment, he closes his eyes and shuts out the world.

Mrs. Richards is in a conversational mood again today. She welcomes the opportunity to talk about the changes in nursing. While checking her vital signs, Dominique tells her about the med room discussion. Mrs. Richards agrees.

Yes, I know what you mean. The public doesn't understand that nurses have to be constantly upgraded and reeducated. They're going to have to become computer experts besides becoming junior engineers. Nurses are with patients much more than doctors are. They're critical to our health. The public doesn't grasp that, either. What they also need to know is that if doctors and nurses are the first and second arms of a hospital, surely food service is the third. I wrote to the hospital administration about this. I warned them about using euphemisms to describe the food, and I said that they shouldn't cut back on quality for the sake of the budget. They can't keep recycling the food. I think I might have had an impact, because I've noticed an improvement in the meat. It's more moist. For me to come back here again, though, they're going to have to do more than that. If they don't, I think I'll move to California, where my daughter is, for future hospitalizations.

By the end of the day, Dominique learns that Arthur has refused the TPN help. Tomorrow, she knows, will mean more problems for him. Although he likes the idea of eating, his poor appetite will act as his own worst enemy in the ongoing battle to keep nourished.

## August 2

Tomorrow never came. Dominique was sick for a week with the flu. This is her first day back. Her return coincides with a rare meeting between the 5B staff and Colleen Lindstrom, this time for the settling of a unit grievance about a job listing in the Outpatient Chemotherapy Clinic. According to the staff, the job was posted as a single, forty-hour position. Three people interviewed for it, and finally it was decided that it could be split between two people. Apparently, the nursing department had changed its mind midway through the process without relaying the news back to 5B. Someone on behalf of the staff reported it to the union on the grounds that it was an example of the withholding of vital information. The staff maintained that more people might have applied had they known that the job could be shared.

Colleen felt hurt by 5B's reaction. She apologized to the group for not informing them of the change in hiring procedure, promised to reconsider the matter, and emphasized that no deceit had been intended. "I can't believe that you'd think that I'd purposefully deceive you," she announced to the group. "I wish someone had come to me about it." The pain of the encounter would stay with Colleen for several days after the meeting. What wounded her the most was the realization that they hadn't trusted her enough to come to her before going to the union.

Upon Colleen's departure, the staff addresses the issue of documentation. Dominique, still weary from the flu, has countless complaints about documentation but not enough energy to voice them. Other nurses express the essence of her thoughts—they are too busy to complete it on time and there's just too much of it.

"I know, I know," says Wendy. "I'll tell them [Nursing Administration] that it's too crazy on this unit now. I'll ask how they possibly can expect us to document dates for meeting patient goals when our patients are so sick. Right after an admission, we can't forecast how long it's going to take to implement our outcomes. We'll review our classification sheets to see how much staff we've said we require. I'm sure that we can demonstrate how understaffed we are, and how stressed we are as a result."

Dominique, perhaps energized by Wendy's outburst of empathy, adds, "It's funny how they want us to take even more of our time to write down how much of our time our tasks take."

Today's good news is that the unit census is very low. Dominique has three patients, only one of whom is her primary patient. Arthur, much to Dominique's astonishment, still resides on 5B. He has requested to be returned to food, but when he gets it, he doesn't eat it. To make matters worse for him, the bowel infection has materialized. Arthur can't be discharged until it's treated. Just prior to the staff meeting, she checked in on him and observed redness and swelling on his nose. Her suspicion that his platelets are low is confirmed later by Diane Dunlop. Dominique is pleased with herself for making the observation. It prevents the administering of another painful lumbar puncture.

Thoughts of Arthur preoccupy Dominique this day. His misery and her career blend into one long shadow. She remembers the personal power she felt almost two years ago when she entered the medical world as a genuine professional, and she can recall the inner voice that told her that she had been granted a special invitation into others' private lives. Some people had been grateful for her presence, had turned to her in need and desperation, while others had withdrawn from her as time and illness advanced. Like Arthur, they increasingly had used her as the target for their frustration. The more control they lost, the more they tried to control her, the more distance they put between themselves and her. Eventually they couldn't remember her name. Then she would find herself withdrawing, too. Mustering sympathy became more difficult.

Perhaps her own bout with the flu and her absence as a consequence have made sympathy more accessible today. Or maybe it's the low census. But now when she enters Arthur's room, her voice is full of sympathy.

"It's just one thing after another, isn't it, Arthur? Just when you think you've got one thing beat, another comes along," she tells him as she places a hand on his brow.

"Yup," he answers quietly. "Yup."

## August 3

Dominique has been trying out a new coping mechanism this morning. She is determined not to expend valuable energy worrying about how much work she has. In an attempt to maintain harmony between mind and body, she moves slowly. She adopts a strolling gait in place of the usual stride or shuffle. So far, she's pleased with the results. By noon she feels she's accomplished at least as much as she does by the same time on days when she's frantic.

The stench from Arthur's room, malodorous in the corridor, is overpowering as Dominique moves closer to the bed.

He greets her with, "I'm a mess. And by the way, where's my lunch?"

"Let me get you cleaned up first, and then I'll go and see. You're supposed to have baked fish today," she replies cheerily.

"It will be cold," he says.

"Well, I guess we'll have to put it in the microwave."

"Then it will be cold and hard."

Ignoring his complaints, she takes the precautionary measures in preparation for the cleanup. She turns him gently and effortlessly onto his side and confronts a seeping mass of loose, orange-colored stool on his body, on the johnny, and on his plastic "chuck" pad. Nothing in her expression communicates revulsion. Some of the stool she places in a plastic container to send to the laboratory to check the progress of his infection. The remainder she transfers to the wastebasket or to multiple washcloths, which soon join the johnny and the bed linen in the hamper. With Arthur in the bed, she quickly and efficiently changes the johnny and the bed linen. Then she props him up in bed for his reward—the microwaved baked fish. He receives it silently.

In keeping with today's vow of calmness, she goes to the cafeteria at 12:30 to fetch a well-balanced lunch to bring back to the lounge. There she meets Ann and her new PCT partner, Sheila, the only PCT on 5B. Sheila is a pretty blonde with a winning smile who is a fairly recent liberal arts graduate of a western university. She has enrolled in Memorial's program to see if nursing is appealing enough to entice her to take advantage of the hospital's tuition reimbursement benefit for nursing school. After two weeks' labor on an oncology unit, she is reminded of the social work she did with hard-core delinquents—they both seem futile. She confesses to feeling shocked at how little time the nurses have to spend with their patients.

"And the doctors are an enigma to me, too," Sheila continues. "I don't see them with the patients very often. They're always in the charts [patient records]. The patients ask me so many questions that I can't help but think there's a communication breakdown somewhere. It seems like there are about sixteen people in between the patient and the doctor. I don't think oncology is the field for me. I get satisfaction out of helping people, but I don't want to feel that it's all for naught."

"Yeh, this is the least popular unit for PCTs," says Ann. "It's easy to understand why. Still, if Sheila and I work well together, and we can demonstrate that having a PCT helps lighten our load, then other nurses will want to take them on. So far, they've been reluctant. They're partly afraid that it will take too much time to train them."

Dominique listens intently to Sheila and Ann, mulling over her own resistance to taking on a PCT. Wendy has encouraged her to do so, but so far, she's refused. She guesses that she'll wait and see how things work out between these two. If all goes well with them, maybe she'll volunteer as a partner when she returns from her LOA.

For the rest of the day, Dominique goes about her business in matter-of-fact fashion. She has two new admissions. One is Mr. Carbone, who was diagnosed several years ago with prostate cancer. He's being admitted now for back pain and severe constipation. His probably will be a short stay, and while he's hospitalized, his nursing care will be geared to pain control. Dominique does not anticipate that she will need to take any extraordinary measures on his behalf.

By 3:45 P.M., she's finishing her report for the evening shift. She speaks into the machine.

Mr. Williams is a young sickle celler. Readmitted with complaints of priopisms [prolonged, painful

erection of the penis]. He isn't in as much pain as he
says. We had him on Demerol, but it was too much
for him. We had to force him to come down on the
dosage. Check with the resident before you give him
anything for pain. He's afebrile [no fever]. Blood
pressure is a hundred thirty over a hundred. He'll go
home in a day or so.

In conclusion, she reels off a string of lab results into the
recorder. Her last words are, "So that's the story on him."

## August 9

Mary Lou has returned to the day shift from her evening-
shift rotation, and she and Dominique are chatting in the
lounge after report.

"Evenings are a better deal. You don't have to draw
bloods, change beds, do baths or charts, and they have the
same number of patients that we do," says Mary Lou.

"Well, at least today won't be so bad. I have four patients, but Mr. Stafford is being discharged. I have a lot of
help today. Peggy is going to work with me. It will give me
time to get caught up on documentation. And now that
you're back, Mrs. Richards has her primary nurse on days,
and I'm off the case. I'll miss her, though. She's fun to talk
to. I can't complain. At least I'm not in the reserves, so I
won't have to go to Saudi Arabia. I'd get pregnant immediately if I thought I had to go," says Dominique in a display
of good humor.

Mary Lou and Dominique head for the nursing station,
where Michael is holding forth about a memo that has come
around soliciting the staff's ideas on promotional slogans
for the media department. He is flanked by several laughing
nurses as he offers suggestions.

"How about, We May Not Be the Best, But We're Definitely the Most Expensive?" His audience likes what they're

hearing, so much so, in fact, that each new slogan he advances contains progressively blacker humor.

"Oh, Michael, you're sooooo bad!" says Maggie.

More laughter.

"So are all of you for laughing," replies Michael, rather pleased with himself for having the last word.

Dominique carries the good vibrations with her as she listens to the chest of her new admission, Mr. Liacopulos.

"Are you from Greece?" she asks him.

"I'm from southern Greece, but I've been in the U.S. for thirty years. I don't know why I have to be in the hospital, though. I've been here before for chemotherapy," he says in heavily accented English.

"What is your illness?" Dominique asks.

"I'm not sure, but the doctor says I'm good."

"You've had some form of cancer, right? Where?"

He points to his chest.

"The lung?"

He nods in affirmation.

"How about your eating and going to the bathroom?"

"Sometimes I can't sleep. I've got too much on my mind. I worry."

"Me, too," says Dominique with a laugh. "We'll get along just fine. I bet you try to sleep all the next day when you've worried the whole night before."

Mr. Liacopulos smiles in agreement. "This leg doesn't feel good. I think they're going to operate on it later."

"You've probably got poor circulation. What about your family? Do you live alone?"

"I've got four big children and seven grandchildren. I live with my wife and my daughter, but my wife is in Greece now."

"I hope you'll get to go there soon. You deserve a trip. I went there once. It's a great country. How's your energy level, though?"

"No good. I retired in 1978. I was a tailor. I became

disabled with a pinched nerve. Since then I've had two operations, one for my gall bladder and one for appendicitis. I don't do much of anything these days."

"Did you ever smoke?"

"Yes, but now I only smoke fifteen to sixteen cigarettes a day. I smoked since I was thirteen. Now I'm seventy-three. I've got diabetes, too."

"Any other pain or discomfort, like sores on your body?"

"No, just my leg."

"Alright, hon, I'll be back later to give you your meds. It was nice talking to you."

"Thank you."

For Dominique, this kind of interaction is the best part of nursing, the part she seldom has time for. She leaves his room with a warm glow and takes a phone call at the station from a nurse at another hospital. The caller seems to be blaming Memorial's staff for Mr. Riley's having aspirated shortly after he was discharged. He had to be rushed to the nearby hospital. "We did a head-to-toe assessment on him before we discharged him. There were no indications that this would happen," Dominique informs the caller. By the time she hangs up, the warm glow is fading. "I don't know what they expect," she says. "You just can't anticipate everything."

Arriving at Arthur's room, she finds Sheila already there. Arthur has pushed his call button. "His cath was leaking, and he wants pain medication," explains Sheila. As she leaves the room, she calls back to Arthur, "Your lunch is here."

Dominique brings him the lunch and tells him that he's looking better today. A faint smile crosses his face in acknowledgment of the compliment. He turns on his side to get more comfortable in readiness for eating sideways.

"Let me give you this shot real quick before you eat," says Dominique, and she gives him the injection. "Have a good lunch. I'll be back to change your IV tubing. I have to do it every seventy-two hours, you know. Otherwise you might get an infection."

Navigating a large weight and height measurement machine down the corridor to Mr. Liacopulos's room is a task she welcomes.

"Hi, I'm back again," she announces as she enters.

His response is a weary one. No doubt he's been trying to recover from the previous night's worry. Reluctantly, he cooperates with her in the face of this invasion of privacy.

"Good, you weigh 149 pounds and you're five foot three. Now you can go back to bed."

"Thank you," he replies.

The afternoon's activities bring her spirits down and yesterday's resolve along with them. There have been new admissions and some reshuffling of assignments. She's back up to six patients. Two female patients are complaining. One of them speaks rudely to her about the heat in the room just after she's given her a lot of special attention. The other one has been in the hospital for a few days but just recently was assigned to Dominique. When Dominique passes her room on the way to somewhere else, she hollers out to her, "Aren't you going to change my bed, and bring me a fresh johnny?" Without a word exchanged by either party, the fresh johnny and the bed change are accomplished.

Dominique shares the afternoon's frustration with Maggie, who whispers in her ear, "Come on Dom, you can do it. You've only got a couple of hours to go."

It turns out to be more than a couple of hours, and it requires a major effort to go about the simple motions of departure when that time finally comes. On the way out, she chuckles over the documentation error she made in Mr. Liacopulos' chart. "Retired taylor," she had written. Someone had looked over her shoulder and pointed out the misspelling, but in hindsight Dominique thinks it might have been better to let it stand as "documentation of burnout."

"Maybe, though, I shouldn't have stayed out until 4:00 A.M. with Mark last night," she reminds herself.

## WEEKEND SHIFT

### August 12, 3:00 to 11:00 P.M.

Mary Lou is right. Weekends are a good deal. There's very little traffic—mostly visiting families, fewer nurses, one or two doctors at the nursing station, a weekend secretary, lots of chatting time in the med room. On this Sunday the census is low, and after she's taken report, Dominique sees that she has an exceptionally short patient assignment roster. Richard, a ten-year weekend veteran on the nursing staff, is with her in the med room.

"I stay home with the kids during the week while my wife works. I take care of all the stuff at home that mothers usually do. Like tomorrow I've got to remember to order fishnet stockings for my daughter's dance class. The schedule works out well for us. I went to a good college on an athletic scholarship, but I was a mediocre student. After a year, I quit. I worked a lot of manual labor and semiprofessional jobs before I hit on nursing. Weekend evening work is the best. There's less stress. The morale is better. Most of the big tasks have been done by the day people. We may administer more chemotherapy and transfusions, but it's not the hard physical stuff that the day shift gets. I like working with women. They're cooperative."

"Well, you may not like working with me today, because I'm in a bad mood. Mark and I had a fight last night about the Middle East," Dominique tells Richard and the newly arrived male pharmacist. "You know what he said? Those Arabs cause all the trouble. I told him it just wasn't that simple, but he's Jewish, so he thinks that everything the Israelis do is right. I don't know if I could spend my life with somebody who doesn't analyze issues from all sides."

"It sure is weird how the United States behaves," replies the pharmacist, whose last name reveals his Armenian ancestry. "Three weeks ago the Iranians were the bad guys. Now it's the Iraqis."

As the pharmacist exits the med room, two more nurses enter and the Middle East discussion is abandoned. All of them except Dominique are standing there talking about their patients and filling up syringes. Dominique is mixing medicines, "because if they're mixed long before ingestion (premixed) they're not as stable." She's ready now to make the rounds on the quiet unit to pass out pills and all manner of liquid elixirs.

Tom is confused when she enters. "Where is my other nurse?" he asks.

"She's off duty."

"Oh, I wanted her to heat up my soup, but now I guess I'll wait to have it later."

"Don't worry, I'll do it for you," says Dominique reassuringly as she hands him water and pills.


Arthur is complaining about his herpes-irritated scrotum and the medication he's been receiving for it when Dominique drops in on him. Dominique returns to the med room to find something to relieve Arthur's suffering.

Carol, another weekend nurse, is in the med room. She's complaining about the conduct of an intern. "He scratches his balls while he's talking to the family. It was so embarrassing, I had to leave."

Dominique laughs with Carol and scurries back to Arthur with a pain medication before moving on to a patient who was admitted on the day shift. He's sharing a room with Tom, and while Dominique is talking to the anxious patient, in the next bed, Tom is making noises obviously intended to get her attention. She continues talking to the patient.

"You seem very upset. What's the matter?"

"I don't know what's wrong with me. Maybe I have a bad cancer. My wife died of it, and it was terrible."

"Have you had a chance to talk with a doctor about your condition?"

"Not really."

"Let me see if I can get him for you."

The doctor whose comportment Carol just recounted is seated at the nursing station. "The new patient in twenty-two is very anxious. Do you think you could look in on him?" she asks.

"Sure, I'll do it right now," he answers with a smile and without any indication of a return of his scratching urge.

Dominique now pays a visit to the female patient who spoke gruffly to her a few days earlier about the room temperature.

"I want to go home," she screams as soon as she sees Dominique. "Why can't I go?"

"You're not stable enough."

"What does that mean?"

"You're still too sick to leave the hospital."

"Well, take this thing off, will you?" The patient points to her johnny.

"I will when I can," replies Dominique.

Exiting the room, Dominique conjectures that the patient's cancer may have spread to her brain.

> The confusing thing, though, is that she's not consistent. She's nice to some people and not to others. Her behavior might have something to do with reactions to medication, too. The doctor thinks she might be allergic to the stuff she's on. I think I'll go look for a possible substitute in the handbook while the doctor is still on the floor. Today there will be time for the two of us to talk about the patient and the treatments that are right for her. I like being able to do that.

On the way to the handbook and the conference with the doctor, Dominique checks on Arthur again. He's still miserable. Now he is sweating. "I'd better take your temperature right now," says Dominique. "You look diaphoretic [sweaty]."

Arthur is too sick to care or understand. He lies passively on the bed. Unbeknown to him, he will soon be making another foray to the X-ray Department to determine if his feeding tube is properly inserted.

For the most part this shift has been kind to Dominique. At the end of it, she feels well organized and complete. Every task is finished on schedule. She's been able to confer with the doctor, get better acquainted with Mr. Liacopulos, and enjoy a six o'clock dinner break. Tom has thanked her for remembering to heat his soup. Her relationship with Mr. Liacopulos has inspired her and caused her to reflect on how much easier it is for her to relate to older people. "They have a stronger sense of self. They're wiser. They've learned to let go of a lot of unimportant things that younger people still cling to," she muses. At 11:00 P.M. on the button, she's on her way to meet Mark. If all goes as she would like it to, he will have grown a little wiser and will have reconsidered his position on the Middle East.

## NIGHT SHIFT

### July 2

There is an eerie feeling on the unit at night. The lights are dim and the air is so still that every patient's moan and groan is audible. To be on an oncology unit in darkness is to feel the inevitability of one's own mortality with an intensity that cannot be experienced during the day, when the sounds from the patients are drowned out by the unending human, telephonic, and vehicular commotion. For the uninitiated observer, a visit to the night shift is as hard on the emotions as it is on the body. "Here but for the grace of God go I," one tells oneself, "and even though I may escape today, tomorrow still awaits me."

The night shift is hard, too, on the bodies of those who don't work it regularly. Dominique tries to minimize the effects of it by staying up late the night before and sleeping as long as possible during the day. Even with this precaution, though, by 4:00 A.M., nausea begins to creep up on her, and it remains with her through the busiest part of the shift, from 5:00 to 7:00 A.M.

Tonight Dominique is the charge nurse, which means that she has administrative responsibilities in addition to her clinical tasks. She must check the code cart (the equipment used for emergencies, such as cardiac arrests), check the acucheck machine (emergency equipment for diabetics), and make the patient assignments for the upcoming day shift. All staff nurses take turns in the charge nurse position, and they are paid a few dollars more per hour when they do so. On this shift there is only one other nurse in Dominique's charge. She is a nightime regular and thus wider awake than Dominique. The two of them will split the unit coverage in half, one nurse on each of the two corridors.

The tape recorder informs Dominique of her responsibilities for the full complement of eight patients that are assigned to her: a thirty-eight-year-old woman with vaginal cancer; a sixty-four-year-old man with lung cancer; a mildly retarded man in his mid-forties who is a drug abuser, HIV positive, and in renal failure; a sixty-two-year-old man with prostate cancer; and a young woman with gastric cancer; and the three primary patients on her side of the unit. The other nurse will cover her other two primary patients, because they are housed on the opposite side.

Dominique begins the shift exhausted, having violated her sleep rule by rising at 8:00 this morning. She needs coffee to get going. She starts off with blood draws. The on-duty medical student wants one drawn immediately on a patient with a low hematocrit. Within fifteen minutes of his request, Dominique has the bloods in the tube on their way to the laboratory. For the next three hours, she draws more bloods than usual for this shift and passes out medications to her patients. It is only her own fatigue and nausea that slow her progress. Most of the patients are groggy and therefore are less inclined to conversation than they would be on the day shift.

Multiple cups of coffee are her antidotes for exhaustion, but eventually they wreak havoc with her stomach. Dominique completes her first rounds of the patients by 2:30 A.M. From then until 5:00 A.M., except for occasional interruptions answering call lights, she works on day-shift assignments and documentation. By 5:00 the dreaded nausea is full-blown, but the medication rounds begin again despite it. She shuffles in and out of every room, waking the weary occupants for their medications, then tallying all of their fluid inputs and outputs on their bedside clipboards. When it's time to give report, she includes the totals in her recorded messages for the day shift. Although she's off the unit by 7:30, she dares not drive without nutritional fortification from the cafeteria. "Night shift nurses on the roads in the morning are a hazard to all the other drivers. It would be so easy to fall asleep at the wheel," she explains.

## August 15

"I overslept. I woke up at ten o'clock, threw on my clothes, and drove in," Dominique tells the other night nurse, Nancy, in the lounge apologetically. Another long list of patients tonight, but the unit is hushed as the shift begins. The voice on the recorder is rushing, sometimes barely audible.

Terrific improvement in Mrs. Johnson. Her lymph nodes and white count are good. The hematologists are thrilled. New admission in room six. Lung cancer. I did the care plan and the functional health assessment. Mr. Shaugnessy in room eight has laryngeal cancer. His bile is light green. He's voiding in his urinal. Needs a dose of milk of magnesia tomorrow.

Mr. Andrews is alert. His mental status is improved. He's going home or to a hospice. [Dominique can't understand the rest of the story on this patient. Something about lack of IV access and an irrigating Foley catheter.] Mr. Bolling in room two has epigastric pain [pain in the front walls of the abdomen]. He's on IV magnesium sulfate. He's NPO [nothing by mouth]. No stool from him yet. He's supposed to save it. He's due for an EKG. He'll be asking for more Demerol. In room four, you've got Mrs. . . . with gleomyosarcoma [a form of brain cancer] in one bed and Mrs. Yount with ovarian cancer in the other. [Again, the details on these patients fade out as the reporter hastens through.]

True to the prediction of the reporting nurse, Dominique hears Mr. Bolling call out for pain medication just as she's exiting the lounge. In the med room, she loads up a syringe with Demerol and takes it to the pleading patient. "OK, a quick pinch, then a little pressure. Now it's over. You'll be fine in a minute," she whispers to the anguished Mr. Bolling.

Back in the med room, she and Nancy chat as they line up their medications in preparation for delivery. Dominique is thinking more about tomorrow than she is about today. Arthur will be leaving for the hospice in two days and she will have a lot to do to prepare him for discharge. She is pleased that finally he has been placed on DNR status. Nancy interrupts her thoughts with complaints about one of the doctors.

"He wants a blood draw right away. He's new. He's concerned about every little thing. He has the I'm-the-doctor, where's-the-nurse? attitude. I tried to tell him that this patient doesn't need acute care at this minute, but he doesn't get it. I've got to go do it now, which really gets my goat. I'm leaving all my meds on the counter for a minute while I'm gone."

"OK. I won't touch them. Don't worry about it," replies Dominique in a soothing voice to her departing colleague. Dominique admires Nancy.

She's the best nurse. She's honest and sincere and has a huge heart. She works so hard, but like many nurses, she can't say no. We try to coach her to say it, and she's improved, but she still gets overwhelmed at times. Then she can't think straight. She's a ripe candidate for burnout. Awhile ago, she worked herself into a state that put her own health in serious jeopardy. I think of her as a perfect example of the undervalued nurse.

Dominique makes her rounds, trying as often as possible to work in the dark, to avoid awakening the patients. As she's hanging the IV drips in Mr. Andrews' room, he awakens in spite of her efforts. "What's that?" he asks, and then, without benefit of an answer, utters, "I have to write out a will." Having apparently said what needed to be said, he returns to sleep.

The hours go by slowly as Dominique refills the IV solutions, dispenses medications, and answers call buttons for painkillers. Mr. Bolling is the worst offender, keeping her on her feet at regular intervals all night. Her nausea comes on earlier than usual and by 5:00 becomes so intolerable that she has to spread herself out flat over several chairs for a few minutes to recover. Against the dictates of her body, she reenters every patient's room for the last time, carrying with her a silent prayer. "Please, God, don't let any of them have a problem, because then I won't be able to leave on time." On this early morning, the Lord has heard her prayer, and so, she believes, has Arthur. Miraculously, even Mr. Bolling has run out of steam.

# HIGH TECH, HIGH TOUCH

## GINA ROSSI, CLINICAL NURSE SPECIALIST, SURGICAL INTENSIVE CARE UNIT

**T**WO FLIGHTS DOWN from the oncology units where Jessie and Dominique are encamped lies the sprawling Surgical Intensive Care Unit, which shares the third floor of the Pavillion Building with the OR. No magic carpet leads one to the SICU. Friends and families of the patients enter through a short corridor that leads them to a comfortable lounge located out of viewing range of the unit. Big metal double doors greet the other visitors—hospital personnel and vendors—within a few steps of the elevator. For them, the initial greeting is hygienic and antiseptic, clean and colorless, like a scene from science fiction. But these visual effects lose some of their significance as soon as one gains entry. Then sound replaces sight as the sensory enticement. A never-ending high-tech symphony of buzzers, beeps, and blips seems, at first glance, to so captivate its audience of nurses, doctors, and patients that their individual identities recede into a kind of never-never land where instruments, not people, are predominant. Yet the SICU has more nursing personnel than any other unit in the hospital except the operating room—over seventy people responsible for the nursing care of sixteen patients (when the house is full) on a unit comparable in square footage to 5C.

Acknowledgment and recognition of faces and personalities come gradually after the auditory shock wears off. Even the layout of the unit favors the visibility of technology over people. Unlike 5B and 5C, the nursing station is not the obvious port of call on the SICU. Gene, the popular secretary, is hard to find, sequestered as he is around a bend and behind a partition. Still harder to find, unless they're out on the floor, are Caroline O'Rourke, the attractive, young, good-natured nurse manager, and Gina Rossi, the older but equally attractive clinical nurse specialist, whose offices are opposite each other on a small corridor off the unit.

To choose working on the SICU is tantamount to living one's professional life on the hospital's fastest track, at the center of the action. Every motion has an aura of urgency, and in point of fact, every patient who is admitted there does represent a potential emergency. No one who occupies a SICU bed arrives with just his or her body and a satchel of personal belongings. From the OR or the recovery room, the SICU-bound patient is accompanied by IV hookups, oxygen equipment, and a watchful anesthesiologist but that is only the beginning. Soon the patient will be attached to a labyrinthian web of tubes and wires leading to countless pieces of machinery—to monitors and pumps, to fluid input and output catheters, to suction tubes, and sometimes to body-warming devices. By the time these procedures are completed, the patient resembles an astronaut landing on the moon. "Sometimes I find myself forgetting that there's a patient there, because I'm so involved in the mechanical stuff," a nurse confesses after an admission.

At the time of admission "the mechanical stuff" requires constant attention by a team of people all watching screens, listening to the signals that emanate from them, and making regular adjustments of equipment in response to the messages they receive. Anything can go wrong at any time, but in general, the combined skill of the people and the machinery make error the exception rather than the rule. It is an astonishing sight, this recurring ceremony between professionals, technology, and critically ill patients. It fills the lay person with humility and awe to be witness to such an extraordinary assemblage of human skill operating under unremitting pressure. For in the final analysis it is the exceptional talent of the people more than the capability of the machinery, as wondrous as it is, that captures the heart and mind of a bystander.

A day or two after admission, in many instances, things change so dramatically that one may be tempted to believe that miracles occur on the SICU. The same patients who only a short time ago were dependent on machinery to sustain them are now sitting up in bed free of most of the mechanical adornments that shrouded them before. They breathe and even speak. Tomorrow they may take a few cautious steps on the arm of a nurse. The day after tomorrow they may leave, bound for the Progressive Care Unit or another part of the hospital. (The Progressive Care Unit—the PCU—is the most likely destination. Patients who go there still require electronic monitoring but less-intensive nursing care.)

The length of stay on the SICU is shorter than it is on 5B or 5C, typically less than seven days. To spice honesty with a dash of humor, one might refer to the SICU as the Here Today, Gone Tomorrow Unit. The joke is not without its grain of truth. Keeping the traffic moving on the SICU preoccupies everyone who works there, but especially Dr. Paul Donaldson, the unit's affable chief. A major portion of his job as the unit's administrator is to serve as captain of the traffic squad. Sandra Wilder is one of his colleagues and one of Gina's good friends. With a mixture of humor and seriousness, Sandra speaks of the traffic flow as "Paul's obsession." "He worries about it night and day. I tell him that he'll drive himself crazy with it. The matter takes care of itself, really. Everyone on the unit has a raised consciousness about moving patients out and bringing new patients in.''

From Paul's perspective, discharging patients from the SICU as soon as possible is a matter of supreme importance. In his words,

> I have valuable human and technological resources there, and I want them used to maximal advantage. When I have patients waiting to come in who can benefit more from those resources than one or more of those already there, I want to make room for the neediest. There are a certain number of patients who can't be moved quickly, who will stay longer than seven days, sometimes for several weeks—the trauma patients, patients with head bleeding, or those who arrive with complications pre- and postoperatively.

Paul Donaldson, Caroline O'Rourke, and the unit nursing staff regard Gina Rossi as one of the SICU's most essential staff members. Memorial's Nursing Department regards her as a most valuable human resource, as do the board members at the American Association of Critical Care Nurses (AACN) and the staff and readership of the *Journal of Cardiovascular Nursing* (*JCVN*). In fact, there are so many individuals and groups who value Gina Rossi that her talents are spread, like sandwich fillings, over the innumerable plates of a hungry throng. She is so knowledgeable, personable, and capable that everyone wants a piece of her—that is the recurrent hue and cry from all of the professional corners of her life.

According to her childhood friends, Gina is one of those rare people who grow younger as they age. When she was in her late teens and early twenties, they say, she looked matronly. Now, at the age of forty-one, she looks younger than her years. It is hard to think of her as the grandmother that she is. The bright-colored clothing she wears, her manicured fingernails, and her smartly cropped brunette hair give

her a youthful appearance. While most grandmothers are
settled into backseat roles, Gina Rossi is in the limelight.
She's a nursing celebrity, a leading player in a professional
theater whose administrative agents are forever scouting
stars. In Gina Rossi, they have found one. She relishes the
glory without letting it consume her or swell her head. The
more notoriety she receives, the more talents she reveals.
Instead of being eaten up by the demands on her, she responds to them as nourishing incentives, as replenishments
of her supply. Each demand propels her to a higher level of
achievement. One moment she's the expert nurse clinician
dressed in scrubs teaching other nurses how to perform
complex procedures, and in the next she's dressed fashion-
ably in street clothes lecturing at a podium to an audience
of nurses, physicians, or engineers. In between these moments are all of the others—the critical care research projects she works on at her desk, the telephonic and written
communiqués she sends about her task force, committee
and editorial assignments, and the informal problem-solving
sessions she holds in her tiny, orderly, file-cabinet–filled
office with Caroline and Paul or a variety of nursing administrators and educators. On top of these duties are the vast
number of formal meetings she attends in the hospital and
outside and the time she spends jetting around the country.
Gina Rossi is so busy with so many divergent activities that
at times it is easy to forget that she owes allegiance to only
one profession.

There is a superhuman quality about Gina that marks her
as a nurse. It definitely evokes admiration and envy in most
people and probably some skepticism in others. At the same
time that she is pulled in every direction, her mood is so
cheerful, her manner so easygoing and seemingly relaxed,
that she appears carefree. One senses, without ever receiving
direct confirmation from her, that she is a good actress, that
she has an uncanny ability to hide her own needs, stresses,
and distresses, along with whatever resentments accompany
them. If the human population is divided at the extremes

between the givers and the takers, she leans so far on the giving end as to be close to a perilous edge. Nurses frequently are accused of a predisposition to overgiving, but in a nurse as psychologically aware as Gina is, it comes as a surprise. Unlike Dominique Raza, but more like Jessie Concannon, the giving part of Gina obscures her vision of the taking part. The net result for both Gina and Jessie is a tendency to be somewhat less clear-sighted about their own needs and about those other human needs that extend beyond their immediate purview. Dominique, although much younger than Jessie and Gina, is more worldly, passionate, and political, and therefore less magnanimous than both of them. This is not to fault either of her senior colleagues but rather to suggest that in her twenty-four years, Dominique already has experienced more of the variety and the Sturm und Drang of life than either Jessie or Gina have.

That measure of worldliness that appears on Gina's debit column is offset on the asset side by an oversupply of expertise. In fact, the word *expert* to describe Gina Rossi's knowledge of critical care nursing or her capabilities as a clinical nurse specialist seems to fall short of the mark. It would not be stretching the truth by much to suggest that she would be portrayed more accurately as a *giant* in her field. Her list of publications on almost every subcategory of the general subject runs many pages, and so updated and sophisticated is her knowledge of critical care technology that she is a regular lecturer on the topic to diverse audiences nationwide. Her technological and clinical knowledge base is as deep as it is broad. It includes a thorough understanding of the operation of and data interpretation from cardiac monitoring systems and intra-aortic balloon pumps (devices to help rest the heart), chest tube drainage systems, the administering of IV vasoactive medications (to open or close blood vessels), and the use of ventilators and defibrillators (machines that restore the electrical rhythms of the heart). In addition, she has special expertise in electrophysiology (interpretation of electrical heart rhythms), hemodynamic monitoring (interpretation of heart pressures—central venous, left atrial, pulmonary artery), and the interpretation of cardiac output (the amount of blood pumped by the heart per minute).

The fact that Gina is a highly visible member of an elite corps of nurses called clinical nurse specialists (CNSs) spells real progress for her as an individual and for nursing as a profession. In and of itself, the role stands as a long-awaited testimonial to the reality of clinical nursing expertise. CNSs are, as the title implies, experts in their field. Not only do they serve an important educational function for any nursing department, but they also represent another open doorway of opportunity for the clinical advancement of ambitious junior nurses seeking more challenging roles. Where once the only chance for upward mobility for a hospital nurse led to an administrative post, the hiring of CNSs signals the possibility of an alternative route up the ladder. Memorial's ten CNSs are well paid and highly trained, all at the master's degree level, in whatever subspecialty of nursing they have chosen. Their work in the hospital revolves around training and consultation for the staff nurses and nursing trainees on their own units and on others when their specialized knowledge is required. Although they are employed primarily to serve other nurses, they frequently are called on by physicians to educate their rank and file as well. Like nurse managers, they have no individual patient assignments, but generally they have more patient contact than nurse managers do, because most of their teaching activities take place at the bedside.

## GINA, DAY TO DAY

By now it must be obvious to the reader that Gina's daily professional life is a multicolored, multidimensional tapestry always in the making. If she adhered strictly to her job description, there would be fewer threads to weave into her work. It would have less variety than it has. Through the combined force of her personality and talent and the blessing of Memorial's nursing administration, she has turned a very interesting job into a fascinating one. Among the three nurses in this book, she is the happiest with her job.

Gina's is an example that should not be lost on nursing administrators anywhere, because there is a tendency in the profession to rein nurses in with ironclad definitions of their duties rather than to allow them to swing as freely and widely as their capabilities permit. The notion that there are gains that accrue from the perception of *work* as *fun* has yet to capture the imagination of most of the profession's top brass. Although there are signs of improvement, there is still a kind of thou-shalt-not-experience-too-much-enjoyment-on-the-job administrative mentality, which stifles the creative and intellectual energy of talented young nurses like Dominique. In addition to these attitudinal impediments are the institutional economic constraints that contribute to short-staffing and hence to heavier work loads, and the ever-looming threat of a nursing shortage. It is a credit to Memorial's nursing leadership that it has permitted nurses of the caliber of Jessie Concannon and Gina Rossi to fan the flames of ambition in their younger charges. The problem is that the Jessies and Ginas are in short supply. Nurses who love their work as much as Gina does are scarcer still.

So while Caroline O'Rourke, many of the staff nurses, and Paul Donaldson may wish that Gina was more omnipresent on the SICU than she is, Gina would be a far less contented and effective nurse if she acceded to their wishes. Her forays into the world beyond Memorial arm her with new ideas and information, which she brings back to the troops at home. They add to her stock of clinical abilities. If she were less skilled at time management than she is, her services to the SICU might suffer more severely. As a hedge against this possibility, she treats the unit as her first priority.

When an emergency arises on the unit or elsewhere in the hospital that requires her presence, she will cancel outside commitments (except for the classes she conducts in other hospitals in the city or prescheduled out-of-town meetings and symposia). For her extracurricular activities, she sets daily goals and accomplishes them in between unit obligations and interruptions from her beeper.

## Staff Meetings

On the SICU, as on the other hospital units, there are weekly nursing staff meetings led by the nurse manager (there, too, the meetings take place in the "bubble"). Gina attends all of these when she's in town. At one such meeting the topic of discussion is a familiar one—the issue of families bothering the staff outside the parameters of visiting hours.

Walter, a highly regarded nurse on the unit, volunteers the opinion that families feel guilty if they don't stay near the patient constantly, even if it exhausts them to do so. "We forget about their needs, because we're so busy with the patients," he adds.

Gina warms to Walter's suggestion. "You're right, Walter. They need a judgment call from us that gives them permission to go home and get some rest. Until they receive it, they're immobilized."

Caroline seconds Walter and Gina and suggests that everybody try to approach families with this idea in mind.

On a different day the staff meeting revolves around another typical issue—coverage during holidays. This meeting is notable because Pauline Irving, the nursing director who oversees the OR and the Critical Care Units (CCUs), is in attendance. At Memorial it is rare to see the nursing directors at unit staff meetings, but Pauline likes to be visible on the units and tuned in to the activities. Her manner is quiet and nonthreatening. She's a good listener, a keen observer, an administrator whose values lean more toward the clinical than the managerial, and the nurse managers and CNSs who work under her appreciate her low-key, participatory style.

Before the subject of coverage is addressed, Caroline brings up the matter of patient transfers and the communication problems that are occurring. She tells the staff that either she or Lois, a nurse in a senior staff position, needs to be informed by the primary nurses about every patient who is being discharged. From this topic, she moves to a reminder to the staff to affix the SICU label to all of the pillows, so that they don't leave the floor, and to another reminder about replenishing the debt-ridden coffee fund. While on the general theme of reminders, Gina emphasizes the need to turn up the volume on the patient monitors. Next she intercedes on behalf of the citywide Intensive Care Unit Consortium, an organization of critical care nurses representing many hospitals that gives continuing education credits for nurses who attend its educational offerings. The ICU Consortium is another of Gina's extracurricular activities. She serves on its planning committees and conducts many of the lectures given under its auspices. Several weeks ago, she posted a sign-up sheet in the bubble for staff nurses to attend a particular lecture, one that she happened to be conducting. Twelve people signed up, but only four attended.

Caroline takes the lead in addressing the problem. "I don't know what more I can do. Two weeks before these events, I try to remind you all that they're coming up. What's going to happen in the future is that if you sign up and don't go, you'll lose a day's pay. It seems only fair to do it this way, since your signatures on the sheet may well mean that other people who want to go will be turned away. Does anybody have any suggestions about what else I can do about this?"

"You can make it harder for people to sign up," suggests Lois, the lone respondent to the plea.

The entry into the coverage matter comes from Walter.

"We need more time off the floor. A twenty- or twenty-five-minute break for lunch would do us all good, but we've got this mind-set that we have to be in control all the time, that we must always be available."

Again Gina reinforces Walter. "I think you should get off the floor. You need some time away."

"Well, speaking of time away. I think we need to start working on holiday coverage now, even though November is two months down the road," says Walter assertively.

Gina, the very frequent flyer, lends a strong second to Walter's motion. "You need to make reservations way in advance if you plan to travel for the holidays."

"In that case, I'd better start making my summer vacation plans now," says Lois sarcastically.

"I'm sorry, but I resent your saying that," answers Walter. "This is an important matter to some of us."

Caroline and Gina concur with Walter and make a mental note of Lois's sarcasm at the same time. Later Lois's behavior will become the focus of some discussion between them. They both respect her professional capabilities, but they sense that she resents each of them, for different reasons. Nurses on other units, too, have voiced frustration with Lois's interpersonal skills. Hard as Caroline and Gina try, they are unable to understand how Lois feels. Neither of them knows whether or not she is aware of her own behavior or its impact. A few weeks after the staff meeting, but before the problem has a chance to develop into a crisis, it resolves itself. Lois resigns.

A return to the general subject of coverage concludes the meeting. Caroline gently suggests that they may want to think about self-containment for the SICU. "They're giving it a six-month trial on the PCU," she tells them. It is hard to tell from her comments whether she is for or against the idea. Here she could have benefited from Jessie Concannon's advice and experience. The older pro would have said to the younger one, First decide what you want for the unit.

Then take the high road and lobby as long and as hard as you need to to get to your goal.

After the meeting, Gina pulls Caroline aside and ushers her into a patient room to check out the equipment.

"I think that at every change of shift, the outgoing nurse should accompany the incoming nurse to check everything out and make sure that everything is working properly. In my old job, we used to conduct report right by the bedside," Gina tells Caroline.

"I wouldn't want to do that, but it would be alright if it took place outside the doorway," replies Caroline.

"Look, people have to realize how important it is. It's quality assurance," says Gina, coming on even stronger than before.

Caroline's silence suggests that she is demurring in the face of Gina's aggressiveness.

The day after the staff meeting, Gina and Pauline are holding their weekly joint meeting in Pauline's office in the Nursing Department. After covering all of the items on their mutual agenda, Pauline comments on yesterday's staff meeting.

"I thought the meeting was very loose-ended," she says. "It wasn't clear how or who would be responsible for resolving the problems."

Her remarks strike a responsive chord in Gina. "I try to use that time to address issues that need resolution, but sometimes it gets sticky for me. I hold back because I don't want to overpower Caroline, but I really feel that she needs to be more assertive and goal directed."

Pauline promises to address the issue with Caroline and give her pointers about strengthening her leadership. She knows that Caroline is a quick learner. The evidence that she is correct comes in subsequent staff meetings, after each of which Gina detects and acknowledges Caroline's continuing growth as a leader.

Although Gina likes the fact that she's not accountable to

the nurse manager, for Caroline, as for other nurse managers, the working relationship between the CNS and herself poses a different set of problems. As peers they need to be careful to avoid stepping on each other's toes, to be clear about differentiating their responsibilities, and to establish a noncompetitive partnership. In Caroline's previous job as nurse manager in another city, the administrative structure placed the CNS under the nurse manager, which meant that she had more control over the person in that position. Here at Memorial, she feels at times that she's more at Gina's mercy than she would like to be. As a result, she meets frequently with Gina to negotiate the scheduling of Gina's time-constrained services to the unit. It's one more job to do for a nurse manager whose staff and budget are almost twice the size of Jessie Concannon's. Granted, she has an assistant, which Jessie does not have, who handles most of the day-to-day staffing and operational load, but she is still left with an overflowing roster of duties to perform.

For all of the potential friction that could develop between them, not the least of which could arise from Gina's stature in the profession, Caroline and Gina are so personable as individuals that they are able to maintain a good friendship, both on and off the job.

## Orienting New Nurses in Cardiac Care

An empty room devoid of a bed but decorated on its walls with stationary hook-up equipment and monitors, awaits the arrival of a cardiothoracic patient from the OR. Gina and Meg wait, too. In short order they will be extremely busy, so they enjoy this idle time. As soon as the patient arrives, Gina will begin orienting Meg, a relatively new staff nurse, about all of the procedures that must be performed on the patient. For the most part, she will let Meg do the work, but she will stand by watchfully, giving instructions when necessary. She anticipates that the two of them and the new patient will be together for the next four hours. Ellen,

another nurse, comes in while Gina and Meg are standing
in the room and chats with them about her husband.

"All along he's been telling me how much he wants to
go to the Rose Bowl, and all of a sudden, after I've already
bought the tickets, he changes his mind. Can you beat that?"
she asks them.

"I'll take your tickets," says Gina jokingly. Then, sym-
pathetically, she adds, "Gee, that's really too bad. I feel
sorry for you."

"The only consolation for me was watching the little
kindergarten kids get off the bus for the first day of school
yesterday. They were so cute and excited. They cheered me
up. If I didn't have my work on the town school committee,
I don't know what I'd do right now. I'm so annoyed with
Chuck," moans Ellen.

The social banter is interrupted by the commotion announcing the arrival of the patient. A man in a blue scrub
uniform, the anesthesiologist, rolls the bed into the room.
Within seconds the cardiothoracic surgeons and a respiratory
therapist appear. Immediately the human action and the
symphony begin. The patient has had an aortic valve replacement operation. Gina tells Meg to hook him first to the
EKG and pressure monitor and then to an SV02 monitor
(which measures the saturation of oxygen in the blood) and
a cardiac monitor. The respiratory therapist then sets to work
hooking up the ventilator to an endotracheal suction tube
(which removes fluid from the trachea). Meanwhile, Meg
is performing other hook-up functions—a chest drainage
tube, an autotransfusion device (it returns blood output back
to the body via a mediastinal chest tube inserted through the
navel to drain excess blood from the chest cavity), and a
blanket warmer. Surprisingly, Meg accomplishes these
tasks without much assistance from Gina. The amount, den-
sity, and tangling potential of the wiring and tubing involved
in all of this truly is astounding, and its successful manipula-
tion seems to make an instant heroine of Meg.

Gina will do the left and right atrial catheter hookups

herself, but later, in a less-pressured circumstance, she will
teach Meg how to do it. In the meantime, Gina needs a
special kind of cable, which is unavailable. She sends the
anesthesiologist out to find one. While he's gone, she and
one of the surgeons joke about the likelihood of his returning
with the wrong cable. "It won't be the first time," says the
surgeon.

To lend more frenzy to an already hyperactive scene,
Gina, the surgeons, and the anesthesiologist watch several
screens, listen to beeps, fiddle with monitor controls, and
check vital signs. After one look at a monitor, Gina decides
to take the patient's blood pressure by the cuff (manually)
to see if it correlates with the monitor's reading of the
pressure. They all act so casual and calm that they make it
appear as if the procedures they are performing have no
relationship to life and death. Gina looks at the patient and
describes him out loud.

"His pupils are pinpoint. He's out of it. He's not going
to wake up anytime soon. His body is cold. Ninety-five
degrees. Is the blanket warmer on him?" Gina's question
is directed at Meg.

"Yes," comes the reply.

With all of the plumbing in place, Gina can take time to
give Meg some pointers. "I always go back to the basics to
make an assessment, so I check the blood pressure manually
and automatically to see if they correlate. You need to
remember, too, to always ask the surgeons where the left
and right atrial catheters are placed. Keep a watchful eye on
the left atrial pressure, because that will tell you what kind
of intervention to use, whether it should be fluids or medications. After you've drawn some bloods and the numbers
come back from the lab, I'm going to show you how to
calibrate the lab's numbers with those on the SV02 monitor."

Satisfied that the patient is stable, the surgeons and the
anesthesiologist leave, but Gina and Meg will remain for
many more hours, watching and attending to him. Tomor-

row, for several days thereafter, and for similar intervals in
succeeding months Gina will repeat this process with other
nurses. These orientations are conducted when a nurse has
been on the unit for at least six months. Learning to handle
new cardiac, or "heart," admissions requires a higher level
of skill than any of the other nursing procedures on the unit.
Until the six-month mark is reached, the nurse will have
been exposed to these cardiac patients only in the latter
stages of their care on the SICU.

### Preceptors' Meeting

If we pretend for a moment that the SICU is an academy,
then Gina is the academic dean, Caroline is the dean of
students, and a small, select group of senior staff nurses
make up the faculty. Apart from providing patient care,
there is probably no more important function on the SICU
than the training of new nurses, nurse extenders, and critical
care nursing students. Aside from the fact that routine procedures are more numerous and complex on the SICU, the
technology changes and expands so often that the nurses are
habitually being trained and retrained. To keep a nursing
staff of more than seventy people up to snuff demands a
consistent and well-orchestrated system of coordination and
communication. It is to this end that the day-long monthly
preceptor meetings are devoted. Gina and Caroline function
as coleaders.

A major part of today's discussion focuses on orienting
PCTs and nurses. Evidence that the use of PCTs is still a
sticky issue at Memorial emerges toward the end of the
meeting.

"Maybe we need more preceptors to help orient the
PCTs, even though I don't think we have to work as inten-
sively with them as we do with nurses," says Gina.

Marion offers an alternative. "Why don't we have an old
PCT preceptor for the new PCTs?"

"No," responds Caroline with uncharacteristic emphasis.

Marion persists. "Nurses are already giving them too much attention."

"And we're putting our own licenses on the line if we don't watch them carefully to make sure they're safe. It's a pain, and it takes so much time," says Penny in an attempt to build momentum.

Gina stops the debate before it starts. "That's just not true. None of you are accountable for their mistakes as long as they are adhering to their job descriptions."

The evaporating steam from the argument leaves a vacuum for Caroline. "The charge nurse on each shift can decide whether a PCT will have a partner or whether she will help several nurses. We don't have to stick to the letter of the law about these partnerships if they don't work at certain times."

"That's right, Caroline. Everybody here needs to try to work on their mindsets about PCTs. Try to overcome them. Use the PCTs in the way that's most workable and helpful. Don't worry about every little regulation." Gina's abbreviated lecture does the trick. The matter rests.

"Let's move on to evaluating all the nurse orientees," suggests Gina.

They move down the list obediently. Nurse A is "wonderful, motivated, and curious." Nurse B gets more "overwhelmed and nervous" than is characteristic of nurses with so much experience (all of it in other hospitals). "She's still got nine to sixteen deficiencies." They decide to assign her to Penny, an especially patient preceptor. Working their way down the list, they are pleased to see how many new nurses are doing well.

Toward the close of the meeting the emphasis shifts from people to paper, from evaluating nurses to evaluating a flow sheet and its adaptability to the new documentation system. The flow sheet is a multiple checklist used as a tool by critical care nurses to document patients' vital signs and all other pertinent clinical information on a continuing basis. It is a crucial and cumbersome record for the nurses who use it and the doctors who read it. Today's dialogue represents one in a series of intra- and interdisciplinary attempts to elevate it to a higher standard of clarity and efficiency.

## Patient Care Conferences

Every Tuesday morning, Paul and Gina hold patient care conferences on both sides of the unit. In truth these conferences are roving meetings of Paul's traffic squad, whose members gather by the doorways of patients who have been hospitalized for seven days or more. The squad, besides Paul, Gina, and Caroline, includes the SICU social worker, the recovery room, cardiothoracic, and PCU CNSs, a respiratory therapist, a physical therapist, a representative from pharmacy, the chaplain, the primary nurses, and the residents in charge of the patients under discussion. As they reach the rooms of the respective patients, it is customary for Paul and Gina to take notes while listening to oral reports from the residents and nurses. Gina does her note taking with a purple pen and matching pad, which never fails to evoke a jesting comment from Paul. When the serious business begins, Paul and Gina have their ears tuned for any potential problems with staff implementation of patient care plans generally and discharge plans specifically. The $64,000 question is, Is everybody doing what they're supposed to be doing to meet the clinical goals that are the prerequisites for the patient's discharge?

In front of room 4 the resident gives an overview of its occupant, Mr. Simpson. "He's got a Tenchoff catheter [one inserted under the skin for the administering of IV medications]. His peritoneal dialysis [insertion of catheter into the peritoneum to eliminate excess of fluid] was stopped and restarted. Two days ago, he was intubated. Now he's extubated. His mental status is confused and worsening. This afternoon, he's scheduled for a lumbar puncture. He's got a GI feeding tube and a high fluid output."

Gina, resting her purple pen for a moment, asks Martha, Mr. Simpson's nurse, about his family.

"They're involved. He's married and has three sons. He tells me he's an attorney, and he certainly talks like one," replies Martha.

Apparently Paul has heard all that he needs to. "He's stuck here for the time being, at least until we can get peritoneal dialysis again. Pretty soon, though, he ought to be able to go to the medical floor for rehab. Everybody got that?"

They all nod affirmatively and move on to Mrs. Peters in room 6. "She's eighty years old and was living by herself until her admission last Thursday. Her sister found her unconscious on the floor. She's intubated, has a ruptured diverticulitis [a rupture in a section of the gastrointestinal tract]. She's septic and has been very sick postoperatively. Her toes and fingers are blue and cold. Looks like she'll lose one leg, maybe two, and all her fingers. She's in bad shape. She does respond to pain, though. I'd say her chances for survival aren't great. We need a code and DNR status on her. There's been no improvement in her condition," explains the resident.

Without waiting to be asked, Darcy, Mrs. Peters' nurse, volunteers, "The weird thing about the family is that the sister who found Mrs. Peters on the floor hadn't seen her for five years until that day. There's another sister, too. They're both out in the visitor's lounge now, but they don't seem to understand much about what's going on."

"OK, here's what we'll do about Mrs. Peters," instructs Paul. "Doug [the resident], you talk to the sisters and see if they are competent enough to make the code and DNR decisions. If they're not, we'll do it for them tomorrow. Eileen [the chaplain], you can talk to them, too, if you wouldn't mind."

The group goes on to two more patients. One of them has been there for two weeks and will have to remain longer.

The other, Paul decides, can be moved tomorrow to the PCU.

Their work completed, the squad heads in different directions. Gina, Paul, and Caroline make their way to the cafeteria together, as they often do after the patient care conferences. There they engage in political discourse over lunch. Election time isn't far in the future, and on the local scene considerable media attention has been paid to government waste. Caroline listens as Paul and Gina raise the banner for lower taxes and the eradication of waste. Today Paul's dander is up about the hard-hatted men he's seen standing around on the street outside the hospital, ostensibly for the purpose of laying an underground pipe. "Did you notice how long they've been there? It's gotta be several months. The job still isn't done. They just stand around drinking coffee and talking. Now if that isn't a prime example of waste, what is?" Paul exclaims.

Gina concurs wholeheartedly and Caroline halfheartedly. Gina's mind is made up on the governor's race. She's going to vote for the candidate who's tough on crime and in favor of cutting taxes.

### Consultation with a Medical Supply Manufacturer

Manufacturers of monitoring equipment used on the SICU send teams of people to hospitals for a week at a time to observe physicians and nurses in their clinical activities and to hold discussions with them about the professionals' use of their products. Their goal is to attempt to learn as much as they can about the work of their products' users. This morning a team of four attractive young men is meeting with Gina in the SICU conference room to learn more about nursing. Paul Donaldson will join them later. Each representative is from a different department in their company—marketing, training, support products, and research and development.

Gina begins with a human-interest pitch. "As nurses we need to take special care to enhance the dignity of dying patients. Sometimes that means breaking the visiting hour rules. We're so busy here that we have a tendency to shun the patients' families. We tend not to like having them around all the time. It means being sensitive to the patient's and the family's needs. One family may be upsetting enough to the patient to warrant restricting their interaction with him, but another family's continued presence may be soothing. A year or so ago, when I was orienting a new nurse in cardiac care, we had a patient who was here for over two months. It was her second admission, and she was going to die. She was too sick to talk. I decided to call a staff meeting to get special permission for the patient to see her new grandchild. Well, she got to see and hold that baby, and I'm convinced that she was clinging to life for just that reason. She had to hold that baby before she died."

The three young men listen politely but become noticeably more animated when Gina directs their attention toward the less personal side of nursing. "My role as a CNS is to be an expert clinician, an educator, a researcher, and a consultant. There's a consensus on those aspects of my job. How much I assume of leadership and managerial functions, however, is murkier. It depends on my assessment of the need and on the expectations of the nurse manager and Nursing Administration. Here at Memorial the CNS holds a staff rather than a line position. Taken literally that means that I have no direct supervisory responsibility. I use my role as a vehicle for influencing people, not as a means of dictating or managing. In that context, I'm a leader. Nowadays a big part of my job is relating to industry. My advice is sought on all manner of medical equipment. I'm an advocate of automation, but I have to be concerned about the cost of it, too. For me, as a nurse, it's hard to make the transition to think of a hospital as a business, but that's the way it is."

Gina's reference to requests for her advice on equipment

sparks the competitive spirit of the man from marketing. "Do you use other companies besides ours?" he asks.

"Yes, we do," replies Gina.

"Well, just remember that we'll accept liability if the equipment is down, and we're always looking for ways to improve it."

"Yeh," says the man from support products, "we're doing all we can to make our products as supportable as possible."

Gina directs the conversation temporarily away from products and back to life on the SICU. "We have sixteen beds here, but the ideal would be ten. The floor is divided into two sides. The nurses call them the high side and the low side [The high side has the high-numbered rooms— rooms 9 through 16]. The nursing staff rotates between the sides. We have a modified version of primary nursing here, but it's not pure, because we have a lot of people on twelve-hour shifts, three days a week. It's hard to maintain primary nursing when many nurses aren't here for the better part of a week."

These remarks are greeted with smiles and nods, and, then, as if she was saving the best for last, Gina says, "This is the highest-tech unit in the hospital. Most of our patients have pulmonary catheters [inserted into the right side of the heart to measure pressure in the various chambers] and are ventilated [intubated]. You may want to rethink the notion of testing more equipment on the Critical Care Unit. While we're getting more high tech, they seem to be becoming less so there. The average length of stay here is four days. Our long-stayers [more than seven days] stay on the average of sixteen days. We've brought it down from twenty-one."

A few minutes into this monologue, Paul Donaldson enters the room. He picks up where she leaves off and gradually redirects the focus back to products. "Cardiac patients use half of our beds. By the time a cardiac patient leaves the hospital, he's been in five or six different beds. We sometimes have gridlock just moving people around. Now,

I have to tell you that your monitors aren't always easy to operate. The EKG and pressure buttons should be separated from all the others. You've got to remember to keep the primary functions simple. You know, *Push, Start*. You people forget that we don't need to be treated like geniuses all the time. We need transport monitoring [monitors attached to patients being moved], but they've got to be cheap and lightweight. They should do EKGs, two pressures. They should have a defibrillator and pulse oxymetry capabilities [to measure oxygen saturation]. We're always sending patients on field trips. Their rides in the elevators are the most dangerous times for them.''

Now the company's men are lapping it up, taking notes, thinking out loud, asking questions, talking about improving the old products and advancing ideas for newer, better ones. The research and development representative is working on an automated flow sheet. Paul plays the devil's advocate for that one. ''Machines can't know certain things. We're going to get artifacts without explanations, and then the damn machine may go down. Flow sheets are good for what's happening today, but we need to be able to look over two weeks' worth.''

The meeting ends just in time for Gina and Paul to take the team on the surgical teaching rounds that are beginning on the unit. The corridor already is jammed with young physicians listening attentively to Clifford Siegel, so the addition of this party to the audience creates pedestrian gridlock.

Later in the week, after the team has visited the morgue, Gina asks them if their visit to the hospital has met their expectations. They agree unanimously that it has. They've gathered reams of information about professional roles, and a trip to the morgue has given them a sneak preview of death. Of course, they are fascinated most by the day-to-day use of their equipment. Their collective impression is that everybody who uses it takes it for granted until it breaks down, and then they curse it. The men are filled with gratitude for the information they've received from nurses and doctors about their technological needs and desires. For Paul Donaldson they reserve honorable mention as the person who knows the most about their products.

## Troubleshooting

Some of Gina's activities on the SICU are unscheduled. Incidents arise spontaneously that prompt her to lend a helping hand or respond to a request. Whenever she can, Gina offers to relieve staff nurses. One day at noontime, for example, she notices that a staff nurse needs a break.

"Go get some lunch. I'll relieve you. Just tell me what's going on with the patient."

"She's Dr. Schiffer's great-aunt. When she wakes up, she thrashes around. There's something funny going on with her blood pressure. I really appreciate your doing this for me. It's been hectic this morning. My other patient got up to go to the bathroom, couldn't get out, and arrested [had a heart attack] in the bathroom," explains the harried nurse.

Gina immediately attends to the blood pressure problem. The results from the monitor and the cuff are different. "There must be something wrong with the plumbing on the arterial line," Gina guesses out loud. Suddenly the monitor signals go off. Gina administers a double dose of Dopamine to elevate the blood pressure. In short order, the patient's pressure is stabilized, but Gina remains at her side until the nurse returns.

On other occasions Gina's beeper summons her off the unit to assist nurses whose patients are having cardiac problems. Nina, the neurology CNS, beeps her one morning for assistance with a female patient in the emergency room. The patient's neurological condition is causing cardiac problems. Gina reads her EKG and determines that the patient is experiencing premature atrial contractions (PACs—irregular heartbeats). "Take some real deep breaths for me so we can get some oxygen into your lungs," Gina tells the patient. Next Nina and Gina compare notes on the neurological and cardiac diagnoses and their relationship to each other. "Make sure she takes deep breaths. Right now she appears to be splinting with her respirations. The PACs are not worrisome at this time," Gina says reassuringly as she departs.

Paul and Caroline both use Gina as a troubleshooter on the unit. In one instance Paul asks her to support him in requesting the participation of the cardiothoracic surgeons at the patient care conferences. She and Paul corner Dr. Ned Schiffer, the chief of cardiothoracic surgery, in the corridor and she puts in the requested plug for Paul's cause. Their combined effort bears fruit at the next conference, where a surgeon from that department is in attendance.

On another matter she plays the troubleshooter with Ned without being asked. In so doing, she knows she is overstepping Lois, whose job it really is, but to her, Lois appears to be too distracted by her own personal problems to attend to the issue. Gina has had her fill of seeing patients come from the OR without their nasal-gastric tubes in place. It's traumatic for them to awaken from anesthesia to be confronted by a nurse who is about to perform an uncomfortable procedure, and Gina feels that it's an unfair burden to place on nurses and patients alike. After some additional corridor finagling, she prods Ned into agreeing to have the residents insert the tubes before the patients leave the OR. "A big part of my job is advocating for one group or another. Sometimes it's for physicians. This time it's for both nurses and patients."

Caroline often consults Gina informally about problems with members of the staff. Presently Caroline suspects one nurse of lying about procedures she's conducted and medications she's administered.

"She lies about some of the things that she does, and she's good at it. It's taken a while for me to catch on, because I'm not on duty when she is and I haven't been able to observe her myself, so I have to rely on other people's reports about her. I've given her a warning already. If I'm going to fire her, I have to build up to it, step-by-step and document each step for the union." Now Caroline wants the benefit of Gina's observations about the nurse's clinical skills.

Gina agrees that she is a problem. "She's been here over a year, and she still doesn't know how to perform some of our most basic procedures."

Gina is helpful to Caroline, too, in the use of computers to make slides for lectures or presentations. Knowledge of computers is another of Gina's areas of expertise. When Caroline has to prepare a presentation on the roles of PCTs and RNs, Gina shows her how to lay out, color code, and print the slides on the computer.

Like Jessie Concannon, Gina and Caroline have roles to play in the business of teaching the new documentation procedures to the staff nurses. There are so many nurses on the SICU that the teaching load has to be split between three people. Caroline schedules documentation sessions and substitute coverage so that small groups of nurses can rotate in and out of the sessions. Gina and Gloria, a clinical instructor in the Nursing Department, share the teaching responsibilities. The three of them meet whenever they have time available to plan the upcoming sessions.

Odds and ends add up to make Gina's daily life complicated and varied. When the SICU staff don't call and the beeper doesn't go off, there are hundreds of phone messages to answer, letters to write, meetings to attend, and lectures to prepare. In the moments she can spare to sit alone in her office, Gina is the personification of the message in telephone company advertisements. She is busy keeping in touch. "I think we should get Sally to emphasize the psychodynamics of critical care in her article before we publish it," she tells her *JCVN* coeditor on the telephone. Or, "I'm just calling to report about my trip to Kentucky," begins an hour-long conversation with AACN headquarters in California.

"Dear Sirs," starts the letter on her laptop computer addressed to a medical supply company, "I've had the opportunity to observe your training tape, and I am writing to voice my objection to the negative portrayal of the nurse in the film. We regret that we will be unable to use your products if stereotypes like this are not corrected."

In the course of a day, Gina's things-to-do list will have a new addition for every deletion and a promise for the next day that a string of foreseen and unforeseen activities will begin anew.

## GINA AT THE PODIUM

The ICU Consortium–sponsored workshop on advanced dysrhythmias (disturbance in the normal heart rate, rhythm, or conduction) draws a huge audience of nurses, a few from the SICU, most from other hospitals in the city. Gina is this morning's lecturer, and she stands at a podium on the stage overlooking an auditorium in a neighboring hospital. In front of and beside her are pieces of audiovisual equipment. She holds a pointer in one hand and a microphone in the other. For this event, she wears a navy blue suit—more conservative than her typical attire.

Gina's contribution to the workshop is a lecture about aberrancy (normal beats that take an abnormal conductive path) and ectopy (premature beats arising from the wrong site in the heart). With the help of visual aids, Gina talks about the monitoring of dysrhythmias. Pictures of erratic waves appear on the screen, and the audience reaction indicates that discernable messages are being sent to viewers. Most of Gina's lecture is delivered in acronyms and technical words and phrases, but occasionally it is punctuated with plain English. "See these beats," Gina says, using her pointer for emphasis. "Well, a while ago some nurses noticed that they looked like rabbit ears, so now we refer to them as 'the rabbit ear phenomenon.'" More technical jargon is interspersed with English. "In electrophysiology you have to remember that nothing is black or white. It's mostly gray. You need to become good detectives. Always be suspicious."

She pauses to invite questions, then introduces them to the second-in-a-group rule, which has some connection to long and short wave cycles. After soliciting and receiving their interpretations of the cycles, she explains that this rule is another phenomenon. "It's called the Ashman phenomenon. Dr. Ashman discovered it and named it for himself. Physicians always do that, but nurses never do," she adds with a laugh. Next she veers her comments toward diagnostic considerations. "We don't need doctor's orders to monitor certain leads to detect aberrancy or ectopy, and we have standing orders for medication administration for premature ventricular contractions. I'll need to show you some more pictures now to help you make diagnoses." Many rabbit ears appear on the screen—some tall, some short, some skinny, some fat. "It's like being at the horse track. You're betting on your diagnosis by looking at the height of the rabbit ears and guessing the diagnosis."

As the lecture continues, more slides appear full of funny-looking waves and others with technical words presented in outline form. Hands rise, frequently belonging to participants who interrupt their own rapid note taking for questions and comments. Gina appears relaxed and confident throughout, as if she could do it in her sleep or happened to be born with a pointer in her hand.

In front of an audience of surgeons Gina has the same ease of delivery. One such lecture is held in a classroom in the Department of Surgery at Memorial. Gina comes with her usual audiovisual paraphernalia. This time the navy blue suit is replaced by a flashier royal blue dress, and the podium places her on the same level as the audience. Most of the approximately fifty seats are filled with surgeons of all ages listening to Gina discuss the intra-aortic balloon pump. She begins by describing the various insertion modes that one

can use with the pump and discusses the indications and
contraindications for inserting them in certain arteries.
"Now just in case any of you are right-brain types, I'll show
you some pictures." They laugh, and then a long list of
insertion possibilities appears on the screen. One item says
"percutaneous" (through the skin); Gina informs the group
that this particular insertion has lots of contraindications,
and she explains what they are. Another slide shows what
a balloon pump "console" looks like, and after that, more
illustrations depicting the balloon inflating and deflating.
These last pictures open up a new topic about how inflation
and deflation affect diastolic and systolic blood pressures.
After Gina has addressed this issue, she activates the flipper
again to reveal another list of possible effects of balloon
pumping. Gina goes down the list with the pointer. It is at
the conclusion of this exercise that she notices Clifford
Siegel dozing in his front-row seat. "Clifford is my gauge,"
she announces to the group. "When I see him nodding off,
I know that it's time for me to stop talking." Once the
laughter subsides, Gina answers requests to review the problems associated with early and late deflation. In her wrap-
up, she chides them. "When we run into problems, that's
when we call in the A team. You know who I mean—the
vascular surgeons. Or we call the anesthesiologists. Just
pass the gas, we say."

No one seems anxious to leave the lecture. They mill
around, asking Gina more questions about all of the terrible
things that can happen with the pump. To the uninformed
observer it begins to sound like it's not worth taking the risk
to use this particular contrivance, especially when, on the
way out the door with the curious surgeons in tow, Gina
admonishes, "Remember now, the balloon mustn't remain
dormant in the aorta for more than one-half hour. If it does,
you may have a thrombus [blood clot] on your hands."

During the course of a year, Gina will repeat these lectures
and present others to many groups, both locally and nation-
ally. At this point in her career, it's second nature, as easy

as baking lasagna. The only distinction is that the former is
business, the latter is her idea of relaxation. Both activities
share the common need to have the right ingredients on hand
and the proper recipe in the head.


## GINA AND PHYSICIANS

Gina and Paul's professional relationship is as close to the
ideal as any relationship between a nurse and doctor could
ever be. All of their interactions are characterized by mutual
respect, collaboration, and easy communication. They are
kindred spirits in their outlooks on patient care and in their
interest in and knowledge of high technology. Although she
has the most frequent contact with Paul, Gina has more day-
to-day interaction with all of the physicians on the SICU
than either Dominique or Jessie have with those on their
respective units. They join Paul to form a long line of her
admirers. Her ability to be so beloved by physicians amazes
everyone who knows her. After all, the history of the interaction between these most proximate of professions is re-
plete with conflict. Nurses have been witness to the darkest
side of doctors, to their do-as-I-say attitude, their superiority
complexes, their outright sexism, their insensitivity. Likewise, doctors have been exasperated by their perception of
the lack of professionalism inherent in some nurses' attitude
that says, I'm too busy to do that, and besides, it's three
o'clock, the end of my shift. Although in hospitals as advanced as Memorial the winds of change have contributed
greatly to the humbling of physicians' stature and the eleva-
tion of nurses', there is rarely a passing day that does not
include some power struggle or other unpleasant remnant of
the old order.

Gina has a sixth sense about doctors that enables her to
bypass every barricade erected to prevent compatibility.
"She gets away with murder with physicians," says Darcy.
"I don't know what her secret is, but we need to learn it."

Gina's secret is that she speaks their language fluently
and never caters to their illusions of self-importance. "When
she makes a suggestion to a doctor, she backs it up with
quotes from articles she's read [or written]. There's none of
this, I have a feeling we should do this, kind of talk. Doctors
want scientific proof that you know what you're doing, and
Gina gives it to us in spades. She's done her homework,"
explains Sandra Wilder.

What Sandra doesn't say is that Gina's scientific savoir
faire coupled with her sense of humor and her refusal to be
deferential earns her so much extra credit with physicians
that in the middle of a potential emergency, she can turn to
the intense chief of one of the surgical services who is
demanding that a nurse stand by the patient round-the-clock
and say, "Harry, I swear I spend half my time calming you
down. You know we're going to take care of it. Everything
will be alright." And the stern-faced Harry will sacrifice his
composure to a momentary giggle. Or, she can be lecturing
to that roomful of high- and low-powered surgeons and get
away with turning the high-powered, somnolent Clifford
Siegel into the group's laughingstock. Instead of arousing
the esteemed physician's ire, she returns him to his senses
in a jocular condition. "Boy, you just wait till I get you for
that one," he promises.

In a waking state, Clifford Siegel is a good observer of
the nursing profession. He is typical of those physicians
who are married to a nurse (as he is) or are the offspring of
a nurse. As a group they are apt to be more knowledgeable,
tougher critics, and stronger advocates than their non-nurse-
related counterparts. Says Clifford,

> When I was a resident, I saw more professional nurses
> than I do now. Today's nurses are competent and more
> highly skilled than they were ten years ago. These
> competent nurses, however, come to work reading
> womens' magazines instead of professional journals.
> They're not as motivated to further their education. I

don't buy the notion, either, that we physicians still treat nurses as handmaidens, but I don't think that nurses are clear that we've grown out of that. I'm in favor of primary nursing. After all, we have primary doctoring. Why should patients have to relate to so many different people? I don't think most physicians would get on a bandwagon for primary nursing, though, because the nursing administrators here and elsewhere are ambivalent about it themselves. It's hard to implement during periods of short-staffing and high acuity, and it's not the cheapest way to deliver nursing care.

Clifford pauses before speaking about Gina.

Gina is exemplary, the antithesis of the negative nurse image. She's professional and competent. She wants to do it all, and she keeps educating herself. Add all that to her sense of humor, her interpersonal skills, her cool composure and performance in the volatile atmosphere of the SICU, and you've got a superior nurse. We need many more like her.

His compliments for Gina are echoed by Jack Atwood, another senior surgeon in the hospital. He knows both Gina and Jessie well, and he compares them.

They're both at the top of the rung—well trained, well educated. Either of them could be a VP of nursing, but Jessie is more aggressive than Gina. Jessie has a mission. She's responsive to the power issues, to making sure that nurses maintain their authority and carry their weight with doctors. She's good for a profession that has felt so downtrodden for so long. Gina's style is different. She's smart as hell, competent as all get out, firm in her convictions, but tender in her approach. The aggressiveness that seems to be in fashion

in nursing nowadays is understandable. I think that
the advances they've made may be an example of too
little, too late, though. They've wasted valuable time
fighting doctors instead of proving their own worth to
the public.


## GINA AND NURSES

Among nurses on the SICU, there is a general feeling that
they are a breed apart from nurses on other units, perhaps a
cut above them. Occasionally they joke about it. "We're
the appliance nurses," they say. Karen, a former SICU
nurse presently home on leave from nursing duty in Saudi
Arabia, reflects their attitudes in a more serious vein. "Intensive care nursing offers the most challenge. You're able
to use a lot more of what you've learned on a day-to-day
basis. There's more variety in your tasks, and you concentrate on one or two patients instead of four or five. On many
units, you just run around repeating the same set of tasks
over and over again."

Up to the time that she resigns, Lois has logged seventeen
years of ICU nursing experience. In describing her most
recent job, she says she functions more like a plant and
equipment manager than a nurse. When she talks about a
nurse's life on the SICU, she goes several steps farther than
Karen.

Nurses who work on ICUs are more interested in
medicine than in nursing, and because they do minute-
to-minute management of the patient, the doctors need
their input more. Then there are all the toys we use.
The more we have, the more we think we need. There
are so many of them, and they are always being replaced with newer ones. You have to keep learning
new techniques of operation and interpretation, just
like the surgeons do. You can get so carried away

with all the gadgetry that you can actually forget the patient. It's a serious occupational hazard. Even if you've spent an entire day by a patient's side, you may not remember the color of his hair at the end of the shift. He becomes a set of numbers. We have a joke around here that our patients are so sick and motionless that we can take care of them for over two hours without seeing a wrinkle in the sheets. It's almost axiomatic to say that being an ICU nurse means that you're a compulsive type. Everything has to be in order, or you can't function.

David, a regular night nurse, echoes Lois's thoughts about the technology on the unit.

We're so busy looking at our machines that we don't see the patient, and they often don't see us. Sometimes it's the doctors who remind us to treat the patients holistically, because they have the advantage of perspective that comes with less-intense involvement. It's possible for some of our heart patients to leave without remembering that they were here. In a way, that's a good sign. It means that we took good care of them.

In both Gina's and Caroline's opinion, Darcy is one of the brightest stars on the unit. She's smart, ambitious, and highly skilled. They rely on her for much of the precepting (teaching) of new nurses on the unit. All of her eleven years of experience have been spent in surgical nursing care, the last six of which have been on the SICU. She loves her work there. "It's never boring. The highest proportion of the work is head, not body, work. We have more autonomy than nurses have on other units. We know more about the equipment than the physicians do. It's really our province. We're indispensable to the physicians, especially the younger ones, who are usually very green."

Morale is high on the SICU. There are grumblings, of

course, but they are relatively minor in comparison to those heard on 5B. Some of the preceptors object to the extra time required to train PCTs, whom they regard as slower learners than nurses. Staff nurses complain more about equipment and interdepartmental problems than about their colleagues. Common complaints are:

- The equipment breaks down and doesn't get repaired soon enough.
- The pharmacy is slow in replacing medication supplies.
- Getting a special order from food services can be a big deal.
- Floats from other units who aren't trained in ICU procedures are more a hindrance than a help.
- High-acuity periods are stressful.

Complaints about physicians are uttered from time to time, but usually in the context of a fleeting moment of intense pressure or in brief, stress-relieving gossip klatches. Two nurses do say that they think Paul Donaldson should be more appreciative of their work than he is.

On the whole, though, the SICU nurses, in concert with their peers elsewhere, express the same standard complaint: too much to do, too little time to do it, too few people to get it done. The difference on the SICU is that the nurses are as apt to fault themselves for their heavy work loads as they are to fault the institution. One frequently hears comments like: "We're codependent. We can't say no. We have to be everything to everybody."

Sitting-around time on the SICU is hard to come by. Nurses don't cluster in the bubble or in the lounge as often as they do on 5B, unless there's been a unit meeting. Occasionally, though, there will be a slow period—a little down time—for the hyperactive staff. At one such time, several nurses gather in the bubble. Part of their conversation is about Gina. Inasmuch as the SICU is like a toy department, no one there would dispute the fact that Gina is the leading toy authority, especially on the "heart toys."

"I think she's brilliant. She knows so much," says Kitty.

"Yeh, but we don't see much of her. I don't understand her role. I think she's supposed to teach us, but she doesn't have much time for that. She orients the new kids, but I wish she was here more. She's so helpful when she is," adds Lucy.

Meg disagrees. "She's been a godsend to me, but maybe that's because I'm doing hearts now. I think she really knows her stuff, and I like her style. She's down-to-earth and relaxed, and never puts you down. You can't bullshit her, either. She asks great questions, and if she doesn't think you know what you're talking about, she'll speak to Caroline about you, but she'll also let you know where you stand with her. I like the way she pushes our professional growth."

Lucy still isn't satisfied. "She pulls herself in so many directions, though. Sometimes she has to go off and answer her beeper when she's orienting you. I have trouble with that."

"Do you remember the day that I had that really sick patient?" They all nod as they listen again to Meg. "Well, she didn't leave my side that day. I was so nervous, and she knew it. I will admit, though, that at times, she has grandiose ideas about how this place should be run. She writes policies about medications that we use every day. She's removed from the reality. Sometimes she wants to mix medications that we don't use. We don't tell her this, because she's so good. It would hurt her feelings. [When Gina learns about the comment on her writing of medication policy, she protests vigorously, saying, "I'd always get the consensus of the clinical staff before I'd write a medication policy."] For some of us it's easier to talk to Caroline, because she's on the unit more."

Other nurses also voice confusion and frustration about Gina's role on the unit. All of them speak of her brilliance, her skills in communicating with physicians, her pleasing personality, and, in the same breath their disappointment at not having more of her. A few nurses, Lois among them, blame Gina for this: "She's a type A personality and an overachiever, a typical adult child of an alcoholic. She's outgrown the job." Still others, like Walter, lay the blame on the academic emphasis in teaching hospitals. As Walter puts it,

> The trouble with the academic types like Gina is that they lose the *trench perspective*. Teaching skills and doing skills are different. The more they move into teaching, the further away they get from doing. You tend to resent it when the CNS comes up to you after four hours of horror in the trenches and suggests that you should try doing something a different way. There's a general feeling that she couldn't have done it any better if she'd been in your position, even with her extra knowledge.

The majority of nurses blame the role rather than the person. They see a disparity between their expectations of Gina, and the Nursing Administration's expectations. From the perspective of the SICU staff nurses, "The Nursing Department wants her out on the road, because it's good PR for the hospital. Besides attracting new nurses to Memorial, they think that her travels will keep them updated on the latest advances in the profession."

Pauline Irving concurs.

> She's a real asset to the institution. She's an innovator in her field. She keeps us current and brings us recognition. When she took the job here, it was understood that we wanted her to keep up with her extracurricular activities. Nevertheless, there is some confusion in the administration about our specific expectations of CNSs. It's a delicate balancing act in terms of how much time they should allot to in-house versus out-

of-house activities. We're not sure exactly what we
want from them.

These comments about Gina and her role are illustrative
of the continuing struggle in the nursing profession to shed
yesterday's bondage for tomorrow's liberation. Gina, and
others like her, are stuck in today's catch-22. Ironically,
physicians at all levels can empathize with her position more
easily than nurses can. Paul Donaldson, as much as he
wants more of her time, does not begrudge her absences. In
medical academia it has long been the accepted practice to
send the senior men (and women) out into the world to
deliver their expert messages while the junior boys (and
girls) stay behind to take care of the patients (for lower pay
and longer hours than those of young nurses). Rarely does
one hear out of the mouth of a junior physician, *I wish that
Clifford Siegel (or anyone else at his level) would stick
around more to teach us all that he knows*. It is assumed
that he will be around when he's around, and won't be when
he isn't, and there will be no suggestions that his absences
are the result of the vagaries of his personality. Medical
administrators, in fact, design rotating schedules for senior
physicians that facilitate their availability for professional
activities outside the hospital.

To be fair to nursing administrators, however, is to state
that finances and unionization contribute as much as the lack
of a clear vision to constrain them in their management of
this endangered role. There are at least three other CNSs at
Memorial who are active in the public arena. To compound
the administration's problems, CNSs, because they are non-
managers, are union affiliated and thus bound by union
prerogatives. Physicians are nonunionized, and most senior
physicians receive the bulk of their salaries from sources
other than the hospital, whereas almost all nursing salaries
come from the hospital payroll. For nursing experts like
Gina to simultaneously increase their ranks and insure the
continuation of their academic and scientific contributions

(both very important for the growth of the nursing profession), the need to find alternative sources of remuneration would seem to be a foregone conclusion. Accomplishing this, however, will require a major collaborative effort between nursing administrators and union representatives, the majority of whom are naturally inclined to be antagonists, not allies. In the meantime, Gina is the victim of a double-bind—the administrative-union stalemate from on high and the staff perspective from below. The staff's attitude that the hand that feeds her is the same hand that feeds them, leads them to conclude that she should spend the majority of her time with them in the trenches. Gina's husband Terry is a longtime observer of critical care nurses. He understands their point of view.

Critical care nurses have to slave. None of them want to be left alone in critical situations, so it's natural for them to want an experienced person standing by to hold them by the hand. It takes awhile before they can develop enough self-confidence to feel that they can work on their own. The truth is, though, that they're not left alone until they have enough training to handle the load.

It's a tough balancing act for Gina, which she acknowledges only when it's brought to her attention—a rare occurrence. Otherwise she behaves as if she's oblivious to it. Caroline believes that Gina's ability to ignore the fallout from the conflicting demands on her time is the natural result of her status.

She's used to being the teacher, the expert, the role model. She stands above the fray. We all know how capable she is. When you've been up on a pedestal for a long time and you've grown accustomed to it, it's easy not to see the resentments that are festering beneath you, but there always are some.

# SORRY, SHE'S
# IN A MEETING

THE HIGHER UP THE ladder a nurse climbs, the more meetings she attends. By the time she reaches the rank of a Jessie Concannon or a Gina Rossi, it would not be unusual for her to spend one-quarter of each working week in meetings. Put her one or more steps above Jessie and Gina and she will spend the lion's share of her time in meetings. Callers grow accustomed to hearing secretaries say, "Sorry, she's in a meeting." The refrain is so constant that eventually the frequent caller will learn to beat the secretary to the punch: "I'm sure she's in a meeting now, but if you'll tell me when it's over, I'll try to call back then."

At Memorial, many of the meetings that nurses like Jessie and Gina attend are held in the Nursing Department headquarters on the fourth floor of the Crane Building. You know you're in nursing territory again as soon as you arrive at another one of those glass bubble rooms. This one is the permanent home of Greg Walters, the Nursing Department's official greeter. Greg has the distinction of saying "Sorry, she's in a meeting" more times during the course of a day than any other secretary. He's the eyes and ears of the place. In a humorous, nonchalant fashion, he tells familiar visitors when the meeting began, who's in it, if it's running late, what kind of moods the participants are in, and who will be attending which of the succeeding meetings. "I wouldn't wait around for her today if I were you," he's been known to say. "She's got another meeting right after this one, and she probably won't even feel like talking in the corridor. It's just too hectic around here."

The staggering number of meetings that administrative nurses attend make it hectic. One cannot help but wonder if all of these meetings are absolutely necessary—if there aren't other vehicles to accomplish the same things.

If one listens to nurses at both ends of the ladder, one hears conflicting messages. Those on the bottom say that "hands-on" nursing is undervalued by the women upstairs, and the women upstairs feel that the downstairs nurses are resistant to changes that are being made in their own best interests. Yet the meetings that are held, except in crises, seem rarely to be concerned with the simmering cauldron down below. Instead they center around the development and implementation of policies, procedures, management practices, and budgetary prerogatives, or on the resolution of interdepartmental dilemmas. Even though it helps to bridge the gap by having staff nurses participate in many of these meetings, there are always some who retain their us-versus-them attitudes. Those, like Dominique, who don't attend invariably hold the more negative point of view. Thus, the potential for conflict seems ever present, and it prompts the outsider to entertain the idea that top-level administrative time may be better spent walking around the units, feeling their pulse, searching routinely for grassroots feedback. As it stands now, the morale on any given unit is largely dependent on the individual style, perspective, and personality of its nurse manager rather than reflective of a broad-based departmental philosophy. Staff nurses see the caretaking functions of nursing, the very functions that attracted them to the profession in the first place, eroding day by day due to an onslaught of managerial and fiscal priorities. And they don't like it.

However tempting it may be to pass off some of these

impressions about the abundance of meetings as criticism, they can stand only as impressions. There are so many changes taking place in hospitals these days (most of which are related to evolving fiscal priorities) that it may be that holding frequent meetings is the best and most efficient way to keep abreast and to insure that nursing interests are well represented. Still, staff nurses are not alone in voicing the fear that their leaders may be too willing to sacrifice high-quality patient care to cost-containment prerogatives. Nurses in higher positions express the same doubts. Nurse manager Joan Thornton is a good example: "I hope our new vice president will lead us back to thinking more about caring for our patients and less about our budgets." It is not yet clear whether, in the long run, the Joan Thorntons in the profession will be marked as the dreamers or the realists. At present there is no argument about the fact that nurses are caught between fiscal incentives and patient advocacy. Ben Callahan describes their current position succinctly: "Ten years ago, nurses didn't have to worry about the cost side at all. Now they have to keep a constant eye on the patient's length of stay."

Jessie, although she dislikes the numerous meetings, believes that it is important to have a voice in departmental and hospital affairs. Stated simply, her philosophy is, If you don't go, you can't complain. She selects those committees that are the most relevant to her work. Many nurse managers choose to spend more time in meetings than Jessie does. For those she does attend, she is usually tardy. She would much prefer to stick closer to 5C. Nevertheless, she is a participant in a variety of departmental meetings and also serves on various hospital task forces and committees. Her style contrasts sharply with that of Gina, who appears to enjoy the ambience of meetings. She's always punctual, well prepared, good-natured, and actively involved. While Jessie fidgets in her seat in one meeting, Gina is thoroughly relaxed in another. Gina's meetings take her everywhere— to the department, to other parts of the hospital, to all manner of home-based and far-flung locations. Jessie tends to regard many of the meetings that take place off the unit as a waste of time. Gina describes the majority of them as "fun" and "very productive."

Jessie and Gina attend so many meetings in so many places that the best that this author can do is offer the reader a glimpse of the sample.

## Nurse Manager Meetings

Even a meeting detractor like Jessie is inspired by Colleen Lindstrom's leadership talent. Blessed with good looks, sociability, a quick mind, and an even quicker wit, Colleen has only to open her mouth to reveal her facility as a manager. She accomplishes effortlessly what it takes most managers to achieve laboriously. Many people, after several years of postgraduate training, still will not learn the lessons that come so naturally to her. Her impact is immediate, and it stays with its recipients long after her meetings are over. Somehow it's impossible to forget the things she says and the way she says them.

An ice bucket left over from a previous function sits on the table of the fourth-floor conference room where Jessie and several other nurse managers are seated when Colleen enters. "What's this?" she asks, lifting the bucket. "Are you giving me the cold shoulder?"

This opener places the group's attention firmly in her grasp. She moves on to business. She asks for feedback from the nurse managers who are members of the hiring committee for the new vice president of nursing. They liked the last candidate the best. Colleen asks for input from everybody present about the qualities that they believe the new vice president should have. Jessie, when she hears that one serious candidate does not have most of her degrees in nursing, volunteers that she thinks it is important for the winner to have a well-established identity as a nurse. The discussion switches to patient care technicians and how well they are being received on the units. On some units the news is good, on others not so good. Colleen confesses that she feels that much of the fallout about them from staff nurses is due to the top-down administrative style of the previous vice president. "Let's get all the bad news out into the open before a new VP comes aboard," she says.

For the remainder of the meeting, Jessie is the center of attention. Once again, she repeats the announcement of her forthcoming resignation. "I'm going back to school to get a Psy.D. in psychology, but I'm not leaving nursing. I'll always be a nurse." Everyone greets Jessie's decision enthusiastically. Colleen, her head half lowered to conceal her sadness, lends her voice to the enthusiastic chorus. There is a chemistry between Colleen and Jessie that empowers both of them, and for Colleen, losing Jessie is like losing a limb.

The group showers Jessie with compliments. She sits scarlet-faced throughout. "Even when you're not around, everyone on your unit talks about how much they like you, how you've been a hundred percent behind them, how you've brought them all to a higher level of nursing," says Lorraine. Joan and Gretchen follow suit. "You have that special character. You've created a vision for your nurses," adds Joan. "There's been more changing on your unit than anywhere else," says Gretchen.

Colleen has the last word. "And the funny thing about it is that you've done more changing yourself than anybody else." Jessie's body language reveals her restlessness. Colleen saves her by changing the subject and rattling off a few requests. "Turn in your time schedules for May and June so we can arrange coverage for meetings. Give me some feedback about where we should locate the new computers for nurse managers. We need some volunteers for the Code Beeper Committee."

Colleen gets the information she wants, along with Jessie's reluctant offer to be on the committee. She's one of the few nurse managers who has been a critical care nurse and knows how to do a code.

Colleen begins another meeting in a businesslike manner. She reads a memo about measles testing for hospital employees and announces that all employees born after 1957 must come up with a physician's documentation showing that they have been vaccinated. The assembled managers moan and groan aloud about having to carry out this order, saying that they have trouble getting people to cooperate.

Leaning forward in her seat, Colleen raises her voice, "Well, that's too bad. They have to do it, and if they don't they can be accused of insubordination." Something in the way she says this invites the ensuing hilarity.

"My mother is very compulsive. She kept records in my baby book about all my shots," declares Wendy Fleming.

"My mother didn't keep a baby book," says Joan Thornton.

"You were probably never a baby," quips Colleen.

Jessie gets a big bang out of this exchange, but as soon as things get back on a serious track, she begins fidgeting again. When Colleen announces that the nurse recruiter position is open and is not listed as a position requiring nursing credentials, Jessie objects strongly. Always sensitive to time constraints, she stresses the screening hours that will be saved by having a nurse in the position. Other people support Jessie's stand, but Colleen neutralizes it by stating that the hospital doesn't have the recruitment needs it used to have.

"I know. It's a sign of the times. It's more cost effective not to hire nurses," nurse manager Rita says woefully.

"I've got an update for you on the VP position. The selection committee's first choice is Dr. Tirrell's last choice. The one he likes is the one with only an associate degree in nursing."

In response to Colleen's news bulletin, Jessie and Rita jump on the bandwagon for a strong nursing background. Colleen, a steadfast champion of change, is more equivocal. "Maybe she doesn't fit because we've grown so accustomed to our own values that we've all hired each other all these years.'' Now other nurse managers who were leaning toward Jessie and Rita just minutes earlier begin equivocating.

At the close of the meeting Colleen advises the managers to take aggressive positions toward the Housekeeping Department if the service isn't good enough.

As they file out, Joan turns to Jessie and says, ''Boy, our profession sure goes out of its way to avoid conflict. We'll take on housekeeping, but when it comes to the big stuff, we back down.''

In the course of any nurse managers' meeting, Colleen, with a simple turn of a phrase, can activate a mood change in the group. She employs this strategy regularly. On one occasion Mary Alice, a very likeable nurse manager, arrives at the meeting five minutes before it is due to end. Colleen is in the middle of an important discussion with the group about whether or not nursing assistants should be permitted to write notes in patient records. As Mary Alice tiptoes toward the opposite end of the table, Colleen's voice trails her: ''I didn't know that we held five-minute meetings.'' Then, abruptly, Colleen returns to the business at hand. Mary Alice receives and retains the message.

## A Clinical Nurse Specialist Meeting

The weekly CNS meetings are held in conference rooms on different units and are distinguished from nurse manager meetings in their absence of a designated leader from the Nursing Department. Coffee, muffins, and pads of paper clutter the table. At one such meeting a regional Clinical Nurse Specialist Conference, to be held in a local hotel, is the main item on the agenda. Gail, the fashionable psychiatric clinical nurse specialist, is in charge of the hors d'oeuvres for the event. She wants collegial opinions about taste, quality, and cost. Everybody has them. Some people remember last year's tasteless hors d'oeuvres. Others think shrimp is too expensive. Stuffed mushrooms are messy, but they're so tasty. Vegetable dips are cheap and healthy. Chicken wings are always popular, although "they're messier than mushrooms." Gail takes copious notes. Miraculously, by the end of the discussion, she manages to sound decisive in the face of the barrage of conflicting suggestions.

Once the culinary matters are settled, Gina asks about the fees that conference speakers will be receiving. She gasps when she hears the figures. "I never get that much. Who do these people think they are?" The group agrees that the figures seem high, but no one present is responsible for procuring or paying the speakers.

Clinical nurse specialists, like all human beings, are not averse to gossip. Every nurse in the hospital is eager for the latest scoop about the new vice president. They want every detail—personal and professional. The CNSs have discussed every candidate's professional qualifications thoroughly in previous meetings. By the time of this meeting, it is clear which person has been chosen. Now the group is looking for a thumbnail personal sketch, an answer to the question, What's she like? Chloe, a CNS who has been a member of the selection committee, tells them. "She's avant-garde. We like her humor. She's a person you can talk to. She's got a big-city flair." Others who have met her attest to her stylishness. One CNS registers the opinion that she likes the way she mixes stripes on the jackets of her suits with other patterns on the skirts. Apparently it is common knowledge that she has lost a lot of weight recently. No doubt this is what enables her to wear so many stripes going in so many different directions. One more thing is certain— she will stand apart from the previous vice president and the current nurse directors. All of their suits are monochromatic.

### The Clinical Practices Committee

The large classroom on Crane 4 is the setting for this committee meeting. Nurses at all levels are participants. They will meet in a big group for the first portion of the meeting and break into subcommittees for the second. Colleen is the chair, and the entire agenda is devoted to the old bugaboo, documentation.

At the podium in the front of the room, Colleen brings the meeting to order. She wants everyone to know that designated groups of people will be circulating on the units to check patient records at random. A sensible person in the back of the room raises her hand to question whether these visits will be perceived as friendly or as search-and-seize missions.

Colleen's appreciation of the question shows in her reply. "Yes, we're going to call the inspectors the docu-police, and all of you who went to Catholic schools should volunteer to serve on the force." Laughter lowers the anxiety level. "Of course, we don't want to make this a competitive thing. We're not going to give out prizes for the best unit documentation. We just want to see where the kinks are and how well the new forms are working." She moves rapidly from this into announcing the various subcommittees, gives each small group a time frame for their tasks, and requests that they report back to the larger group at the end of an hour.

Jessie is on the planning subcommittee for "outreach to the floors." When her group has relocated to a small classroom, Sarah, a CNS, offers to lead the meeting. Within fifteen minutes, several methods for implementing the outreach have been advanced and one method has been selected. The unfinished business is when, who, and how many committee members will visit which floors. Sarah suggests that this task may require a second meeting. The mere hint of another meeting prods Jessie into action. Every muscle in her body indicates that she is hell-bent on getting the job done then and there. "Let's get our date books out right now, and then let's divide up the floors among ourselves," she insists with her own date book already in her hand. For the next half hour they arrange the logistics of the outreach, and they complete their assignment ahead of schedule.

Gina is on the Chart Review Subcommittee, which is meeting several weeks after the docu-police have made their rounds. Everyone comes to the meeting loaded down with patient records that they have removed from their units. Nicole McClean, another nurse director, and Colleen are coleading the meeting. They've come with a list of criteria to evaluate and score the documentation. Gina is thrilled to discover that the SICU has done well. Wendy Fleming is disheartened to find no nursing notes at all in a record from her floor. The total tally from all of the units yields discouraging results.

"Why don't you try taking a few nurses at a time and running through the instructions until you've reached every nurse? That's the way we did it, and our scores were high," Gina offers cheerfully.

"We can't afford to be complacent. We've got to get tough about this," says Nicole, her voice reflecting the seriousness of the matter.

## The Materials Distribution Committee

In the bowels of Memorial's buildings are scores of administrative offices. The Materials Management Department occupies a suite of rooms in one of these subterranean locations. Jessie, along with several other nurse manager representatives, serves on the Materials Distribution Committee, whose function is to evaluate the distribution of supplies to the units. Pillow talk is recurrent in these meetings, because pillows are always winding up in the wrong places. One unit or another is sure to be too short or too long on pillows. Jessie admits that her unit could be better about labeling its pillows. "We all know how I feel about pillows. I hope we don't have to talk about them anymore today."

Cost cutting ranks a close second to pillows as an item of concern for the group, and the department has its own cost-cutting jargon.

"We want to make an impact on utilization," explains Mitch, the committee's chair. "We need your help to provide incentives for people to use supplies more efficiently. We've got to keep within our budget frames. In this last period we didn't do so well."

"Well, we don't have enough forms for the storage room," Jessie tells Mitch.

"We're working on that now. We're going to establish a Forms Management Committee, and don't worry, nursing will be represented."

Jessie sighs at the thought of having to serve on another committee.

Jim from the Materials Management Department announces that the hospital is seriously considering hiring an outside vendor to take care of all supplies. "This should streamline our operation."

Mitch is going to publish another Materials Distribution Center catalogue, and he needs nursing feedback on how to describe and organize the items in it.

"I think you should send out a questionnaire with a deadline for return to all nurse managers to get the information you need. The unit secretaries can help," says another nursing representative. Her suggestion receives the unanimous approval of the assembled congregation.

"I'll tell you a story now. I've resigned. I'm going back to school." Jessie's announcement is delivered this time in a rather jolly mode, undoubtedly the result of a sudden realization that her departure will exclude her from the new Forms Management Committee. It throws her listeners off guard. There's an awkward silence.

Jim rises to the occasion. "No kidding. Wow, that's great for you. I sure hope they'll recruit someone of your caliber."

### The Institutional Review Board

Memorial's affiliated medical school is attached to the hospital by several pedestrian bridges. Traffic between the hospital and the medical school moves across the bridges in a steady stream throughout the day. One Thursday morning, Gina joins the throng on her way to the Institutional Review Board meeting. The board meets in the medical school in a large penthouse room with tall windows, affording an excellent view of the city. The lofty location of the meeting hints at its importance. Seated around a giant table is a group of men and women, only a few of whom are wearing white coats. The board, as soon becomes evident, is charged with reviewing all of the research proposals submitted by Memorial's and its affiliated medical school's staffs that involve the use of human subjects. Its members are a mixed group of health care professionals, lawyers, and community representatives who examine the proposals according to safety, procedural, and legal criteria. Gina is one of the two nurses on the board.

Each participant comes to the meeting with an enormous packet of proposals that he or she has read previously. Some of the professional board members will be responsible for oral presentations explaining the salient points in the proposals. The authors of the proposals are not permitted to attend these reviews unless the board has specific questions that only they can answer. For today's meeting, a day-long event, Gina must deliver the presentation for one of Jack Atwood's proposals. (The presenter must have knowledge of the author's specialty area.) The content of the proposals is strictly confidential.

As usual, Gina's performance is polished, clear, and articulate. She recommends a few changes in wording but otherwise finds no fault with the proposal. The board, however, puts her on the defensive in a few areas. They question whether the study is "intrusive" to patients, whether certain drug tests are necessary, and whether the location of the research is explained adequately. Clifford Siegel, another member of the board, does his best to bolster Gina's cause by addressing these concerns. It's no go. The board postpones a decision until these issues can be explained to their satisfaction. Gina and Clifford are discouraged. They hate to see important research delayed. Gina blames herself for not having anticipated the board's reactions. For the remainder of the meeting Gina listens and contributes to other people's presentations, but the sting of the morning's rejection stays with her.

From whatever vantage point one looks at the proceedings that occur here, there is no denying that they leave a lasting impression. The mere fact of the board's existence should send a heartening message to every potential consumer of services in teaching hospitals. As Clifford Siegel, in his infinite wisdom, put it after the meeting,

> Those lay people on the board raise issues on behalf of patients that narrowly focused researchers would never consider. We're lucky to have them, and they work hard. It's important to have the right balance, though. Today there weren't enough medical members in attendance. That's just a fluke. The complex details of research are hard for lay people to grasp. The longer they serve, the more they know, but you need a healthy representation of researchers to explain the fine, technical points.

## The State Council of Nurse Managers

The state's Council of Nurse Managers is holding its annual meeting in late June. This year Jessie cannot attend, because she and several of her friends have rented a summer cottage for a week's vacation, but two of Memorial's other nurse managers are there—Judy LaVigne and Ron Ramsey. Judy is the nurse manager of the PCU. She already has been elected as the next president of the council, having made a name for herself as a leader in the fight staged by the Nurses of America to put pressure on the media to present a more

positive and realistic image of nurses. So successful has this
effort been that the TV program "Nightingales" has been
taken off the air. Judy has received local and national recognition for her part in the campaign. Ron's is a lesser claim
to fame, but around Memorial Hospital, he stands out as
one of only two male nurse managers, and here again at the
council meeting, he is a visible minority.

An audience of well over one hundred nurse managers is
seated in the conference room of the seaside resort where
the meeting is taking place, awaiting the appearance of
the guest speaker, a nurse. The group varies slightly in
sex and greatly in age, shape, size, and style of dress (everything from shorts to business suits) and reflects homogeneity
only in whiteness of skin. Finally this year's president
comes to the podium, makes a few announcements, and
then introduces the speaker as a health systems consultant.

The group warms to her immediately. She knows nurses,
and she knows how to home in on their most glaring vulnera-
bility, the one characteristic that would have sent Jessie
through the ceiling had she been there to hear it named—
the occupational hazard of being more giving to others than
to oneself. The speaker has all of the jargon, too—"codependent," "dysfunctional," "rescuer"—and she wraps it
in a package of metaphor and humor until she has reluctant
volunteers coming forth talking about their personal
"wants." One woman confesses that she wants to publish a
book on management strategies for nurses. Another divulges
that she wants her hospital to give nurses more authority.
"See," says the speaker, "when you stop trying to fix
everybody else, stop trying to rescue them, stop being codependent, then you can go after what you want." She goes
on to say, "Nurses are always walking around with backpacks full of unmet needs and unfulfilled wishes. It weighs
them down. It's loaded with resentment and disappointment.
You keep lugging the backpack because you think that if

you take care of people enough, more than enough, someone someday will take care of you.''

Her remarks are greeted with knowing laughter. They're in the palm of her hand now. It's time to unpack the backpacks, and here's how it's done:

> You don't go around anymore with the idea that no one has to worry about you because you'll get satisfaction in your next life. You do learn to say no, because if you don't, yes is meaningless. You get power through creativity, not through control, and the more creative you are, the more power you get. Don't say nurses don't have power. Go get it. Get a vision, and go after it.

Sustained applause follows her as she leaves the room.

At 11:30 A.M. the morning meeting concludes and the participants file out for before-lunch cocktails. Strawberry daiquiris at five dollars per drink are the rage. A stack of bills sits on the bar. People with pink drinks mingle in groups around the bar and on the adjacent deck until lunch is served at noon.

The lunchtime conversation is lively. Judy and Ron compare notes with nurse managers from other hospitals, and then the talk turns to nursing in general. Liz, seated opposite Judy, says that she thinks nurses are always nurses even when they're not nursing. They're always worried about someone else. She volunteers that lately it's been her new dog who worries her. Every time she lets the dog out, she wonders if he'll come back with a venereal disease. Do dogs get venereal diseases? She's not sure. She must remember to ask the vet. And what if the dog chooses the wrong mate, a canine partner who is beneath him? While Liz is joking about her dog, Judy whispers to Pam, a young woman to her right, that there is a writer at the table. "I hope you're not going to suggest that nurses are blue collar like that other writer did," Pam says, turning her attention to me.

Tell your readers how hard we work, fifty to sixty hours a week, and how much responsibility we have, how professional we are. Tell them that we often don't get the credit we deserve, like when the medical supply salesmen come around and we give them our ideas about products. You know what happens. They turn around and use our ideas to make better products, and we don't get the credit or the money. That's partly our fault, to be sure. Now we're learning to be more careful.

Pam's last remark would have made the morning's speaker proud.

### The AACN Certification Task Force

On a steamy Saturday morning in August, Gina arrives at the downtown hotel where the task force is holding its two-day meeting. The sixteen task force members are critical care nurses from all over the country. Two representatives of a professional testing company also are present. Their collaborative effort is devoted to ensuring that the certification examination for adult critical care nurses is always in line with what they do in their jobs. Another exciting part of the task force's work is to develop a proposal for two new certification programs in neonatal and pediatric critical care nursing. Once their work is finalized, proposals will be submitted to the board of directors of the AACN Certification Corporation for approval.

The gathering begins in the spirit of a family reunion. Baby pictures are passed around. Ogles of delight can be heard from one end of the table to the other. Even the men show pictures of their babies. Everybody is eager to catch up on the news about everybody else.

Merriment is soon displaced by business. They are now in the final stages of their work together, and they are eager to package it. Earlier they sent a questionnaire to twenty-five hundred critical care nurses throughout the United States. They instructed respondents to describe their experiences caring for critically ill patients in terms of uniqueness, frequency, and type. Specifically they are looking for common uses of equipment, medications, and nursing interventions in adult, neonatal, and pediatric critical care. In order to qualify to take the examinations, they believe that nurses should have a significant number and variety of critical care nursing experiences. (This means that a nurse should have cared for many critically ill patients and administered a wide range of treatments.) A nurse who is new to the field would not meet their qualification standards. Although certification will not be required for every critical care nurse, those who elect to receive it will gain recognition and greater opportunity for advancement. Some will receive financial rewards as well. The primary goal of certification is the protection of the public. To promote this worthy objective the group rallies around the maxim that nurses who are delivering critical care should have sufficient knowledge and experience.

In proposing two new certification programs, their task is threefold: (1) to determine if there are enough experiences to justify an examination; (2) to determine if separate exams in each of the three subspecialties or one inclusive exam for all of them are indicated; and (3) to agree on the format of the exams. Between task force meetings the testing company staff have been busy collecting and assembling data from the questionnaires. Much of today's and tomorrow's meetings will be devoted to their explanation of the findings. By the end of the weekend the group will have learned that there are enough experiences to warrant giving the examination and enough *different* experiences to justify three separate ones, and they will have blueprints of examinations to present to the AACN Certification Corporation board.

Gina's task force friends take advantage of her temporary absence from the room to talk about her during a break in the meeting. She is held in high esteem, and they see her as a role model. Not only is she very advanced in her field, but she's one of the most popular lecturers on the critical care circuit. People flock to hear her speak. And as if that weren't enough, she is one of the best group facilitators, researchers, and leaders in the field. Her star is still rising, they say.

# AFTER HOURS

**D**ESPITE THEIR DIFFERENCES in personality and temperament, Jessie, Dominique, and Gina are like one another, and possibly like their colleagues everywhere, in two significant ways. They delight in the after-hours company of other nurses. These close bonds appear to be born as much from need as from commonality. At the end of a day, most professionals, businesspeople, service workers, and artisans will have gone about their daily affairs without so much as a glimpse or thought of death, but nurses will have thought, seen, and felt its constant presence by the end of every day. No one, not even physicians, will have been exposed to it so unremittingly. The departure from an atmosphere of pain, misery, and mortality to one of fellowship and frivolity begs for a transitional phase. Nurses like Jessie, Dominique, and Gina frequently find it in end-of-the-day drinks with other nurses who speak the same acronymic language and who understand, often without the necessity of language, that the shadow of death can be as real as the radiance of life. Whether they are single like Dominique and Jessie or married like Gina, nurses make social time for one another in their schedules.

Dominique, because she is the least experienced and stands closest to the bedside, feels the weight of human suffering most acutely.

My friends who aren't nurses just don't understand what my working life is like. For them, death and dying are distant experiences. How can you stand it? they ask, as if I'm a little crazy for putting myself so close to it. Maybe they're right. They have no idea how impossible it is for me to walk off the job one minute and party the next. The patients' pain is still too vivid, and my own physical and emotional exhaustion demands that I take time out to gather a second wind.

By the time a nurse has accumulated enough experience to reach Jessie's or Gina's position, they have had so many trials by fire that they have built vital defense systems to protect them from intense, personal wear and tear. Often it is the climate of emergency and high pressure that is apt to precede death, more than the death itself, that takes a toll on them. They have learned to accept the inevitability of death, to regard it more as destiny than tragedy. They mourn it, but they don't personalize it. They understand that disease can be a force more powerful than human ingenuity and modern technology combined. So the kind of self-confidence that comes with repeat performances removes them from the tendency to question whether fatal outcomes might be the results of their own commissions or omissions. Even with only a year and a half of experience, Dominique has seen signs of change in herself.

In the beginning, I was heartbroken when one of my patients died, especially if it was someone I liked a lot. I thought if I'd only done this or that, maybe he or she would have lived. Now I may still think that there were things I could have done, but I know down deep that that isn't true. I struggle more these days with feelings of futility than with feelings of grief.

Funny that after long hours of caring for others, nurses can be so willing in their social lives to pick up right where they leave off, to make themselves so available to administer to the woes and worries of friends, relatives, and lovers. Strange as it may seem at first glance, this is the second common denominator between Jessie, Dominique, and Gina, and one that they share with many other nurses. No sooner are they out the hospital door, than they are doing something for somebody else. Hardly a week goes by when Jessie isn't listening to her friends' problems or buying them gifts she can't afford for all manner of major and minor occasions. Dominique, the least selfless of the threesome, nevertheless cancels recreational activities to come to the aid of troubled friends. Gina, despite her hectic professional schedule, doubles as a sympathetic ear and a hostess-innkeeper. At the very moments when common sense would presume that they are most needy of nurturance, they are the nurturers. Lesser mortals cannot help but wonder, Has the me generation passed them by? Do they believe that nobility is synonymous with giving and ignominy with receiving? Or are they the walking, talking, living, breathing codependent prototypes of pop psychology?

None of these questions yields a black-and-white answer. The gray answers are written into and embellished by the characters' personal stories. Only one strong clue, contained in their common occupational biography, sheds light on all of the questions taken together: a daily diet of other people's misery eventually provides sufficient nurturance to the nurturer. The closer she comes to the suffering of others, the further she travels from her own. Usually the only conscious reason she voices for choosing to be a nurse is her desire to be helpful to suffering people, but that is partly an illusion. What she doesn't know and doesn't say is that continuous caregiving is a selfless activity that affords her an extra layer of protective coating against experiencing her own personal pain. Still, hers is a kind of grand illusion. We, the public, are the beneficiaries of such selfless generosity, and we ought to be more grateful.

Because, historically, nurses have given more to society than they have received, it is heartening to see them uniting now to champion their own and their patients' interests. Let us hope, though, that in the advancement of the cause, they avoid the worst of physicians' self-promotional errors—too much zeal in the personal pursuit of luxury items, not enough zeal for the health and welfare of the neediest. No matter what strategies we as a society devise to counter it, the truth is that capitalism and caring for the sick are incompatible marriage partners. It's impossible to justify dispensing care in the same way that we sell fancy cars, by restricting delivery to those who can afford to be sick as if they belonged in the same league as those who can afford to buy the latest luxury sedan. Nurses nowadays are comparable to dissatisfied spouses. They know that the marriage isn't working, but they're not sure why. Some of their uneasiness about all of the fiscal hullabaloo that whirls around them in whatever hospital they find themselves is due to their suspicion that all patients, regardless of means, get the short end of the stick and that the poorest patients get the shortest. "In the long run," explains Dominique, "all patients suffer for the shortness of the supply of nurses and for the inadequacy of the health care safety net, but the impoverished patients suffer the most."

## THE GANG

Jessie, Dominique, and Gina each have their female gangs, friends they've known for a long time. Jessie has two gangs. One is her family; the other is a huge assortment of friends, many of whom are nurses. Dominique's and Gina's are a disparate group of childhood friends, but each of them has her gang of nurses, too. Gina, like Jessie, sees a great deal of her extended family, mostly for Sunday and holiday visits, but unlike Jessie, nine times out of ten the family gatherings take place at her house. Gina's and Jessie's lives are chock full of ritualized celebrations. Dominique's life has more room for spontaneity. All three seem to favor socialization over solitude. Rarely do they say that they look forward to time alone. Even though each of them spends many intimate moments with just one person, the overriding impression that they leave is communal and interactive rather than private and introspective. Dominique, as introspective as she is, uses the group as a sounding board for self-analysis.

No one comes better prepared for gang affiliation than Jessie. She was born into a family gang and to this very day remains an active member. Every year there are numerous gatherings of the Concannon clan, and Jessie is present for most of these events. On July fourth it's Jessie's, her sister Claire's, and her brother-in-law Dan's turn to host the annual holiday family bash, to which a select group of friends also are invited. They're all there—her parents, sisters, brothers, their spouses, her nieces and nephews, her paternal grandmother, a handful of her nurse gang, more spouses and babies. Beer and wine flow freely. Dan stands over the grill. Dad alternates between watching television and socializing. Jessie dashes around picking up babies and toddlers and chatting with everyone. So do Claire and Mom. Grandma sits in the kitchen, taking advantage of one of the few privileges of senior citizenship—the right to let everyone come to her. Dinner is buffet style. The guests spread out on the lawn, in the sunroom, and in the kitchen. When the meal is finished, a mad flurry begins. Most of the adults and all of the children rush to cars to drive to the town's annual circus celebration. The circus is Dan's special mark on the event. He's passionate about circuses. Maybe it's because all of the color and the pageantry far above the ground bring proper balance to his life as a casket salesman. "Underground novelties," he calls his wares.

It's sweltering inside the tent and everybody sweats profusely, including the elephants and the tightrope walkers. Even in the tent, Jessie is the consummate nurse-hostess, checking on everyone's comfort level. After the circus, the children with cotton candy stains around their mouths are accompanied back to the house by sweat-soaked adults. Dad is asleep in front of the television and Grandma is reclining on a couch. Soon the returning revelers join with those who've remained behind in a circle around an extraordinary cake. It has white frosting, horizontal lines of strawberries, and a square of blueberries in the left-hand corner. The wine and beer and coffee chasers flow on into the evening.

Dominique discourses, dances, dines, and drinks with her friends. Any boyfriend that happens into her life will not only have to adapt to her, he also will have to work his way into her circle of friends. Her friends, lest the reader has forgotten, are her surrogate family. Woe be it to him who is her lover to step too heavily on their toes. He, too, must discourse, dance, dine, and drink with them. "Mark was rude to Cleo last night," Dominique tells Katie one morning in the nurses' lounge. "She was trying to be friendly to him, and he just ignored her. I was so mad. He told me that he was just tired, but I said that that was a poor excuse. I said that even though I'm exhausted almost every night, I'd never act that way around his friends."

Dominique is out of her house as much as she is in it. Her social life is a jumbled stew spiced with different combinations of human ingredients. Sometimes she and Mark go to gathering places in the city or on short trips with her friends or his, or the two of them take weekend biking and camping trips alone. At other times she hangs out with her friends without him.

Dominique and her friends share a common concern for the world around them. They see it spinning backward, not forward, and they believe that their generation is expected to do something about it. They wonder how they can possibly help stem the raging tide of violence and poverty. The burden seems too heavy. For Dominique, volunteer work in underdeveloped countries feels like a more significant contribution to the global burden than working on an oncology unit. It drives her crazy the way people just sit around and talk about what needs to be done, then don't do anything about it. There's no peace for her if she doesn't act on her beliefs. Yet on the days when the burden is unbearable for her, Dominique thinks that it might be a good idea to do something totally uncharacteristic. "Like maybe I could become an actress, or just open a career book and pick something out at random."

In Gina's immaculate, sectional-sofaed living room, her old friends chew the fat along with their take-out Chinese food. They remember their old boyfriends, the parties they held together, the night Larry got so drunk they had to carry him to the nearest bed, and the time Gina told Paul Raymond that Sharon wanted to go out with him (she never did). And they remember Gina's mean-spirited paternal grandmother, who was always yelling out the window at her, saying she couldn't stay outside because she had to clean the house or take care of her little sisters. They break into hysterics recalling the poor woman's funeral and how one of her male relatives walked to the casket chanting under his breath, "Ding, dong, the wicked witch is dead." They remember feeling sad when Gina left college to get married. She always was an overachiever, a person who sacrificed her own ambitions to fulfill other people's needs. They remember a chubbier Gina taking care of everybody—her sisters, her mother, her father, her aunt, her first husband, and all of them. Once she even gave a favorite recipe to her first husband's second wife, and later she entertained the two of them in her home. "No doubt about it. She's going through the pearly gates when she departs this world," says Lil.

Now, Gina may be a slimmer supernurse, but her friends retain their image of her as an overachiever who settled for second best. In their eyes, she's still a frustrated doctor.

One senses that it is difficult for them to comprehend how
a nurse can attain Gina's notoriety. From all appearances,
the exalted position that she enjoys in her field has not
tempted them in theirs. They are schoolteachers, day-care
providers, and secretaries. While Gina jets from coast to
coast making her mark on the health care industry, they go
to Disney World for fun. They arrive by boats and planes,
have their favorite restaurants in Orlando, and accumulate
enough air miles to get there free the next time. In between
the junkets and the jobs, they have been loyal to one another
all these years. They've been the shoulders to cry on for
divorces, illnesses, and sundry other mishaps and misfor-
tunes, and they've been one another's celebrants for remar-
riages, anniversaries, births, and birthdays. Once upon a
time, they walked to school together. Now they walk together through all of their sadnesses in hope of finding their
happily ever afters.


## HOME


Dan Mosley, Jessie's brother-in-law, is fond of telling visitors to the home he shares with Claire, Jessie, and his
daughter Rebecca that when he married Claire, he got three
of her sisters in the bargain. At one time or another in his
married life with Claire, he has lived with every member of
the Concannon family except her parents and three brothers.
"Jessie is the Last of the Mohicans."

So Dan, his wife, his daughter, and Jessie, make a home
together in the suburbs. Rather than see their domestic circumstances as odd or out of place, they regard it as a source
of entertainment. Jessie's idiosyncrasies and her role in the
affairs of the household are favorite topics of conversation
for Claire and Dan.

"Sometimes she chooses not to have any common sense.
When she doesn't want to do something, she'll feign not

knowing how to do it. She'll act like an airhead,'' says Claire.

"Yeh, I have two nicknames for her: 'Space' and 'Twit,' and she answers to both of them,'' adds Dan.

Claire thinks it's amazing the way Jessie stays so upbeat all of the time. "She has hundreds of friends and never has conflicts with anybody. She can't find anything bad in anyone. Lots of people demand her time and her ear, and she doesn't mind. She gives and gives and gives. She's a confidante, even to old boyfriends who have jilted her. The patients don't seem to get her down, either. I like to hear about them, and she likes to keep me posted. Their stories seem very sad to me. Dan doesn't like to hear about them. He leaves the room. The only time Jessie gets tearful is when someone yells at her, but no one here at home does that. We all like each other a lot, so there's not much reason for her to be sad around here.''

Jessie laughs at their descriptions of her and interrupts with one mild protest: "It's not true that I give all the time. I get a lot back.''

In spirit, if not in body, the presence of Claire and Jessie's father lingers in the air around the three of them like oxygen—invisible, inescapable. Dan says that his father-in-law never liked him because he was divorced. "Now he tolerates me. Before, he wouldn't speak to me.''

Claire doesn't disagree but delivers a halfhearted defense of her father. "He thinks that once you're married, you stay that way. Those are his values.'' Claire adds, "He thinks that Jessie's weird, but he'd never tell her that.''

She is quickly seconded by Dan. "In his book, the only thing a nice girl from a nice family can do is work for a few years, get married, buy a house, and have babies. That's the norm, and you're supposed to conform to it. You haven't done that, so you're weird. And this business about going back to school makes you extra weird. You should stay right where you are, keep moving up and collecting bigger paychecks.''

"Those are his true feelings," say Claire and Dan in unison. Claire supports her side of the debate with a recollection from her own biography. "Remember when I wanted to work for his company, and he wouldn't let me because I was a girl? It didn't matter what my skills were. Girls weren't supposed to work in their fathers' companies."

If nice girls are supposed to be married, so are pretty girls. Jessie Concannon, a pretty girl, now a pretty woman, isn't. She says she would like to be, but one can't be sure if she lets herself look inward enough to ask the relevant psychological questions about why it hasn't happened.

Dominique is single, too, but her unmarried status has an edge of youthful advantage that Jessie's lacks. On the surface it would seem that her painful childhood may become a tether on her future, but looking at her now, that possibility appears unlikely. An observant child may be able to disengage from his or her abusive parent more easily than a similar child whose parent's behavior looks less vivid through her childish lens. Dominique could see her father's problems, and more than either of her siblings, she has been able to put him in proper perspective. She remembers the relief she felt when her parents divorced, and she entertains no illusions now about her father's chances for rehabilitation. Much to his consternation, she visits him infrequently, and then only for brief encounters. Throughout her life, she has steadfastly rejected his attempts to regulate her social and sexual life in accordance with his fundamentalist Muslim beliefs about women. From adolescence into young adulthood, she has gravitated toward kindly, liberated men. She expects them to be good to her.

Although Dominique now resides with her mother and teenage brother, it hasn't always been that way. Throughout college and for a short time thereafter, she shared city apartments with various friends. Her return to her family nest is the result of economic necessity. Dominique is in a position to help her mother pay the rent. She lives there in haphazard fashion, with one foot in the door and the other one out. She does this not for lack of loving them but in the desire to maintain the measure of independence that she regards as vital to her continued growth.

The mixture in Dominique's background of British, American, Muslim, and Irish Catholic influences have left their mark on her. "I think one of the reasons that I'm always questioning things is the result of having had to adapt to so many cultural and religious concepts and values. I'm not a religious person now, but I have come to favor the Muslim point of view over the Catholic one, and I feel prouder of my American heritage than my British one. Even though I don't like the male chauvinism that is characteristic of Muslims, I like their idea that God is inclusive, not exclusive. They don't have the Catholic notion about being the chosen people. There's none of this stuff about God's punishment for bad thoughts. God, in their view, is benevolent, nonpunitive, and nondiscriminatory. The conception of God as a source of positive energy appeals to me. This perspective is pretty recent, though, because both of my parents presented me with scary pictures of God. Now, just as I am beginning to feel settled into a point of view, along comes the Middle East situation. It bothers and confuses me. They make it seem as if their wars are waged in the name of God, when in reality they're waged in the name of money."

Middle Eastern roots, further removed than Dominique's, are part of Gina's heritage, too, though at this stage of her life, they are barely apparent. If she leans toward any ethnic identification, it is toward the paternal Italian-American side rather than toward the maternal Lebanese-American one. Her husband's ancestry is Italian, and reminders of Italy appear in the Rossis' cooking and in their routine Sunday family gatherings, but not in their religious practices. Gina's larder and her deftness in the kitchen provide the family clan with an abundant variety of Italian specialties, from pastas to pastries. Terry, too, can whip up a terrific tomato sauce. Before they sit down to eat, the four-generational family spreads itself out on the porches that extend from the rear of the house and onto the acres that surround it. Terry takes some of the children on tractor rides. The others ride bicycles or play games on the lawns. Gina, her sisters, and her daughter supervise the playing children. An assortment of husbands mill around the property as the old folks watch the activities from the porches. Notwithstanding the presence of men, the scene has a maternal quality.

Gina has it most of all. She is a devoted grandmother, a devoted mother, and as devoted a stepmother as her three stepchildren have allowed. "I think that the story of Cinderella has done more damage to the image of the stepmother than anyone cares to admit," Gina says frequently. "The stepchildren assume before you step into the maternal role that you're going to be wicked and unlovable. With Terry's two oldest children, I never could make an inroad, but with Jeff I've been able to." Jeff, Gina, and Terry live amiably under one roof now, and Terry is as much a father to Kendra as her own father is. Initially, however, the blending of the two families did not go smoothly. "It was a rough ride for almost four years. The kids raised holy hell in the house during their adolescent years, when Terry and I were newlyweds."

Since the three oldest children have moved out, Gina and Terry have had time for themselves. Because both of them travel in their work, they have recurrent separations and reconnections. It's a comfortable life-style for both of them and gives Gina time alone with Kendra, who lives nearby. The mother-daughter relationship is closer now than ever. There are bedrooms, furniture, and toys upstairs for Gina's two grandchildren. Her house is their second home.

Gina and Terry entertain their many friends as often as they do their families. Because Terry is a health care vendor, he knows many of Gina's colleagues almost as well as she does. Thus, their social life is an easy convergence of their individual professional and personal spheres.

Off the job as well as on it, Gina seems more content than either Jessie or Dominique. Part of the explanation for this lies in her age and station in life, but another part seems attributable to her nature. She appears as one whose experience has bid her to take the lumps of life in stride. If being a caretaker is her birthright, then she accepts it and enriches it with professional ambition.

## HUSBANDS AND LOVERS

"Jessie has a real talent for picking the wrong men," says her best friend Trina, a nursing administrator in another hospital.

When she was in college, she gravitated toward older men—men who leaned to the wild side. I think that somewhere in her head, she had the idea that she could tame them. In her twenties, she went through a few agonizing romances. One man was a real charmer. He had a blue-blood background, was a real athletic, jetsetty, outdoorsy type with a roving eye. She fell hard for him. Even though he treated her unfairly, she was always willing to forgive and forget. There were other guys after him, but they, too, were unrealistic choices for her. Lately there hasn't been anyone.

Dominique is highly selective about her men. They have to meet her standards of comportment and share at least some of her desire to make the world a better place. Mark, her current boyfriend, is in his early thirties and is an optometry student. He is attractive, personable, and very attentive to Dominique, though not always in just the way she wants him to be. His stable, small-town, Jewish origins are the antithesis of her unstable, urban, Irish Catholic–Muslim origins. "I come from a small town in Pennsylvania," says Mark. "My father is an optometrist there and my mother is a homemaker. I wouldn't mind going back there to settle down."

This difference in their backgrounds fuels the tension as well as the fascination in their relationship. It dominates the conversation one night at dinner, when Dominique is looking especially sexy and appealing (so much so that she has succeeded in turning the heads of all of the men on the street outside the restaurant where she and Mark are meeting).

"One thing that you told me a little while ago really bothers me," says Dominique. "All along I've been thinking that you're so liberal. You say you are, but then you tell me that you're a Republican. That's bad enough, but the reason is even worse. You say you registered Republican because that's what your parents are."

"See, that's how you like to start fights," Mark responds. "I'll admit that I'm not as political as you are."

"Well, at least we have a couple of things in common. Neither one of us is religious, and we both want to do volunteer work," replies Dominique in an attempt to defuse the argument. "You've grown up having a lot more comforts than I've had. You've never had to struggle about money, and you probably never will. That's why I have trouble tolerating your moodiness sometimes. It seems so spoiled. You fuss about being too tired, too hungry, or too hot. I'm not sympathetic about that stuff. And then there's the difference in our age. Because you're ten years older than I am, I'm always afraid you're going to say that some of the places we go to are too wild, the music is too loud, or that you're too tired to do this or that."

"Dominique, you didn't feel comfortable when you visited my family. You didn't think that they could understand the struggles you've had, and you didn't think you could ever have a close relationship with them like you had with your last boyfriend's parents. I think you judged them too quickly. After all, you only spent a couple of days with them."

"If you and I ever got married, I'd probably visit with

them on holidays, but I can't picture myself getting close to them," responds Dominique. "You're readier than I am to chill out and get married. You know that you'd like a comfortable house in the country and a couple of cars. I haven't thought that far ahead. I don't even know what direction I want my life to take right now. People my age are trying to figure out what they're supposed to want. I'm sure I'd freak out if I was married and had a kid, and I haven't the slightest idea about the kind of house I'd like to have. I'm always wrestling with what I should do next. I have to have goals."

"Yeh, I think you ought to relax more. You give too much and you come up empty too often. That's the trouble with nursing. I respect you for doing what you do, but I think it exhausts you. You're always stressed and hyperactive."

Finally their conversation sweetens. Dominique changes the mood by saying, "I like your eyes and your smile, and I think you're great looking. You're a good guy, and you're supportive to me. I guess I like it, too, that you don't go way out on a limb about anything. You're steady."

"I like the way you look too. I think you're pretty, a good person, someone who cares about other people, and you like to do a lot of different things. You're good at planning ahead and you're fun to be around."

"Gina and I owe our relationship to the intra-aortic balloon pump. She was my student long before I married her," explains Terry. "In the beginning all we talked about was balloon pumps, but then I got divorced and so did she, and now we both teach people about balloon pumps. I sell them; she uses them. Another nurse fixed us up, but our romance was a long-distance one, because when we started dating, Gina was about to go to school in the South, and I had three kids to raise here. It helps our relationship that we're both in the medical field. We understand the pressures of each other's work. She doesn't seem very stressed to me when she comes home, but we leave each other alone until we get acclimated to being together. We still talk a lot about balloon pumps. She can talk to me about bad situations at work, and she knows that I'll understand what she's talking about. I like the fact that she's independent and has her own career goals. She's a nice lady, and she's motivated. I couldn't stand it if she was a clinger.''

For Terry, marriage to Gina is the best medicine that the doctor could have ordered. They speak the same language and enjoy the same things. Neither of them is as relaxed as they'd like to think they are. ''He tells me that I can't relax, can't sit and look at the apple blossom tree, but I think that he's the one who can't relax. Despite what he says, I do sit under the tree and look at it. He's the one who's always puttering around. He never sits still. Look at him. He smokes like a chimney. Doesn't that tell you something?''

''We're not religious, and we're about the same politically, except maybe I'm a little more conservative than she is. Our financial situation is good. There's no stress there. We're putting a lot of our money into retirement, and we have enough left over to do the things we like. Gina's not a superlady. She's a general, all-around kind of person. Entertaining is fun for her. Gina likes to put on a big feed. The results of it are right here,'' says Terry, laughing as he points to his rounded stomach.


## A WORD ABOUT CODEPENDENCY

Whether or not they begin their caregiving roles as children, as Jessie and Gina did, or as adults, like Dominique, a diverse professional work force of over two million nurses is unjustly stereotyped when lumped together as ''codependents,'' just because they are employed as caregivers. Nonetheless, when the guest speaker at the state Nurse Managers' Meeting described earlier speaks of the codependent character of nurses, her words resonate with her audience. The characterization may appear to fit as perfectly as custom-tailored clothing—so perfectly, in fact, that its flaws escape attention—but there are flaws. The problems with the label are its derogatory connotation, its facility for being overused and misused, and its inherent cynicism. In the lexicon of pop psychology, codependency is seen as the "illness" of giving care in lieu of receiving it. It has its usefulness when employed as a diagnostic tool to help spouses (usually female) of alcoholics or other addicts (usually male) refrain from endless, self-sacrificing servitude to their sick mates, thereby "enabling" the continuation of the addiction. It loses its usefulness when it is applied to everyone who delivers care voluntarily or professionally. Then it includes mothers, housewives, and all manner of female helping professionals. Eventually the word is used so loosely that there's not a woman alive who is not afflicted with the disease to some degree. The word's most insidious characteristic is its implication that somehow we women should—and can—repair ourselves to perfection.

None of us, male or female, is dealt a perfect familial hand in life, and to an extent that goes far beyond our personal control, we all make do with what we get. Very often the missing cards contribute as much to the enhancement of our creative potential as the ones we're dealt. Some people become lawyers because their families gave more credence to facts than to feelings. Other people become captains of industry because their families instilled in them the idea that making money was life's essential mission. Still others choose nursing because their families assigned them apprenticeships as family caretakers. All of them, in some measure, offer a service to society, and nurses provide some of the most indispensable services in our civilization. In nurse manager Judy LaVigne's words, "You don't become a nurse if you want to get rich, but you do become one if you want the satisfaction of knowing that what you do for a living makes a difference in people's *lives*."

# THE LONG GOOD-BYE AND THE SHORT GOOD-BYES

## JESSIE'S WORK OF ART

**T**HE DAYS HAVE passed quickly. By the end of May Jessie feels as if it were just yesterday that she announced her departure. She hasn't thought much about what it means to her to be leaving 5C. August still seems a long way off. Mostly she has been concerned with practical matters surrounding her return to student status—the loss of her $55,000 salary, the need to supplement borrowed money with part-time income, the interviews for the required psychology internship placement that she must procure as part of her training. The financial implications worry her the most. Her concerns are shared by her father. "I don't know how she's going to manage," he says wistfully. "Even when she was making good money, she spent more on everybody else than she did on herself. She's much too generous. She's not a saver. Now she's giving up a good salary and financial security to be a poor, struggling student."

"He wouldn't say this to her face," says her sister Claire, "but I know that he thinks she's crazy to be doing what she is."

At times Jessie, too, thinks she must be crazy. Thirty-four years old and self-supporting yet foolhardy enough to arrange her own marriage to a bank. Nevertheless, she is determined to go through with it, come what may. Jessie believes strongly that her study of psychology will open new and as yet undiscovered doorways for her as a nurse and for easing the pain that cancer patients and their families suffer. And now the month of May has come and almost gone. The unmistakable signs of summer are in the air as Memorial's employees move outside to eat their lunches on the benches in front of the Pavillion Building or on the small plots of grass bordering the medical school next door. Jessie's reawakening to the reality of her departure comes like the warmer weather, gradually but inevitably.

Leaving here feels scary all of a sudden. It's like everything I've worked for might change when a new person comes. I suppose I should be satisfied that I've touched some people's lives, but it's hard to accept that it could all be different here after I'm gone. Let's say you do a piece of art—a painting. You can work away at it, and then you finish it. It stays forever the way you made it. Sure, maybe it gets a stain or two, but it's still there.

Jessie's fears about the changes are shared by most of her colleagues, but even as late as the end of June, the nurses, especially those working regularly with her on the day shift, are still in the denial stage. Marty Rosenbaum, as well he might, senses the mood on the unit.

There's no doubt about it. They're denying it, and she feels guilty about leaving, so she can't enable them to share their feelings with each other and with her. There's a group fear that the floor will fall apart. Jessie, after all, has brought them full circle from a warring gang to a happy family. When she arrived there, it was an angry place with a lot of disgruntled nurses. Jessie was knowledgeable and worked well with people.

Jessie became the good mother, the teacher, the empathizer, the martyr for them. She spoiled them rotten. At times, she was so overinvolved that it would drain her, and then when things didn't work out, she'd get upset and be down on herself. In this last year, I've noticed that she's been able to pull back a little, to stop expecting herself to please everybody, like the way she admits that she doesn't like or want to perform some of the administrative duties that come with the job. I think she's making the right move. She's empathic by nature, and that quality wears well in our field.

When he finishes speaking, Marty's expression reveals a hint of appreciation for having the opportunity to think out loud about the impact of Jessie's move. Eventually he will be one of the major players in helping to pick up the pieces on the unit.

Although he may be the most attuned to the collective unconscious on 5C, Marty is not alone among physicians who are worried about the impact of Jessie's departure. The others are apprehensive not only for the nursing staff but for the medical staff as well. The senior fellows and residents on David McGuire's medical oncology team are as saddened as they are concerned about her loss. Says one team member,

She's made this unit so pleasant to work on. It's amazing that she's been able to do that, considering the potential for depression that exists here. She's such a happy person, so thoroughly knowledgeable about oncology and oncology nursing, so good with people. The morale here is better than it is anywhere in the hospital. We will miss her terribly, and we're afraid that this place will never be the same again. We'd like to be able to participate in selecting her successor. It's very important to us, but it's entirely possible that the Nursing Department won't ask for our input.

Hal Bloomfield, too, is aware that he has feelings about Jessie's leaving.

I haven't been here very long, and for me to be able to say that I will miss someone as much as I think I will miss her after having known her for such a short time is a big compliment to her. I've just never seen a unit run as well as that, and I've never seen a head nurse who knows so much and who cares as much about the staff and patients as she does. It's almost an impossible act to follow. I think it will be tough on her successor. She'll be tested constantly.

Predictably, Jim Morley is a dissenter among the senior doctors. "I know she runs a tight ship up there on 5C. Things go smoothly, but people come and people go. The world goes on. I don't think that the place will fall apart because Jessie's leaving. Institutions are bigger than the individuals who work in them." Perhaps he is silently entertaining the wish that someone will emerge to fill Jessie's shoes who shares his own persuasions about nursing.

The southerly breezes are blowing gently as June rolls into July, but still the nurses aren't buzzing much about Jessie. They go about their work and pop in and out of her office as they always have, but they linger less now. A veil of self-sufficiency cloaks the unit, interrupted now and then with a comment about the future. "I wish we knew who was going to take Jessie's place. I don't like not knowing," are the usual refrains. Plans are afoot for a series of farewell parties, but the nurses handle these in much the same fashion as they do their routine tasks, and in actuality, planning parties *is* routine for every nurse. There is always someone celebrating something—the birth of a baby, an upcoming wedding, a milestone birthday, a graduation, a permanent or temporary departure. Already this year there have been several parties in the bubble on 5C and several more in restaurants and clubs, like the Nurses' Day shindig at the comedy club. Nursing parties resemble ritualistic family gatherings. Everybody comes, everybody contributes, and there's always too much to eat. For Jessie's farewell the nurses on 5C have hired a room in a suburban restaurant, where they will host a large surprise party. Abby has sent out invitations and ever since has been collecting money to defray the costs of the extravaganza, twenty dollars per person. Later Jessie's fellow nurse managers will host a party for her, as will the Nursing Department.

The nurse who seems the most visibly affected by Jessie's departure is Toni. Shortly after Jessie announced her plans to the staff, she strongly encouraged Toni to apply for the nurse manager position, but Toni has resisted. "I'm getting married in October. I still don't have my master's degree, and I know I could never be as dedicated as you are. I'm just not ready for it," she told Jessie.

So now, a month before Jessie is to leave, Toni is out of the running. Other candidates are being considered, but so far, no one has been hired. Toni, therefore, has agreed that she will answer the call to be the acting nurse manager until a permanent one is found. It is her way of thanking Jessie for all she's done for her. "She's made me love being a cancer nurse. She's such a strong nursing advocate. She stands behind us one hundred percent. I don't know how to describe this special quality she has, but it's had an impact on all of us, whatever it is." Tears come to Toni's eyes as she speaks about Jessie.

When we came here, we were all young and very leery about working on a cancer floor. She taught us so much about death and dying. She helps people die. Now it's second nature to me to do that, too. She's an ally for people always. Other nurse managers are not as accessible as she is. I know she'd like me to apply for her job, but I like my free time too much, even though I'm so appreciative of her recognition of my leadership potential. Nursing seems like it's the most important part of her life. I don't know how she feels inside. She's such a private person.

In private, all of the 5C nurses attest to Jessie's impact on them. Abby and Mary Lynn share Toni's feelings about Jessie's positive influence on their individual decisions to remain cancer nurses. Abby now thinks she might like to become an oncology nurse manager like Jessie.

She's brought me full circle. She kept motivating me and helping me overcome my weaknesses. Maybe I got interested in cancer nursing because I had had a malignant melanoma removed from my leg a few years ago, but I don't think that that was sufficient incentive to keep me interested. I think Jessie has everything to do with keeping me interested and enthusiastic about making a career out of cancer nursing.

The "assertive" Mary Lynn feels that she has taken full advantage of Jessie's people skills and has learned from her to keep her disagreements with doctors away from the listening range of her patients. "Jessie has the experience, the authority, and the education to garner respect. I learn from her example. She's so resourceful. She has given me increasing responsibility and made me recognize my capabilities."

Marcy, another of the young Turks who came to Memorial around the same time Jessie did, is less favorably disposed to a career in cancer nursing than her peers and only slightly less complimentary about Jessie. "Everybody loves her. She's always making sure that we're happy. She overextends herself, and I think people take advantage of that sometimes. If any of us want a day off, she'll call twenty replacements for us until she finds one. The first year she came, she worked New Year's Eve herself so that everybody else could have the night off.''

Paula on the day shift and Lydia on the night shift are the two old-timers on the unit. The former is as guarded in the expression of her feelings as the latter is forthcoming. They've seen other head nurses and nurse managers come and go, and in some ways Jessie's departure is for them a part of the natural order. It's not that Paula isn't appreciative of Jessie's contributions. She, like her more junior colleagues, recognizes Jessie's extraordinary capabilities, but perhaps she has had less need for them than the younger nurses have. An exceptional nurse in her own right, she has, at Jessie's instigation, been the recipient of a nursing award for excellence granted by the state nursing association and has enjoyed hospitalwide acclaim as a result. Had Jessie been a less confident nurse manager, she easily might have been threatened by a woman of Paula's stature. Instead, each has given the other the respect that she is due, and their relationship thus stands as an exemplary model of professionalism.

Night nurses like Lydia are subject to all of the feelings of exclusion that come with working the graveyard shift. Removed as they are from the bustle of daytime activity, it is easy for them to feel that they are a finger-in-the-dike crew that merely holds things together until the day people arrive. Although they are paid more per hour than day shift personnel, often their contributions to patient care are downplayed or overlooked by the daytime authorities. For Lydia to say, then, that Jessie is the best nurse manager she's ever worked for in her twenty-four years of nursing experience (fourteen of them on 5C) is no small accolade. Jessie's imminent departure is upsetting to Lydia, however inevitable she thought it was.

I get so emotional about it. She made us [the night people] feel like we were just as important as the day people. Before she came, I never participated in hospital committees or activities, but she motivated me to do it. She changed the time of staff meetings so that we had a chance to meet with her and the day staff. Whenever I've done something as a favor to her or to the unit, she thanks me with a personal note making mention of the specific contributions I've made.

She's the most objective person I've ever worked with. Nurses are often accused of wrongdoing by other hospital workers, especially doctors, but she never assumes that these accusations are correct. She asks for reasons why things happened the way they did. She makes sure that someone is at fault before she determines that a complaint is valid. No one has done more to get us out of the handmaiden role than she has. She insists that we get respect, even going over physicians' heads when she thinks it's necessary. She has an uncanny ability, too, to find your strengths and draw them out. Often you didn't even know they were your strengths until she discovered them. Of all her qualities, this capacity to bring out the best in everybody is her most outstanding one.

We have to face it—no one is going to be able to fill her shoes. I think the modern emphasis on management did her in. Her heart wasn't in the budget stuff. She believes that nurses and patients should have everything they need. We do everything we can to help keep her budget in line, but it's hard. We believe, as she does, that the patients come first. My biggest fear now is that we'll lose all the good nurses we have because they'll lose their incentive to stay once Jessie is gone.

Some of the doctors don't like us, the old-fashioned docs. They think we're too bossy and that we act like we know the patients better than they do. They're the ones that get mad at us if we tell patients the truth about their illnesses. The better doctors, though, really appreciate how much we care. A few of them try to send all of their patients to our unit.

Sometimes the patients can be just as disrespectful as the doctors. They regard the hospital as a hotel and tell us that the ''service'' is terrible. My answer to that is that we give care, not service. Caretaking, I'm afraid, is still low-level stuff in this society. Even though nursing is much improved over what it was, it's still considered woman's work, and that gives it low status in the public mind. With the high cost of health care, many patients probably don't think we're worth what we make, especially if they see us as ''service workers'' rather than ''caretakers.'' So, even despite the existence of people like Jessie, who set such high standards for the profession, I wouldn't want my daughter to be a nurse.

Lydia's college-age daughter has heeded her mother's advice and does not plan to become a nurse, but Jessie's ''daughters'' on 5C, with the possible exception of Marcy, seem intent on following in ''mother's'' footsteps. There are no rumblings from any of them about leaving. Jessie's days are numbered, though. The last Saturday in July has arrived and the devoted daughters are hosting their farewell fete. Most of Jessie's family comes along with most of the nursing staff, Hal Bloomfield, David McGuire, and the members of the medical oncology team. A former 5C nurse has flown many miles to be there. Colleen is the lone representative of the Nursing Department.

Guests mingle in their party clothes and introduce their mates or spouses to one another while they sip cocktails and sample hors d'oeuvres. Jessie makes sure she chats with everyone, telling them all how nice they are to come. And so it goes, until the finale, the evening's climactic moment, is upon them. Then Jessie is presented with a leather briefcase and a check from all of the nurses, secretaries, PCTs, and nursing assistants on the unit, and a group photograph is taken of all of the unit nurses together with Jessie at the center. There is a word of thanks from Jessie to the gathered throng, but no long speeches, no sentimental verbal journeys to close out the evening.

Two weeks later, on August 9, Jessie's next-to-last day, the Nursing Department gives its party for her. Like most departmental functions, this one takes place in the Crane 4 conference room. Food service has arranged a pink nonalcoholic punch and healthy snacks to be served buffet style at 4:00 P.M., as is the usual practice for events of this nature. People file in and out to say good-bye to Jessie, telling her, each in turn, how much they will miss her and wishing her good fortune, until finally a small group of hangers-on is assembled to listen to Colleen present Jessie with a funny coupon book full of promises to be cashed in at later dates— dinner at Jean Pirelli's, drinks on David McGuire, a week's supply of peanut butter crackers and Diet Coke. Jessie, looking lovely in blue linen, gratefully accepts the coupons with a broad smile and a face as red as her hair. She likes it this way. No fuss, no fanfare. A few days later a staff nurse on another unit who knows Jessie remarks, "Wouldn't you know it? One of the best nurses they've ever had, and they send her off just like they would if she was graduating from a Catholic girls' school. They don't want to make a hero out of anyone, especially if she's a fighter like Jessie is."

Memorial's president, Dr. Tirrell, when he is informed that Jessie's farewell party was a low-key, little-publicized departmental affair, says,

> It's an example of the tendency on the part of Nursing Administration to handle things themselves. They don't come to hospital administration for help at certain times when our assistance might be useful to

them. If there's a departing nurse who has made exceptional contributions to the hospital, it would be
nice if we could be on hand to acknowledge and reward her for her work.*

On her last day, August 10, Jessie leaves in the early
afternoon, but up to a few hours before she's due to leave
it's been business as usual. She and Toni go over last-minute
details that have to be taken care of in preparation for her
stint as nurse manager. Toni struggles through the process
teary-eyed. Afterward Jeanette has some questions about a
medication, and once again she, Jessie, and Susan convene
to solve the problem as if it was just another day. But the
most gratifying accomplishment for Jessie's last day is her
meeting with Ben Callahan to go over the draft of the unit
booklet for patients that has been on hold for so long. Ben
has been a longtime admirer of Jessie's professionalism. His
admiration dates back to a day more than a year ago when
he witnessed Jessie calmly holding 5C's patients and staff
together while nonunit personnel restrained a patient who
had lost all self-control. Before the crisis was contained,
the patient succeeded in starting a noisy and potentially
destructive rampage. Now, on her last day, it pleases him
to be able to assure her that the long-awaited first draft of
the booklet will be ready for review and editing next week.

Another farewell party takes place at 2:00 P.M. in the unit
conference room. Everybody comes, from all three shifts.
Food is abundant and the mood is low-key. Conversation is
forced, but there is less anxiety than there was in July,
because Jessie's successor has been hired and will assume
her duties after Labor Day. Also, a new clinical nurse specialist has been employed to perform the oncology education

---

*According to Colleen Lindstrom, Dr. Tirrell was invited to this
event. "Nursing Administration sends him invitations to all such
occasions, but he rarely attends."

function for the staff—a role that Jessie was able to manage alongside her nurse manager functions. Thus, two people will be hired to replace one.

During her final hour Jessie remains in and around the nurses station. Everything is running smoothly, no stone has been left unturned, but the pace is lulled. Lucille confesses that she feels lousy. She tells Jessie that she wants her standing near, "So I can see your face as much as possible." Jessie dutifully stands next to her while she dials admitting to make sure that Mrs. Jefferson, a former patient, is "coming back to me" today.

Gloria, Paula's PCT partner, and Lucille talk quietly to one another, and when Jessie moves away momentarily, they both express their sadness. "I wouldn't be where I am now if it weren't for her. She encouraged me so much. We're going to miss her something awful," says Gloria.

"Yeh," answers Lucille, "we'll have to give it a good try, but it's not going to be the same here. She brought us so far—all the way to this point where there's all this caring and loving, and in a minute, she'll be gone."

And in a minute, she was.

The first snowfall of 1990 comes between Christmas and New Year's, in the middle of two spurts of unseasonably mild weather. Jessie is enjoying a short break from almost four months of graduate school and has just returned home from a few days at her parents' house, where the entire Concannon family gathered to celebrate the Christmas holiday.

I'm more relaxed now than I've ever been. There's no question that being a psychology student is a lot less stressful than being a nurse. I have to laugh when my fellow students talk about how stressed they are. From where I sit, it strikes me that the job of a professional psychologist or full-time psychology student is far less taxing than any nursing job. To earn money for school, I'm working part time as a per diem staff nurse, and I can feel the difference. Nurses are on their feet all the time. It's exhausting.

As Jessie speaks it becomes evident that some ambivalence has crept into her thoughts about remaining a nurse after she receives her psychology degree. "I still feel strongly about maintaining my identity as a nurse, but I like a psychologist's schedule better. At times I feel guilty when I start thinking about how much easier it would be. In a few years I'll be forty. There's something to be said for a more leisurely pace. Getting to work at nine A.M. seems like such a luxury."

Adapting to the academic side of the psychology program has been easy for Jessie, but the clinical work has been more difficult. Two days a week, she serves as a psychology intern in a residential treatment program for troubled adolescents.

I love all the theory that I'm learning in school, but I've had some trouble with the practice part. When I was a nurse, I didn't feel that my professional and personal selves were any different. My goal has always been to make people comfortable. Now it seems that I'm expected to make people *un*comfortable. I'm supposed to pry into their personal business, stir up their emotions, and interfere in their lives. That's very hard for me. I thought that practicing psychotherapy would be second nature to me, but it isn't. In addition, I've found out that there isn't just one way to do therapy, there are twenty different ways. That has been a startling discovery.

In the first written clinical evaluation that Jessie has received from her supervisor, there are compliments aplenty about her academic ability and her popularity with clients, fellow students, and clinical colleagues. There is also a notation about her transitional struggle. "She's had trouble moving from a fix-it mentality to a process orientation. [The phrase *process orientation* refers to the practice of focusing on and attempting to understand the verbal and nonverbal communications in a therapeutic relationship. Essentially it is a passive stance rather than a directive or "fix-it" stance.] The shift has been difficult for her because of her long experience and training as a pain reliever."

## DOMINIQUE AND THE GLOBAL BURDEN

By mid-October, just as she's about to take her leave of absence, Dominique's spirits have lifted. Four new nurses and two PCTs have been hired on 5B, and Wendy Fleming has appointed Dominique as preceptor for one of them. Except for the first two weeks of her preceptorship, when her own patient census was very high, she has been able to enjoy a more leisurely pace on the unit. Teaching Nell, the new nurse in her charge, has been so gratifying that Dominique has changed her mind about taking on a PCT partner. Wendy will assign the next new PCT to her after she returns from her leave.

I've really enjoyed the last five weeks. I've liked being in a leadership and teaching position. It's been surprising to me to discover how much fun it is. At first I was nervous about it, but once I got into the swing of it, it was great. There have been a lot of nursing students around, too, and I've been able to help with their training. I'm glad to be leaving to do my volunteer work, but I'm not jumping for joy about it the way I would have been if things were as bad as they were during the summer. I'm leaving in a really positive frame of mind. Nell has done very well, and that reflects favorably on me.

Nell has warm parting words for Dominique.

She's been a great teacher. She's very open and easy
to know. It would have been much harder for me to
relax if she had been the intimidating type. I was more
attracted to working on this unit because of the warm,
family-like atmosphere than because it was an oncology unit. Dominique made me feel right at home. It's
a good place to start a nursing career. You learn a lot,
and they make it comfortable for you to express your
feelings about death and dying. Of course, I also like
the fact that I don't have to work on weekends very
often.

Dennis Bauer, a young, attractive medical resident who
knows Dominique, drops by to say good-bye to her on her
last day. He's interested in doing volunteer work, too, and
she has brought him some information about a volunteer
program for physicians. At certain times when Dominique
and Mark have been fighting, she has fantasized that Dennis
might be a romantic possibility. If Dennis has had similar
thoughts, he has not revealed them. Instead he has taken the
position that it's better not to date your colleagues.

It's too much of the same stuff. Medicine, medicine,
medicine. You hear it all day long, and when you get
out of here, you want to think about something else.
You want to learn new things. Doctors and nurses
don't date much. Some of the residents date each
other, but even that is less prevalent than you might
think. I think Dominique is a great person. I admire
her altruism. She does an excellent job, though she's
not the most high-tech type. She doesn't know tons
of medicine, but she's got a great way with doctors and
patients. Generally she's good-natured and helpful to
everyone. Unlike many nurses, she doesn't look at
her job as just a nine-to-five obligation. That's the

difference in outlook between nurses and doctors. Doctors perceive themselves as the ones with the real patient obligations. We don't think we can just pick up and leave when our time is up.

Sister Eileen, the hospital chaplain, also stops in on 5B to wish Dominique well. Like Dennis, she admires Dominique for her interest in volunteer work. "It really says a lot about her that she can be so enthusiastic about delivering service to very needy people under very difficult working conditions. She gives the physical presentation of a young girl, but she has the competence of a woman. She's highly attuned and sensitive to people's feelings. She reads body language and affect very well."

No one is more appreciative of Dominique than Wendy Fleming. As conditions on the unit have improved, Wendy has been able to do more to reward Dominique and to make her job more satisfying. Dominique's role as preceptor is the result of Wendy's initiative. When Dominique returns from her leave, Wendy intends to continue prodding her to assume additional responsibilities. The bonus for Wendy is that Dominique feels more positive about her and about working on the unit now than she did initially. Wendy, however, has been unwavering in her admiration for Dominique. "Dominique adds an extra dimension to nursing. She comes with more baggage, worldliness, and life experience than other nurses, so she's that much more sensitive to all the different cultural and psychological attitudes that patients bring with them to the hospital."

Dominique's last day on the job ends on a triumphant note as she receives grateful applause from a class of nursing students who have spent the afternoon in the 5B bubble listening to her lecture and demonstration of the latest model IV access system.

It feels good to leave with success under her belt. True, there have been disappointments. Tom and Arthur, her two youngest patients, have both died—Arthur shortly after dis-

charge to the rehabilitation hospital, and Tom following
another short stay on 5B. But all in all, the successes and
satisfactions outweigh the disappointments. Now she can
even allow herself the privilege of looking forward to returning to 5B.

On the Sunday following her departure the 5B nurses give
a farewell brunch for her at a local restaurant. It's a relaxed
send-off, more like an excuse to get together than an official
fete. Two months hence, Dominique will be back on 5B.

In the sweltering heat of Santo Domingo, 5B seems far away
and long ago. The flies and the heat and humidity stay with
Dominique and her nine volunteer companions on the long
bus ride into the Dominican countryside. En route to the
village where they will be residing for two weeks, the sce-
nery is verdant and mountainous in some places and sordid
in others. Cars in need of fuel are being pushed in long lines
at gas stations along the way. Dominique is told that it may
be several days before any gasoline is available. The poverty
that she sees in the towns they pass through overwhelms her.
People stand on unpaved streets surrounded by litter and flies,
or they stand in the doorways of tattered concrete blocks that
serve as homes. Already she knows that disease lurks behind
every doorway and then spreads without mercy in a giant
sweep through streets, villages, and towns. She is thankful for
the one day that will separate her from her work.

In the rural rectory where she is housed, there is no
electricity, so Dominique's journal reflects the uneven pen-
manship that darkness inflicts on the writer. The notes,
recorded at bedtime, are barely readable, so Dominique
deciphers them orally for me:

> When we arrived, we busied ourselves organizing the
> medicines and supplies that they will take tomorrow
> to a clinic in a remote area of the country. Later, the
> priest gave us an official welcome, and hosted a dinner
> for us in the rectory. Afterwards, he took us to visit

the orphanage attached to the rectory. It was filled with children too sick to be cared for by their parents. We helped put them to bed. We bathed them, played with them, and tucked them in. We were all pretty sad when we went from the orphanage to our own beds. Between our sadness and the street noise, sleep was hard to come by. The noise was deafening. There was the roar of mopeds, the constant beat of merengue music, and the intermittent clanging of church bells.

The next day the group has to make a long journey by jeep through the mountains to the clinic. Hundreds of people are lined up, awaiting their arrival. The clinic is a tiny one-room building furnished with one table. There Dominique begins diagnosing and treating patients. In her journal, she describes the experience:

We acted like doctors. We had no laboratory facilities to help us diagnose. We had to rely on our eyes and ears. We treated fungal infections, parasites, urinary tract infections, and as many pain symptoms as were treatable. By the end of the day, we had only seen half of the people. We stayed another day, and still were unable to treat everybody. The patients were wonderful to us. In all of their own misery, they were still able to think about us. They brought us home-brewed coffee all day long.

On another day they journey to a clinic nearer to the rectory. The poverty is more grinding and the diseases are more prevalent than in the previous location. Mobs of people greet them wearing black bracelets that signify hope for relief from disease. Babies have red ribbons tied around their wrists. They treat as many people as they can, but it is impossible to do justice to the task at hand.

They go from village to village for two weeks. Some of the journeys are treacherous and take them over winding, narrow mountain roads, through mud-filled gulleys and rocky canyons. The diseases and the plights seem to worsen along with the traveling conditions. Dominique's journal reflects the pathos.

We got to one clinic where 160 people were waiting for us. As usual, there was no privacy for patients in the clinic. One woman had a boil on her vagina. Many men complained of impotence, and some of them needed penile examinations. One of the saddest scenes was a woman in her fifties who arrived in great pain on the back of a burro. She had a huge abdominal mass and was bleeding. She had uterine cancer which had spread to her brain. If I'd seen her at home, she would have been given an IV morphine drip immediately, but we didn't have any equipment like that at the clinic. No sooner had she entered, then in came a baby weighing less than her birth weight who had a serious respiratory infection. There were no ambulances or other means of transportation to get the woman and the baby to the hospital, so we drove them ourselves. When we got to the hospital, they didn't have the right medicines there, either. They put the woman on IV fluids, but they had no morphine for her pain. We went to the pharmacy to buy medicine for the baby, but there was no morphine to be found. Because there was a national strike by then to protest the country's lack of essential services and commodities, and the rectory was supporting it, we couldn't provide money for ambulance service for the woman and the baby to return home after their hospitalizations. At least we saved the baby. It was hard to accept that the best that we could do for that poor woman was provide her with public transportation money. She lived a long way from the hospital.

Two weeks after her Dominican experience Dominique and her boyfriend Mark join a group of optometry students and practicing optometrists to volunteer in providing glasses and eye care to Mexicans in Cancun and the Yucatán. The Mexican government, in appreciation for their help, accommodates them in hotels in both areas. In Cancun they are housed in a beachside hotel, where all of their meals are prepaid. They have very little time to bask in the sun, however. The two thousand pairs of glasses they have brought with them have to be distributed to needy people in the city and in the rural area in the Yucatán. Dominique knows nothing about optometry, but after a very brief orientation, she is left alone in the two clinics to which they are assigned to match the prescriptions with the glasses in the crates and then to fit them to the wearers.

This was a totally different kind of experience than the Dominican one. I wasn't involved in treatment, but I certainly had to learn a new skill very rapidly. It was a real challenge. I didn't even know how to read the prescriptions at first, and I certainly didn't know how to adjust the frames. I only had one tool to use to make the adjustments. I was surprised at how quickly I caught on. The optometry work brought immediate gratification to the volunteers and the patients. The patients were so appreciative about regaining their eyesight. There's so much unemployment in Mexico that they would never have been able to have the glasses without our help. It was an instant-cure experience. You knew immediately that you had helped them and given them a new lease on life.

Dominique is convinced now that volunteer work will be an annual occurrence for her.

I can't imagine not having it as a regular fixture in my life. The two experiences taught me that I could meet big challenges. Coming back home for the holidays was an adjustment. Christmas, with all its materialistic glitz, just didn't mean as much to me, not after all the misery I saw. I feel very good inside. I know I've touched people's lives, and I can see that I've gotten other people to want to follow my example. I've already gotten one nurse to offer her services. I'll get others, too. I've accomplished my goals for this year. I'm going back to 5B, but by April I hope to have my goal established for the coming year. It will probably mean going back to school for a master's. By then I hope to know when and in what field I want to get it. No matter what, though, I'll volunteer again next year.

## GINA AND THE CASUALTIES OF WAR

In September of 1990 Gina anticipated that her life in the coming year would be much the same as it was then. She would be busy on the SICU and somewhat busier with her extracurricular responsibilities than she had been the previous year. Most of her time in the next twelve months was already allotted in her appointment book. Someday she would return to school for a doctoral degree, but that remained a distant goal to be fulfilled at some undetermined time when the spirit moved her. From past experience, she knew that she could trust the spirit to propel her forward.

But life is unpredictable. It is January 1991 and America has gone to war in the Persian Gulf. Gina's spirit has started rumbling.

I can't just stand by and do nothing if we're going to have casualties in the field, so I've volunteered to go to Germany with the Red Cross as part of a team sponsored by the Society of Critical Care Medicine. Current plans call for wounded soldiers to be sent to hospitals in Germany before they're sent home. This could put a huge burden on German hospitals. It's impossible for me not to go if they desperately need people who are skilled in critical care. Paul Donaldson and Pauline Irving have volunteered, too. We'll have five days' notice to prepare ourselves for a two-week stint there.

Gina is convinced that she must be on hand if men and women are going to be hurt in service to their country. She feels that the very least that she can do in payment for their service is to offer them hers.

## TO CARE OR NOT TO CARE: THAT IS THE QUESTION

At the end of one of her more stressful days, Dominique turned to me and said, "You know what the title of your book should be? *To Care or Not to Care: That Is the Question.*" I knew what she meant. For weeks I had watched her energy barometer drop from a high at the start of a shift to a low at the end. Exhaustion and stress were such intrusive visitors to her daily life that they sometimes made her feel that she had nothing left for *caring*. It bothered her when her own needs seemed to supersede those of her patients. "How can I be a nurse, much less an excellent one, if I feel this way?" she'd ask herself repeatedly. She was not alone. Many of her young colleagues experienced similar self-doubt. It existed alongside a growing recognition that caring, if it is to find sustained expression in feeling and in professional activity, requires a personal energy supply that depends for its existence on institutional and societal replenishment. At the same time that the recognition was growing, the replenishment was diminishing. Too few nurses, not enough money, more and sicker patients, and who cared anyway? Do politicians care? Do hospital administrators? Some of them perhaps, but not enough to make a difference. Do voters care? Do patients care? To Dominique and many of her colleagues it looked as if *not caring* was spinning so far out of control that if nobody else was going to care, why should they? But put the nagging questions to sleep for awhile, and in the morning these nurses *care* again. Can't get away from it. It always comes back, this caring business; like it really never left, just felt like it did. It's in a nurse's bones and blood.

For Jessie and Gina, it was the same. Nursing and caring were synonymous to them, too. Gina thought a book about nurses ought to be called, *The Caring Business* or *The Business of Caring*. She and Jessie, it was true, divided their time between hospital business and delivering care. Jessie had more doubts about whether the two activities were compatible than Gina did. Their working days usually were longer than Dominique's, but they were less exhaustion prone. They had time off from caring. Only after Jessie had entered graduate school in another field, did she realize how tiring it had been to be a nurse. It wasn't the business part that took the toll, it was the caring part. Even so, after a half a year of school, Jessie could not say she was going to become a psychologist. She was still a nurse at heart. Nursing is what you do when you care. Can't get away from it.

Nurses will go on caring for us because it's in their bones and blood. The caring *feelings* that they have for all our suffering will always be there, but their ability to perform some of their caring *activities* will be compromised. To continuously give care necessitates receiving it. Nurses have to ask for our support, not with the worn-out and unheard language of the victim (many Americans refuse to believe that there are any victims), but with confident voices, loud and clear, coming over radio airwaves and television screens and from newsstand headlines. We will have to respond then, loud and clear, with votes, voices, and cash on the line. Their care of us is *our* business. Will we respond? *That is the question.*

# NONFICTION PERENNIALS
## FROM ST. MARTIN'S PAPERBACKS

25 THINGS YOU CAN DO TO BEAT THE RECESSION OF
THE 1990s
Alan Weintraub and Pamela Weintraub
_____ 92646-4 $3.95 U.S./$4.95 Can.

THE PEOPLE'S PHARMACY
Joe Graedon
_____ 92962-5 $6.99 U.S./$7.99 Can.

HOW TO STAY LOVERS WHILE RAISING YOUR CHILDREN
Anne Mayer
_____ 92715-0 $4.99 U.S./$5.99 Can.

76 WAYS TO GET ORGANIZED FOR CHRISTMAS
Bonnie McCullough & Bev Cooper
_____ 92940-4 $3.99 U.S./$4.99 Can.

YOU CAN SAVE THE ANIMALS: 50 Things to Do Right Now
Dr. Michael W. Fox and Pamela Weintraub
_____ 92521-2 $3.95 U.S./$4.95 Can.

# EXPERT CHILD-CARE ADVICE AND HELP—

## from St. Martin's Paperbacks

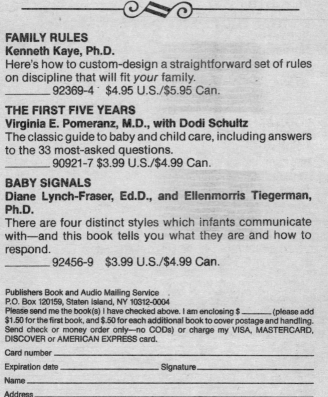

**FAMILY RULES**
**Kenneth Kaye, Ph.D.**
Here's how to custom-design a straightforward set of rules on discipline that will fit *your* family.
_____ 92369-4   $4.95 U.S./$5.95 Can.

**THE FIRST FIVE YEARS**
**Virginia E. Pomeranz, M.D., with Dodi Schultz**
The classic guide to baby and child care, including answers to the 33 most-asked questions.
_____ 90921-7 $3.99 U.S./$4.99 Can.

**BABY SIGNALS**
**Diane Lynch-Fraser, Ed.D., and Ellenmorris Tiegerman, Ph.D.**
There are four distinct styles which infants communicate with—and this book tells you what they are and how to respond.
_____ 92456-9   $3.99 U.S./$4.99 Can.

# LANDMARK BESTSELLERS
# FROM ST. MARTIN'S
# PAPERBACKS